White Lies
and
Stakeouts

Susan Alison

For Melanie xx

Chapter One
(Ignorance is Bliss)

"OKAY, MOOCHER," Liz shouted. "You just STAY THERE and be a good dog!"

Moocher looked puzzled, but keen, as always. He butted his head into her knees and licked the back of her hand reassuringly.

He also looked around him as if to query the wisdom of having this conversation in the downstairs bathroom at the back of the house. He sniffed the air, too, as if to savour the freezing cold breeze rushing in through the open window.

Liz patted him and he wagged his tail. He knew she'd have her reasons. Thus encouraged, she cleared her throat and took a deep breath:

"OKAY, MOOCHER!" she yelled again. "Have this rawhide shoe to chew while I'M OUT and NO-ONE ELSE IS HERE – to keep you company while you're all ALONE!" Her throat was getting sore, but Liz wanted Granny Smart to know she could come in now and use the bathroom.

Moocher threw his rawhide bribe over his shoulder. It narrowly missed landing in the loo; it hit the wall with a satisfying 'thwack' and fell to the floor. He pounced on it as though it was about to run away, and while his back was turned, Liz was off, tearing down the hall, yelling, "BYE, BYE MOOCHER. BYE, BYE!"

Once on the path outside the front of the house, she stopped. Fat rain-drops trampled her hair and crawled down her neck. She stood staring all around, but not really seeing.

It seemed odd that Malvern Road looked just the same this morning as it had yesterday. But – how could it possibly look just the same now that she knew a granny lived in her shed?

Chapter Two
(One Smart Granny)

"You're telling me I have a granny living in my garden shed? Is that right?" Liz had pronounced each word very carefully.

And Melanie still said, "Yes, Liz. That's what I'm telling you, and no matter how often you want me to tell you again, I'll tell you the same thing."

Liz heaved a huge chest-expanding sigh, shut her eyes, opened them again, took another deep breath, then stopped. She was getting dizzy.

She drew out a chair at the breakfast-room table and nodded her most reliable lodger towards it. "Sit down, Melanie." She sat down. Liz sat down. Moocher threw himself onto his back under the table. The floor groaned and black hair-balls rolled around like tumbleweed in the draught he created.

"Right," Liz said. "This granny. She doesn't happen to be just any old granny, does she? Oh, no, she just happens to be the granny from across the road?"

"Yes," Melanie said.

She looked anxious, which wasn't like her. Melanie was usually bright and cheerful, bouncy and optimistic. Not anxious.

Liz could feel the same anxiety spreading across her own face. "No, not just *any* old granny. You're saying we have the granny who belongs to one of the most influential lawyers in Bristol. The granny who belongs to a famous actress."

Melanie's face hardened. "Not *belongs*! Don't say *belongs*. She doesn't *belong* to anyone except herself."

"I'm sorry. You're quite right. However, we *are* talking about the granny who's been splashed all across the tabloids because she went missing a few weeks ago, aren't we? The Smart Granny."

"Yes."

"In my garden shed?"

"Yes."

"Right. Let's sort this out, then." Liz stood up and tried to make her way to the back door, but couldn't even get into the kitchen. Melanie had planted herself in the way like a determined keeper deflecting a shot on goal.

"Excuse me," Liz said, stepping to one side.

Melanie also stepped to that side. "No, you can't go out there," she insisted. "She mustn't know you know."

Liz retreated and sat down again. She wasn't prepared to take on Melanie. She would lose. "If that's the case, why did you tell me at all?"

"Because I can see you're beginning to notice things. You were puzzled about footprints on the floor the other day, when it was raining. You said it made you feel spooky."

"It did. Because I knew no-one was in. You mean she came in through Moocher's door? She came in through the dog-flap? To use the loo or something?"

"Or get some water, maybe, or wash, or to get a warm-up. Also, at some point," Melanie added, "you'll go out to the shed and then you're **bound** to notice. The only reason we've got away with it for so long already is that you're the least enthusiastic gardener this side of the Pennines."

Liz noted the 'we' but chose to ignore it, at least for the time being. "This isn't some sort of practical joke?" She was conscious of a pleading note creeping into her voice, but was unable to change it to joviality.

"Would I lie?"

"Okay. I believe you. Ohmigod. She must be freezing out there. Why's she out there? Why's she living in my shed?"

"She had to get away from those awful people that call themselves her family."

Liz's head began to feel as though its rightful contents were draining out to be replaced by mouldy yoghurt.

"Those **awful** people had me to dinner the other night. They weren't awful at all. And they're worried sick about where their Granny is, for God's sake. We've got to tell them."

"You can't! You must promise me you won't tell them."

"Melanie, please be reasonable. How can I not tell them? They're my friends."

7

"They're not! They're acquaintances at best. And they've been having the whole street in to dinner. They're trying to feed their way into acceptance."

"Well, they succeeded with me. They had lobster – mmm – lobster. And they had home-made lemon meringue pie – mmm – home-made lemon meringue pie. And they had ..."

"Liz – this is about more than your belly!" Melanie looked at her as though she'd found a slug in her mouth.

Maybe she was right about them. Liz knew she hadn't been the only one from Malvern Road to sit at Tallulah and Graham Smart's dining-table and be regaled with tales-in-the-life-of-a-soap-actress, and yummy food, and tales-in-the-life-of-a-highly-successful-lawyer, and yummy food. Lots of yummy food. She flinched as Melanie waved her hand in front of her face and put paid to her brief food-dream.

"They're really worried about where their granny's gone," Liz said.

"She is not *their* Granny. And they are *not* worried. It's all an act. Or rather, they might be worried, but it won't be over Granny's welfare. It'll be because of their so-called reputation if the truth were to get out."

"The truth?" Liz felt weak. She couldn't handle the truth! She dreaded what was coming.

"They have treated her so badly," Melanie said. "They have stolen her house and all her money. They did it while she was sick after her husband died. It's disgusting, but I don't know how we can get it back for her."

It was painfully obvious that Melanie was close to tears. Her face had gone all blotchy, which was quite pleasing to Liz, because hers did that too. "Hey, hey," Liz said. "Whatever it is, we can fix it. We're the fixing sort. You know that."

Melanie gave a wavery little smile. "Yeah, I know. That was another reason to tell you. We didn't want to tell you before in case you felt obliged to shop her."

Okay, now was the time. With great misgiving Liz queried it: "We? You keep saying 'we'."

"Yes, 'we'. I couldn't have kept it quiet all this time by myself. I mean, me and Laurel and Jason and ..."

"What? All this time everyone in the world has known about this, except me?"

"Not everyone in the world. Just most of your lodgers, that's all."

Liz knew without being told that Danny didn't know. Danny couldn't keep a secret. Everyone knew Danny couldn't keep a secret.

She sighed. And asked anyway, just to see if her not being told was as bad as she thought it was. "Does Danny know?"

"Of course not! Danny can't keep a secret!"

That made her feel better. Slightly.

"But the others had to know or we couldn't have kept her safely in your shed, could we? We've had to take it in turns to provide her with food and get her in for a bath and stuff like that …" Melanie's voice tailed away. Liz wondered if it was because of the horror she could feel changing the shape of her own face as she tried to imagine how someone, especially a granny, had managed to live in her shed all these weeks.

"Has she been there all the time since she disappeared?" Liz demanded.

"Pretty much," Melanie admitted.

It was a horrible thought. The weather had been foul in that time – not just wet but really, biting cold. It wasn't a deluxe shed. It was your bog-standard-for-chucking-things-in type shed.

"And is she really okay?" How could she possibly be okay?

"Considering we, or to be precise, Laurel, found her sleeping rough in the centre of town, she's much better off than she might have been. The trouble is, we don't know what to do next. We can't work out how she can get back what's rightfully hers. And she can't really go on living in your shed for the rest of her life, can she?"

"No." Liz was glad they could agree on something.

"So, what do we do next?"

"And I'm not allowed to know that she's living there?"

"No, she'd be terrified. She would leave when we weren't looking if she knew you knew. Especially as you *seem* to be quite friendly with Tallulah." Melanie paused before adding: "But you can't really like the woman, surely?"

She looked at Liz as though an unsanitary event was about to occur. Liz tried a smile, but it didn't work. So, she said: "No, certainly not! She's obviously a very shallow piece of work, that one." She had her fingers firmly crossed out of sight on her lap.

Melanie beamed. Liz beamed back.

"However, she can't stay in the shed," Liz said, still deliberately beaming.

Melanie scowled. Liz flinched, her rictus grin disappearing like a belch in a typhoon. "Melanie, it's too damn cold for *anyone* to stay out there, let alone a granny. She'll have to come into the house. And then we'll have to sort out what to do when we know the full story ..."

"We already know the full story!" Melanie looked suspicious again.

"Okay, when *I* know the full story. And have taken some advice. Maybe from Hugh."

Ah ha! Liz had said the magic words. Melanie's face not only cleared but also suddenly shone with relief and optimism again. "Ooh, Hugh. Of course. He's just the person we need."

Well, that's nice. If you don't happen to be his ex. Which Liz was. But there was no doubt that he was an extraordinarily useful chap to have around if you were in trouble. And, for the sake of a granny, Liz was prepared to have him around. He would know what to do. In the meantime, where was she going to put Granny Smart? There was no way she could stay in the shed a moment longer.

Liz expected Melanie to go straight off and get the granny now that the magical Hugh was in the equation, but she didn't. After a few moments of what was apparently some highly energetic thinking she said, "No, it still won't work. If she knew you knew she would leave and then I dread to think what would happen to her."

"You've said that already."

Melanie fixed her with a sharp stare. "Nothing's changed, Liz."

Liz fidgeted in her chair. "But, why would she leave?"

"Because she wouldn't feel that she could stay if you knew. She'd be convinced, for one thing, that you would tell Telly and Grabber."

"Telly and Grabber?" Liz muttered faintly.

"And," Melanie continued. "She wouldn't want to be a bother either. She would feel she was imposing if you knew. No, it won't do. You must promise me you won't let her know you know."

Liz reached for her biscuit tin and found it empty. Melanie got hers down and slid it temptingly in front of her. Hmmm – it was bulging at the seams with custard creams and chocolate fingers. "Okay," Liz said. "I won't let her know I know. But I want you to take the hot water bottle from under the sink and make sure you fill it up every night. And there's some blankets in that old cupboard in Wayne's room – take them out to her. But it can't go on like this for too long. There has to be an answer that suits everyone."

"Thank you! I knew you wouldn't let us down." Melanie grinned at Liz and suddenly enveloped her in a hug that sent cascades of custard cream crumbs down her front. Just as suddenly she gabbled something in her ear and shot off, running down the hall, and slamming the front door behind her.

Liz was alone except for her trusty dog who wanted his belly rubbed, a granny in her shed who believed she didn't know there was a granny in her shed, and her usual, reflective, logical and laid-back thought processes:

Ohmigod! The Smart Granny's living in my shed!! Ohmigod!!!

And then Liz had been overcome with the need to let Granny know she could come in now if she wanted, hence shouting at Moocher to STAY THERE, even though he had no intention of going anywhere, and so here she was lurking outside her own front door, getting soaked to the skin in the rain. The very cold, very wet, relentless rain.

Chapter Three
(Mapmaker)

Mapmaker slogged up the road from where he'd finally managed to get his car parked. It had been another heavy eleven hours at the office with back-to-back transatlantic conference calls. His American counterparts never seemed to stop for breaks. The business end of the video gaming industry, whilst paying him extremely well, had nothing playful about it at all.

The rain was steady, but he found it soothing more than irritating, knowing he would soon be home in the warm and dry. He looked forward to a relaxed afternoon and evening working on his new game idea, and updating his journal and map. He might need to top up his energy levels with a quick nap first, followed by a large malt whiskey and a takeaway supper. Yes, that sounded good. He quickened his steps.

As he passed number nine, he saw Liz Houston skulking outside her own house. Where her hair wasn't sticking out in dripping rats' tails, it was plastered to her skull in an urchin-look, and the way she was hunched over, her hands deep in her pockets, he could tell she was cold. He couldn't begin to imagine why she was suffering like that just outside her own home. Maybe she'd lost her keys. He couldn't do anything about it if she had, and he knew there were multitudinous people living in that house so one of them must be around soon.

Not wanting to look like he was hurrying away from her, he didn't quicken his steps. He did try to lengthen his stride, though. He didn't want to get embroiled in anything Liz Houston had going on. He'd heard enough about her wild schemes and scatty ways to want to race across the road and run like hell in the opposite direction. He managed to stop himself doing that, at least.

He had way too much on his plate already. He might feel the need to know who everyone in Malvern Road was, but that didn't mean he had to get involved in their lives. Nor did it mean he wanted them to know him, or anything about him.

Chapter Four
(Angela Gets In)

Liz noticed the chap from the middle flat at number twenty-nine. She knew he had carefully avoided catching her eye. She knew he was trying very hard not to break into a sprint away from her. She didn't blame him. She must look like something that had drowned at sea and washed up on a muddy beach. Also, she was well aware of how odd it must look for anyone local who spotted her there, lurking outside her own front door. It defied rational explanation.

Idly, she watched as a car unsuccessfully tried to manoeuvre into a space big enough to accommodate Wales. It was a small, powder-blue coupé model with alloy wheels and little frilly-edged, brocade-covered cushions on the back seat – actually, Liz couldn't see the cushions, but she knew they were there.

When the full significance of what she saw dawned on her, Liz leapt for cover behind the wheelie bin and peered carefully out. The travelling sofa was still shunting back and forth, trying to get closer to the pavement. Liz didn't believe she'd been seen by its driver.

She sidled along behind a few rain-laden bushes that could have been placed there for her convenience, flipped around the corner, and was hidden from sight as she unlocked her front door and dived for safety. She wanted to rush out and yell at Moocher that she was back so Granny would know, but there wasn't time. She had to get under cover before the sofa-driver – her sister, Angela – had any suspicion that she was in, and yelling at the dog might just give her away.

Liz decided on a hiding place just in time before the assault on the front door began. She curled herself up as tight as she could in the space she'd chosen, only to find her human hedgehog act in danger of being thwarted. A load of fat seemed to have materialised from somewhere and collected around her waist. It was difficult to breathe and remain curled up that tight. She clenched her teeth and waited it out as best she could.

Then Angela changed her tactics and, leaving the front door, she wielded her handbag like a cudgel on the bay window instead. She used such force Liz was afraid the glass would give up and fall out of its frame. Then Angela would be able to get in. And then Liz would be discovered skulking under her own table, behind the rather nice gold chenille tablecloth she'd got from the second-hand shop across the road.

And then she'd never hear the end of it.

"Silly girl, Liz," Angela would say. "No need to be afraid. It was only me."

Well, yes. That was the problem.

Then Angela would say: "You know, it's far too easy to get in your house. You ought to do something about it."

Quite so.

Liz was distracted from her imagined conversation with Angela by a sudden, urgent compulsion to sneeze. She couldn't allow it to happen! She breathed deeply, very fast. That didn't stop it. That just made her feel sick. She grabbed her nose, but the sneeze came anyway and tried to get out of her ears, leaving the contents of her head feeling pulverised. Still, at least that danger was now past.

It really needed cleaning under this table. Liz supposed she ought to do it. After all, even though it was a communal room, and if it's a communal room then any of her lodgers should do their bit of cleaning, she was pretty sure none of them hid under the table. Therefore, she should do it. Drat.

A restful silence had fallen, but her sister had the cunning of a hungry fox, so Liz stayed as still as she could. She tried to stop breathing, too, conscious that Angela also had the hearing of a bat. Liz listened hard, trying to ignore all the noises in her head left over from the sneeze-explosion.

Then she heard the hurried pad of paws coming down the stairs. Moocher must have been napping up there. Ohmigod. He was going to come running in and betray her!

Liz froze. Maybe he wouldn't find her. He raced down the

hall, claws muffled by the carpet. Then came a sharp pattering as he hit the bare floorboards of the breakfast room, followed by a more distant, but still distinct, clattering on the concrete floor in the kitchen.

Liz knew he was in the utility room when she heard the crackle and rustle of a heavy-duty bag as he pushed his nose into it, accompanied by a few explosive breaths like a stamping horse. He always did that even though he knew he couldn't get at the dog-biscuits inside. He cantered back towards the front of the house, scratched on the sitting room door then ran into the front room. And out again.

Of course, he couldn't be expected to find her straightaway. He'd only just got up from a snooze. None of us are at our best when we've only just got up. To be fair.

Then he chased back up the stairs. Liz could hear him thundering about all over the house, an excited 'wuff' escaping him every now and then. He thought it was a game.

And then she heard the 'clatter-thunk' of the dog-flap in the back door. As Moocher was upstairs snuffling about, this meant that one of her lodgers, Wayne probably, had forgotten his keys and had to go round and in through that way. Moocher heard it too and came stampeding down the stairs to see who was there.

But, it could also be the granny who didn't know Liz was back inside. Ohmigod. Now what?

Liz decided she'd stay under the table until all was clear, but she was out of luck. Moocher came bouncing in and flung himself at her golden chenille as though he'd known she was there all along and was only pretending to search the rest of the house.

There was no getting away with it. Liz returned his sloppy lick with a hug and climbed out of her hiding place to be confronted by the horrible sight of her sister, hands on hips, feet as far apart as her elbows and a smirk on her face.

"How did you get in?" Liz demanded. She needed to know to prevent any future recurrence.

"Through the dog-flap, of course," she said. "What am I supposed to do if you won't let me in?"

"You did not crawl through the dog-flap, Angela!" Liz wasn't going to believe *that* any time soon. Angela was the last person who would stoop to doing such a thing. Well – maybe not absolutely the *last* person – Their Mother would be the very last person, but Angela would be so close to the last you couldn't get a sliver of something sliverish between her and Their Mother.

"I *did* crawl through the dog-flap! What else could I do? You wouldn't let me in."

Liz eyed her usually perfectly turned-out and immaculately-behaved sister. She appeared to be telling the truth. And yet, Angela would never do such a thing! It gave Liz a peculiar feeling to think that she might have.

What the hell?

She returned to the attack: "What made you so sure I was in? You're not one of my lodgers – you can't just go forcing your way into people's houses."

"It's *your* house, isn't it?"

"Yes, but that doesn't give you any right…"

"I know you'd like to forget it, but you *are* my little sister and if I feel the need to see you then I should be able to see you. Your friends next door agreed, which is why they let me through their place and into their garden so I could get over the wall and in through the dog-flap."

Liz wanted to argue with this, but she was tired and didn't feel strong enough. And Angela hadn't even got to the point of her visit yet. But she made a mental note to ban everyone next door from letting her sister through their house again.

"As for being sure you were in," Angela said. "Your car's parked outside."

"I could have walked somewhere."

"It's pouring down with rain."

"I could have worn a wetsuit."

"You don't have a wetsuit."

"See. Now. That's what's wrong here. What makes you so sure I don't have a wetsuit?"

"I would know if you had a wetsuit," Angela said. She threw her poor, battered handbag down onto the settee. Then she removed her posh raincoat with the bits of fur around the neck – all straggly now – and flung that down to join it. She looked like she was staying. "This is stupid. How do we get into these silly, childish, arguments?"

"They're not childish," Liz said. "Anyway, you started it."

She thrust her hands into her pockets, stuck out her bottom lip and caught sight of herself in the mirror above the sideboard. Oops. She sucked her lip back in, whipped her hands out of her pockets and in her haste to act as if she really was thirtyish, offered Angela a cup of tea.

"That would be lovely," her sister said.

Damn.

Chapter Five
(Mapmaker)

Mapmaker locked his front door behind him with some relief, helped himself to a single malt, one of his few self-indulgences, and flopped into his favourite chair. He'd spotted it – a late 17th century oak wainscot chair – in an antique shop when he was on the Isle of Islay at the same time as he'd first formed his lifelong, but respectful, relationship with malt whisky.

He'd been fascinated by the chair's shapely physique, its intricate carvings and the story told in the inlaid picture of a dog in the back panel. But what he really loved was the little verse carved beneath the picture, which said:

> *I made this chair for you*
> *because you constantly purloined mine.*
> *This is my chair now you're gone*
> *because in it you'll always live on.*
> *You were the best dog.*

He thought this would probably be the closest he ever got himself to having a dog, and he was okay with that. The thought of the responsibility of a living creature made him feel quite queasy, but he was happy to enjoy the ethereal presence of someone else's without the hairs all over his clothes and the messes of all sorts he did his best ***not*** to imagine.

The chair had cost him more than the car he'd had at the time, but since he'd bought it, he'd taken it everywhere with him, completely happy to hire a little trailer if his current vehicle didn't have room for it.

Intending to do some work, Mapmaker pulled out the laptop he used for game design, but only glanced at it before reaching for his Malvern Road journal. This was more of a draw these days than the world-building for his latest game.

He took a sip from his glass, savouring the whisky, appreciating its sweetness, its smoky warmth that could keep at bay the effects of any cold, damp weather. Some days he added water, which seemed to bring out reminiscences of ancient times living in a croft by the sea.

Today was more of a business-like day, though. Today he had new information.

Chapter Six
(Angela's Awful Announcement)

"Now then," Liz said, having successfully moved Angela out of the front room without too much argument, and got her seated at the table in the breakfast room, tea cups at the ready, biscuits tastefully piled on a plate.

"Why were you so desperate to see me, Angela? It's hardly your normal entry, is it? How would the good women down at the bridge club feel if they knew their star organiser had been crawling, uninvited, through other people's dog-flaps?"

"Why don't you find out?" she said. "We've got a meeting tomorrow afternoon. You're welcome to come along."

She had Liz there. She knew her sister wouldn't come along to such a meeting for all the villas in Spain. "I'm busy tomorrow afternoon, I'm afraid," Liz said. "What a shame. So – why so desperate?"

"Two things. One is that you've been holding out on me about the people across the road." The look on her face suggested that Liz had betrayed her big-time.

Liz had no idea what she was talking about.

"And the other thing?" Liz prompted. And just for the smallest measurable amount of time she felt sick all over. Because Angela's face now registered a look such that Liz had never seen on it before and she knew Angela was going to tell her she had some terminal disease.

"I, I need …" That was as far as Angela got before breaking off and looking all around the breakfast room as though she'd never seen it before. She looked at it so minutely Liz was sure she'd be able to recall its drawbacks in all their fascinating glory three years hence.

"What? You need what?" Liz's voice was sharp even to her own ears. Moocher leapt out of his basket in the hall and ran to her, forcefully pushing his nose into her hands, convinced she must be telling him off. She patted his head and pulled his ears, crooning, "It's okay, Mooch. It's okay."

"Well, really. There's no need to shriek," Angela said in her usual, patronising, big-sister voice. Liz decided she couldn't possibly be about to slip off this planet, after all.

She kept her cool, although that tone of voice was like a stick in a wasps' nest to her, simply asking, "What do you need, Angela?" And was amazed to see a faint flush of pink colour her sister's face. Bad enough that her immaculate sister would crawl through a dog-flap to see *her*, but if whatever it was could make her blush as well, then there was something seriously astray.

"What I need is, well, is …" Angela started crumbling a custard cream directly onto the table. No, this couldn't possibly be her sister who insisted on a plate if given a boiled sweet. Some alien must have taken over her body.

"What I need," she said again, "is for you to tell me why you didn't let me know that the woman who moved in across the road from you is a famous actress!" She glared at Liz, daring her to yell: "Liar!" But Liz humoured her and let her get away with this evasion for the time being.

"She's not *that* famous, Angela," Liz said. "Anyway, I didn't know straight away. Somebody else had to tell me."

"Even so. You could have phoned me when you did know."

"Why?"

"Because how many famous actresses do you know? She might like to play bridge. Or she might like to be more involved with the local community."

"Hang on a minute," Liz said, "this isn't *your* local community!"

Angela looked at Liz as though she'd made a telling argument. Her mouth opened and shut twice. Then she said, "I really need some help to stop Robert finding out about the affair I'm having."

Liz actually felt the earth judder.

Her eyes forgot to blink. The clock on the mantelpiece lost its tick. She heard a tin can rattling along the street outside, driven by a forlorn wind. A door banged, and banged and banged in her head. Someone's garden gate squeaked in protest. She imagined tumbleweed rolling down a deserted, apocalyptic Malvern Road.

"That does it," Liz croaked. Clearing her throat, she leaned in what she hoped was a threatening manner, towards this person sitting in her breakfast room and said, "Show me some identification! Now!"

"Don't be silly," Angela said.

Liz obviously had to practice her threatening manners. "I simply don't believe this is my sister saying what I thought she just said. Tell you what, say it again. Go on, say it again. I expect it'll come out differently this time." Liz hoped. And prayed.

Angela leaned towards her. Liz listened. Keenly.

Her sister said, "I really need some help to stop Robert finding out about the affair I'm having."

Yes. She *had* said what Liz thought she'd said. "Have you been checked over, recently? Had your middle-age MOT? Are you out of your mind?"

"Plenty of people do it," Angela said.

"Plenty of people do it? Is that the best justification you can come up with for having an affair? I tell you what – there's not plenty of people married to a wonderful man like Robert. What are you playing at? I thought you two were the match made in Paradise." Liz felt tearful. She felt betrayed. She'd thought Angela and Robert and little Johnny were as happy as fleas on an unbrushed dog. As a family they'd seemed to be the epitome of solidarity in a world built on rapidly shifting values.

"Yes, plenty of people do it," Ange insisted. "How can you know? How can you know what goes on behind closed doors?"

"Well, if I can't know then why have you come to me in order to protect what's going on behind your particular closed doors?"

"Because you'd know about these things."

"You've come to me because you reckon I know all about having shady, double-dealing, behind-your-back affairs? Well! Thank. You. Very. Much. Not!"

"All right. All right. Don't you go getting all hoity-toity with me, Elizabeth!" Angela sniffed. "You *are* divorced." She sniffed again. "AND now separated as well." She thought about that and added: "Having got back together again. But not married. And now separated. Again."

Being divorced appeared to mean Liz was a scarlet woman. It seemed as if getting back together again and then getting separated was even worse.

"What!" That was the extent of Liz's outraged vocabulary. Liz knew her sister couldn't help it. In the same way that Angela couldn't help thinking that the art of housewifery was about covering a salmon with quarter slices of cucumber and a thin sliver of stuffed olive for its eye. Or that folding napkins into recognisable cathedrals, or that the art of concocting a flower arrangement with some nuts, cinnamon sticks and a pine cone was of paramount importance in a woman's life, and that if she couldn't cook a decent meal for her husband every evening then she deserved every infidelity she got. She couldn't help it. She was brought up by Their Mother. She really, really couldn't help it.

Of course, Liz had been brought up by Their Mother, too, but she'd spent most of the time believing she was an alien hatchling dropped off in the wrong place, so it didn't do her as much harm as it did Angela. Their Mother had also thought Liz was an alien hatchling dropped off in the wrong place. It was the only thing they'd ever agreed on.

And, there was only one thing to be done in this ridiculous situation, and that was to tell Robert immediately. He would fix it. He would get hold of the adulterous, slimy-git-weasel-turd responsible for Angela's temporary insanity and sort him out. And he would sort out Angela as well. He'd just lay down the law with her and she'd fall into line again and be grateful for it.

Yes, that's what Liz had to do. She had to find out who it was and see Robert straightaway.

"So, anyway, who is the lucky man?" she enquired in a I-don't-really-care-but-I-feel-I-should-show-some-interest sort of way.

Angela's carefully emphasised eyebrows seemed to arch sneeringly at her. "I'm not going to tell you, Liz. You'll run straight off and tell Robert in that touching way you have of believing he can sort everything out."

"Oh my God! How could you think such a thing? Anything you tell me is in full confidence. I'm so offended that you should think that, Angela." Liz jumped up and stalked to stand in noble posture by the mantelpiece.

Rats!

Angela gave her one of those annoying I-know-you-better-than-you-know-yourself looks and Liz was relieved to hear the front door slam. Melanie came bouncing into the breakfast room. She always bounced. Other people would have walked.

"Hello Angela. How are you?" she enquired.

"I'm very well, thank you, Melanie. How are all your affairs going?"

Melanie stopped bouncing. "All my affairs?"

"Yes, I'm hoping to draw on your experience. Of course, I'm only having one paltry little affair, but even so, I'm sure I can pick up some hints and tips from you, dear."

Ohmigod. The sooner Liz could get Angela out of affair-mode the better – and the more likely she was to keep her most reliable lodger.

"Take no notice, Melanie," Liz said. "Angela's drunk."

Melanie automatically looked at the clock above the fireplace.

"Yeah, I know it's early," Liz said. "But she's going through a strange phase."

"Take no notice, Melanie," Angela said. "I'm not drunk. Liz is jealous, that's all."

"Jealous! Of you?" It took Liz a moment to find any more words: "Anyway, surely you don't want to tell everybody. I thought the point was to keep it secret from Robert."

"Yes, but Melanie won't tell."

"She might if you carry on being so damned offensive."

"Don't worry, Liz," Melanie said. "I have nothing to be ashamed of …"

"I'm not saying you do."

"… that's why Angela can't offend me," Melanie finished.

Oh. How nice to be so rational.

"So, Melanie," Angela said, "Any advice?"

Melanie grabbed a handful of biscuits and headed for the

back door. Granny Smart! Liz had forgotten all about her with the advent of Big Sister and her Awful Announcement. It must have been the shock. In fact, her head felt like an empty cave. Yes, it must be shock.

Also, she was fearful that Robert might soon be free. He wasn't supposed to be free.

Liz had always half-fancied Robert. She'd always known her little, totally secret, imaginary indiscretion would come to nothing – because he was happily married to Angela, and because Liz didn't want it to come to anything – not really – it was just a lovely little dream to have *because* it wasn't going to happen, and because he was such a dream-guy, like whoever was playing Mr Darcy these days.

"I'm afraid I can't help you, Angela," Melanie said, halfway out of the house. "I've never been able to do the two-timing thing. I have tried. But I failed miserably. Sorry." And she was gone.

She was only being as honest as Melanie is. In fact, the very word, 'Melanie' could be used instead of the word 'honest' and everyone who knew her would immediately know how very honest that was. But Angela had a look on her face as though someone had rapped her on the shins with a thorn-covered truncheon.

Liz almost felt sorry for her. Until she remembered how unfair her sister was being to Robert and to little Johnny. And then she couldn't quite work out whether she felt anger at Angela or pity for this person who must be a crazy, mixed-up person, given she didn't want Robert to know, so she must want to keep him in the long run. What on earth was she playing at?

Liz's long-held fantasy-fancy faded and disappeared in the harsh glare of her sister's deadlock. Damn. Robert was no longer a safe fantasy. Now she'd have to find someone else to lech over whilst knowing full-well nothing would ever come of it.

Angela straightened up in her seat. Liz tensed. Rightly, as it turned out.

"You know, Liz," she said. "It's only as your loving big sister that I say this, but you must start to do more exercise and eat less rubbish." She leaned forward, picked up the plate and flicked the biscuits on to the floor. A volcanic eruption exploded under the table and a great, black, hairy tornado flew out and ricocheted around trying to stuff another biscuit into his mouth before he'd finished the one he already had. This tactic resulted in great gobs of half-eaten gunge and gouts of crumb being sprayed around the room.

Angela shrieked and jumped back. Her chair fell over and hit the floor with an ear-ringing crack.

Liz yelled. "Angela! You know damn well no-one feeds my dog without first asking me. Biscuits are bad for him. They'll rot his teeth and make him fat!"

"Better him than you," she yelled back.

Well, she'd walked into that one, Liz thought. She didn't attempt an answer. She was too busy trying to collect as many biscuits as she could before the cookie-wolf got them and sent them to canine bellyland.

Liz was dismayed to find herself wheezing a tad with the bending over. She remembered how difficult it had been to roll up under the table and breathe at the same time. Maybe Angela was right. Angela *was* right. Liz had put on weight and not even noticed. She would have to do something about that, or how would she be able to hide from unwelcome callers in the future?

Melanie had appeared, no doubt attracted by the sound of furniture being thrown about. She helped restore order. Moocher slunk out to his basket looking extremely pleased with himself.

"I'll take myself off, then," Angela said. "Thanks for the tea." She, also, had a curiously pleased expression on her face. What the hell?

"You off to see lover-boy-git then?" Liz felt compelled to ask, angry for Robert and still hoping she might find out enough to give him a clue.

"At least *I* have a lover," Angela said.

Ooh. Nasty. "*And* a husband, don't forget," Liz said.

"If you weren't so chubby, you might be able to get yourself a lover!"

"I might. If I wanted one," Liz said.

"You're jealous," Angela said.

"Don't be silly."

"Pack it in, girls," Melanie said.

They packed it in and Liz saw Angela off her premises without another word, but the way Angela looked her up and down made her feel like a side of beef hanging in a butcher's walk-in freezer. Maybe she meant a side of pig. Unfortunately, her sister was right, though. Liz had to do something about it, and she would.

Tomorrow, probably.

Feeling like an overweight bruiser, she practiced a suitably menacing expression in front of the mirror. This wasn't difficult, as she imagined she was facing Angela and her bit of muscle-fluff. Then she went off to collect some rents. She managed the houses on both sides of her own and sometimes the tenants in the one belonging to her old neighbour, Lydia, were not as forthcoming with the dosh as she would like. Being one to look on the bright side, she thought her excess poundage might come in handy in such a situation. It might add more weight to her demands.

Ordinarily, she knew she would have gone off chortling at the pun, but at the moment Liz thought she must still be in shock about having a granny in her shed and having a more-than-ordinarily insane sister. Flab, or shock – it all helped, and she extracted the rents with hardly the need for a snarl.

Being on a roll, she decided to get the rent from Philippe, the tenant in her other old neighbour's house on the other side of hers, although she never needed to snarl at him. He was always amenable. Too amenable for her taste. She preferred her men to fight back. So, despite him being a wealthy restaurateur who lived in the 5-bedroomed house all by himself, he wasn't on her list of 'possible men'. Although, to be fair, her 'possible men' list was very short these days.

Through the kitchen window she spotted Philippe out in his garden. It was as she went out the back door to speak to him that she suddenly wondered exactly why Angela had inflicted herself on Liz in such a dramatic way. She wasn't *that* keen on her, and she hadn't, in fact, asked Liz to do anything, say anything or *not* do or say anything. Liz couldn't understand why Angela had told her about her cupcake lover at all.

She must be Up To Something.

Chapter Seven
(Mapmaker)

Mapmaker savoured another sip of malt. He didn't usually drink alcohol so early in the day, but he felt the need of something familiar and reliable in his system. As soon as he'd made the entry into his journal and updated his map, he would have a snooze and sleep it all off. It had been a heavy day.

He'd not only been working hard, but he'd gone for a five-in-the-morning breakfast to a local café he'd been delighted to discover opened at such unsocial hours.

However, much to his dismay, he'd seen someone he recognised as a neighbour approach his table to collar him. His initial apprehension had proved wildly incorrect. She turned out to be highly entertaining, and informative. He'd had a hard job trying to keep up with her, and envied her the energy which seemed to shine from her.

Now that he was back at home, he was anxious to record the nuggets of information she'd bestowed on him before he forgot any of the details.

Mapmaker looked forward to meeting her again now he knew she haunted that café, the only one on the Gloucester Road which didn't have fancy coffee machines that snorted and wheezed, and tea bags on strings, or saucers to put a mug on; the only café he'd found in years that still had sugar in glass dispensers with a chrome spout, and plastic squeezy tomato and brown sauce bottles on the table, not to mention being open at that premature hour of the morning.

Mapmaker fished the map from its special drawer. He uncapped his ink pen. He liked to use his fountain pen for this task.

To him it signified that this job was that much more imperative than any other. It also meant that he was very careful not to make any mistakes, because it made such a mess if he did, and then he'd have to start again.

He needed to focus like he'd never focused before in order to keep the outside world from getting in. As long as he could concentrate really hard on all the little things he did, he could keep himself stable and safe.

He lowered the gold nib to the parchment. In italic lettering he filled the gap on the map of Malvern Road for number 22:

Enid Holdsworthy, 80+, cat.

Pushing the chart to one side, he pulled over the journal and wrote:

Number twenty-two: Enid Holdsworthy (owner) – chief informant, 80+, lives alone, collector-of-stories, black cat called Whitson. Gardens, front and back – overgrown. House neglected. Sleeps during day; roams at night; has breakfast in Greg's Grub at 5am.

He could now record what she'd told him – if he could get it sorted out in his mind. Mapmaker stared at his notes and then, on a bit of recycled paper he sketched it out in an attempt to get his head around the various relationships for number nine, Malvern Road, Liz Houston's house.

After a while he reached for the map and in the relevant space for number nine, he wrote:

Liz Houston, 30+, 2 x lodgers, dog.

In the journal he wrote:

Number nine: Liz Houston (owner) – accountant, 30+, landlady with lodgers. House needs work; uncleaned windows. Dog = Moocher = Border collie.

Lodgers: Melanie (known for honesty), 30+; Wayne – tax specialist, 30+ (Melanie and Wayne an item?)

Frequent visitors: Hugh (Houston?) – Liz's ex-husband; Liz's sister.

Then he remembered the small, powder-blue car with alloy wheels he'd just seen outside number nine. He was pretty certain that was the sister. He filled in the other details about Liz's sister that Enid had given him: Angela Rowbottom was a wannabee social climber; she had a son, Johnny, and a husband, Robert.

Mapmaker had got the impression from Enid that the two sisters didn't get on very well. There was also a mother, but Enid hadn't seen her in Malvern Road recently although she did used to visit, so maybe Liz had fallen out with her.

He carried on with his notes in the miscellaneous column: Liz's back garden backs onto the garden belonging to Mrs Noakes who has a tortoise called Tinkerbell that is always getting out.

He paused thinking about Enid's uninhibited mirth whilst telling him about the huge dog flap Liz Houston had in her back door and how she made potential lodgers prove they could get in and out of the house by limboing through the dog flap before she allowed them to become lodgers.

He smiled again, thinking of it. He was going to have watch out for Enid's fertile imagination! No one would do such a thing!

Apparently, Liz Houston's windows being filthy was a security measure – her theory was that if the windows were so dirty you couldn't see through them then obviously the occupants of the house were not just lazy, but broke as well. Therefore, burglars wouldn't be at all interested.

He went back to making notes – the back garden contains an 8x10 foot shed, small pond, big apple tree; alley down the side of the house between number nine and number eleven; front garden = shrubbery.

Mapmaker couldn't see how Liz Houston could bear to live in a house with so many other people in it, although, at least at the moment, there were only two others, but also what appeared to be a succession of people coming and going – he shuddered at the thought and glanced appreciatively around his own room, glad it was empty but for him. And his chair. Not having to deal with other people gave him welcome time out from the world.

Going back to the map he noted that the police, according to Enid, made quite a few visits to number nine …

Chapter Eight
(A neighbour's problem)

"Good afternoon," Liz said. She peered over the wall into next
door's garden. It was almost as messy as hers, which was a relaxed
anything-goes sort of garden, not a regimented one like next door's
used to be before Philippe moved in.

In fact, Moocher was doing his, I'm-a-gold-prospector-on-
the-Klondike bit at that moment, digging like fury – just to prove
how relaxed her garden was. He stuck his dirt-encrusted nose in
the air when he heard her voice.

It flashed across her mind to wonder if Granny Smart could
see and hear her, but Liz knew she had to ignore it. She had to
pretend she didn't know there was a granny there at all.

"Good afternoon!" Liz said again.

Philippe flinched but looked up from his minute inspection
of the ground he stood on, frown furrows still deep on his
forehead. "Hello, Liz. Who says it's good?"

"Ooh, grumpy. I didn't say it **was** good. I was **wishing** you
a good afternoon."

"Humphff."

"Not a good time to visit, then?"

"Oh, do you want the rent? Why not come round and have
a coffee while you're at it. I've got some of those Italian biscotti
you like."

Mmmm … Philippe's coffee. Philippe's biscuits. Liz
clambered over the wall and then hauled herself back again to put
Moocher's old beer crate in position so he could come over too.

They sat in some grandeur in Philippe's front room with

tiny cups of very strong coffee and yummy almond biscuits to dunk in it.

"What's up, then?" Liz asked. They'd already dealt with the rent.

"My windows keep getting broken," he said.

Liz turned to look at his bay windows.

"Not these windows," he said. "The restaurant windows."

"Which restaurant?"

"All of them. That's the point. If it was only the restaurant on Park Street, or only the one in Westbury, or only the one on Whiteladies Road, then I would accept it as being par for the course. But it's all of them. The first time it happened was a while ago. It is a thing that does happen so I didn't think anything of it, but just in the last couple of days there've been a couple more."

"What about everyone else? Are all your mates' restaurant windows getting broken?"

Philippe shrugged. It was one of those fabulous, sinuous shrugs that quite took Liz's mind off the problem. So, when he said, "No more than usual," it took a second or two to work out what the conversation was about.

She took a deep breath and reminded herself that she didn't fancy him anyway. She just wished he wouldn't shrug around her.

"You think it's personal?" she asked.

"It looks like it." There was that shrug again. No wonder females aged between four and ninety-seven got all coy and flustered around him. Except her, of course. If the window-smashing was personal, it was probably some cuckolded husband or dumped boyfriend.

"It does seem odd that it's all three restaurants," she agreed. "What are you doing about it?"

"I just keep getting the windows replaced and hope that it stops soon. I can't think what else to do."

"Anything nicked?"

"No. Just the windows broken. They don't appear to be entering the restaurants at all."

"When does it happen?"

"Must be early hours of the morning."

"What about keeping watch for a few nights and seeing if you can catch them?"

He shrugged. (Yikes!) "Seems a bit impractical, Liz. There are three places …"

"How often is it happening?"

"About one window a week."

"Good grief! What do the police say?"

"Not a lot. They're 'keeping an eye on the premises'."

"There's enough people between these three houses, Philippe," Liz said, gesturing behind her to take in her own house and the one the other side of it, too. "And you'll have other friends. Surely, we can mount a watch for a night or two. Worth a try, don't you think?"

"That's very good of you, Liz, but it seems too much of an imposition."

"Nah, it isn't. Not if you're going to supply us with flasks of expresso, loads of biscotti and maybe the odd pizza or two." Philippe, although a somewhat reserved character, had proved to be very generous in the past when it came to his neighbours' projects, sponsorships and the like. Liz was sure his neighbours would be happy to reciprocate.

He hesitated, but somehow Liz didn't think it was the thought of the supplies. She thought it was more likely to be the idea of getting that involved with all the lodgers of the other two houses. He wasn't a very outgoing person, and maybe he found it a little daunting.

"Done!" he said and held out his hand. She took it and they shook on the agreement. His smile was worth it. Now all she had to do was round up all the people she'd volunteered for the effort.

Chapter Nine
(Mapmaker)

Mapmaker considered the records he was keeping on his
neighbours – he wasn't sure why he needed to record if someone
owned their own house or rented it, but he'd always rather have
more information than not enough.

He had deliberately chosen to use a loose-leaf journal so
that if he had to change anything, he could do it without making
too much of a mess. He didn't like mess. He liked to work in a tidy
and methodical fashion.

He checked his notes for the house either side of Liz
Houston's. There was just a low brick wall between nine and
seven. And between nine and eleven. He wondered if all the back
gardens on Malvern Road were only accessible through the houses.
He wondered if that information was useful. He sighed and noted
down about the walls. It would seem that, if required, someone
could access the rear of other properties merely by jumping over
those low walls. They wouldn't all be like that, though. And some
would have trellis on top of the walls so it wouldn't be easy
without creating an obvious trail of devastation.

He needed confirmation of the information he had for the
occupants of number seven. According to Enid they were all
lodgers – Liz Houston managed the house and its tenants for the
owner. Enid had entertained him with the story of the owner who
was, apparently, a robber of old, fond of disguises. He'd had to
escape when he'd been found out. He had fled out of the back of
his property, through the gardens out there, and away. No one had
heard of him since. He wondered if that was true or whether it was

another example of Enid's colourful imagination.

At number eleven, now owned by Liz's ex, Hugh Houston, lived Philippe, the guy with the restaurants – two, or maybe three restaurants. It had a scruffy front garden, although within it was a tiny, dead square lawn. He didn't know about the back garden.

Apparently, Hugh Houston had bought the house fairly recently at a time when he and Liz were making a go of it together. That attempt appeared to have not lasted very long.

Mapmaker didn't know where Hugh was now, but if he was no longer one of Mapmaker's neighbours then he wasn't relevant.

His Malvern Road map was depressingly empty. There were so many other houses about which he had no clue what was what and who was who. He didn't like the feeling of not knowing who was around him. It made him anxious. He would have to crack on and find out!

He half-turned to stare out of the window, not that he could see much from where he was sitting. Absently, he ran his fingers across the carved words in his chair. He shouldn't have avoided Liz Houston. He was going to have to be more sociable, more involved with the locals. It was hard for him to do it naturally. He'd always been engaged in his own world; his own imagination and creativity were more than enough company for him.

His mother always used to say he had his head in the clouds. She never said it unkindly, but she did worry about him crossing the road and climbing trees more than most mothers because she knew he was not necessarily particularly present when crossing the road or up that tree. He was more likely to be in Avalacia, one of his made-up worlds, or riding Boschinata, his dragon crossed with a minotaur-like steed, across the Plains of Ash. The road in the present, or the tree, would barely register on his consciousness.

And yet, somehow, he had survived, possibly *because* of his imagination, and that was quite apart from the fact that his imagination more than paid his bills now.

But maybe it was time he tried to be more present in *this* world, in Malvern Road in particular. He was going to try to come completely down to earth. It was about time!

Chapter Ten
(Stakeout)

Liz rallied the troops more easily than she expected. Considering that slouching around in cars keeping an eye on a pane of glass wasn't the top of anyone's list for a scintillating time on a Saturday night, it was gratifying the number of people happy to help.

Long after dark had fallen, she was trying to get comfortable in her car. It wasn't a very comfortable car to slouch in.

Laurel, in the passenger seat, was one of the tenants next door and had a reputation for knowing a little about a lot. Liz was finding out how true that was.

"Did you know that the expression 'stakeout' comes from the idea of staking out a goat to attract a lion?"

Laurel's hoarse whisper jerked Liz back from a land dangerously close to the marshes of slumber. "No," she whispered back. "I didn't know that. What I do know is that if you carry on whispering as much as you have been, your throat is going to wear out."

But Laurel ignored her. "Doesn't make sense though, does it?" she said. "We're not trying to attract a lion. We're not trying to attract anyone. We don't want anyone to see us. That's why we're being all clandestine and hiding in the car. So, why does this word for surveillance come from staking out a goat to attract a lion?"

"Good point," Liz agreed wearily, knowing that if she tried to simply not answer at all, she would merely be asked again. And again. "It doesn't make sense."

"No, you're right. It doesn't make sense. None of it makes

sense. The word 'stake' for a start is to do with sums of money, booty, gambling, maybe for sticking in a vampire's heart, or for tethering goats."

Despite her best intentions, Liz lost it. "For God's sake, Laurel, can't you keep quiet for a while? Not even for a short while?"

The answer was immediate. And pertinent. "No, I can't," she replied. "If I kept quiet, I'd fall asleep. You'd fall asleep, too. It's only me keeping us awake. As it is, Moocher's already asleep."

They looked over their shoulders at the back seat. There was Moocher, their standard bearer, their mascot, their furry hero – flat out. He breathed heavily, but quietly. Every now and then he twitched. In his dreams he was probably on a rescue mission to save the world and impress that pretty little Border collie he'd been fancying just around the corner from them. Fat lot of good he'd be if they saw the window-smasher. There wouldn't be time to wake him before the villain got away.

"It must be nice being a dog, don't you think?" Liz said. "Not a care in the world. No worries about a roof and meals and paying the bills. Well, if they're in an okay place, I suppose. If not, maybe not. No, maybe not. Anyway, I won't be falling asleep any time soon. I'm dying for a pee."

"So am I actually. What do you think people do when they're on a stakeout and they want a pee?"

"Dunno. Maybe they have those bags they strap to their legs and just let the pee all hang out into that."

"Yeuch! You mean they have a catheter."

"I can't say I'd thought it through that thoroughly," Liz said. "Maybe they just get out of their car and pee behind it."

"But anybody could come along!" Laurel looked horrified.

"Perhaps, if it's your job to do stakeouts all the time, you don't drink for a few hours before your shift and then you don't need to pee at all."

"Well, it's not my job and I have to pee. What are we going to do?"

"We can't leave. What if the window-smasher turned up just when we left?"

"I think the espresso might have been a mistake. I don't think coffee should be drunk if you're on a stakeout without any pee mechanism."

"On reflection, I think you're right. At the time it seemed like a good idea to keep us awake."

"It *is* keeping us awake. Full bladders usually do. Any of those biscotti left?"

"No."

"Any pizza left?"

"No."

"It's no good. I *have* to pee."

"Trouble is, I don't think it's a good idea for either of us to go off on our own and leave the other one behind," Liz said. "He'd be sure to turn up then. So, it's both of us or neither of us."

"Oh, surely you can't think whoever it is – he or she – would harm us, do you? They're only smashing windows. That's a far cry from beating up stake-outers."

"I just don't think we can be too careful, Laurel. They could be capable of anything. How would we know?"

"For a start, they're giving me a hand. Sort-of."

"That's a strange thing to say. How are they giving you a hand by depriving you of sleep and stretching your bladder further than it should be stretched?"

"You're forgetting my profession," Laurel said.

Criminy. Laurel wanted her to think as well, even in the dead of night. So, Liz gave it some thought and finally realised. "Ohmigod. You mean Philippe is giving you the work of re-painting the windows every time they're smashed?"

"Yup. That's it exactly. He has to have them newly signwritten every time. Why shouldn't it be me that does it as it's my job and we're neighbours and we, er, we know each other?"

Laurel tailed off lamely enough to alert Liz's something's-up antennae and she was on to it like a St Bernard down a helter-skelter. "What do you mean, '*know each other*'?"

For the first time in hours Laurel actually fell silent which merely excited Liz's interest even more.

"Come on, Laurel. What did you mean? You can't say that much and then no more."

"Oh, well. I suppose it doesn't really matter now. Philippe and I had a thing going for a while." Liz watched as Laurel briefly dropped her face into her hands before straightening up again, her hands now clenched on her knees. "But it ended," she whispered.

An extraordinarily sharp sadness filled the car. Moocher whimpered in his sleep. Liz felt uncomfortable. "I didn't know you and the Master of Sexy Shrugs had been an item," she said, rather feebly.

"That's because no-one knew. No-one was supposed to know. *He* didn't want anyone to know. I expect he's like that with everyone so that no-one ever knows what a total bastard he is!"

Oh, dear. Liz felt even more uncomfortable and said the first thing that came to mind. "If he's such a total bastard how come he's giving you the jobs, then? Why would he do that if he just wanted his wicked way with you when he isn't getting his wicked way anymore?"

"Shhh ... Someone comes," Laurel suddenly whispered. "But, don't forget. No-one knows about me and him and I don't want anyone to know."

"Okay," Liz whispered so softly she couldn't even hear it herself.

They sank further down into their seats. Liz tried to stop breathing. It seemed so noisy. She was also conscious that any movement made fabrics rubbing against each other startlingly loud in the night. Laurel wore a particularly loud jacket. But now that the time had come, now that the window-smasher approached, silence as thick as a lorry-load of foam mattresses reigned and they waited for what would occur.

And Moocher farted.

Ohmigod. Here they were in a hermetically sealed car and her dog had just farted. They would never come out of this alive. Liz tried even harder not to breathe, but that didn't last long. Then she did breathe and had to try very hard not to choke and gasp and make any dying noises to attract the window-smasher's attention. She heard a strangled cough from Laurel's direction and that did her in entirely. She started to laugh. She found that trying to keep the mirth silent merely produced the most porcine-sounding snorts which in turn fuelled the desire to laugh even more.

She looked up and saw three heavily jowled canine faces peering into the car. They appeared transfixed as though they'd discovered a cage full of two-legged cats. Liz could see the whites all the way around six irises as their eyes seemed to grow larger and larger. Then she saw one of them turn to another and say something and that was when she realised that it's true that owners grow like their pets, and only one of these creatures was really a dog.

Maybe it was expresso-induced delirium or the lack of sleep, but that finished her off. There was no way her bladder would be able to keep everything in one place under that sort of strain. She just *had* to have a pee. Laurel's hysterical cackles bursting out through her fingers didn't help.

Liz sat upright, waved at the startled faces, started the car up and zoomed home. They raced into the house. Liz ran upstairs to the bathroom, Laurel and Moocher carried straight on through the house – Laurel to the downstairs loo, Moocher through the dog flap and into the garden. No doubt with a quick woof to Granny Smart while he was out there.

They used the facilities, rushed back out into the night, leapt into the car, rocketed back to their post again and found Philippe, sitting on the pavement surrounded by shards of glass, picking at an enormous box of chocolates.

He looked up as they approached and offered them the box. "I brought these to thank you for all your efforts," he said.

They'd deserted their post, and in their miniscule, barely-worth-mentioning absence, the window-smasher had come to call.

Chapter Eleven
(Mapmaker)

It was Saturday night and Mapmaker was looking forward to having a lie-in the following day. He was tired. Malvern Road wasn't yet familiar enough for him to feel at home. He couldn't relax.

Plus, he was working hard at his business. It was going through quite an expansion – the kind of expansion that, if he could keep it together and get where he intended to go, he could back off a bit and virtually let it run itself. But he needed to keep on top of it for now. So, he couldn't relax on the work front, either.

He pulled out the map and the journal and stared at them until his vision blurred.

It was his mother who first called him 'Mapmaker'. When small, he'd make maps of the house he was in, sometimes the room; he'd make maps of the garden, and the shops they went to; he'd created mind maps before he even knew they were a thing. They'd started small, got bigger and more complex, went through a phase of becoming board games and ended up becoming even more multifaceted video games which now gave him a good living.

The only other significant woman he'd ever had in his life, Sarah, didn't like the term, 'Mapmaker'. He suspected it sounded too basic for her. He also suspected she'd have tried to find any alternative to anything that had originated with his mother. She'd tried to call him, 'Cartographer' for a while. Of course, that wasn't going to work. It was inaccurate and stupid, and didn't slide off the tongue so smoothly.

Sarah.

It was a long time since he'd thought of her. He realised

this might be the first time he had thought of her – or the loss of her – without feeling down.

He was pleased about that. He'd moped enough. He reached for the notes he'd made when he saw Enid. He'd already transcribed most of them, but there was the house on the other side of Liz Houston's, too, which he knew was full of lodgers.

Number seven – Laurel, Danny, Jason …

He knew there were more, but as it was a rapidly changing population, Enid wasn't sure of the others. When he'd asked, she had said she'd find out, seemingly pleased that she had a 'assignment' to fulfil. He hadn't told her why he wanted the information – then again, she hadn't asked. She was very much a 'live and let live' person. He liked that.

He capped his pen, but then realised there was another gap he could fill in – uncapped his pen and wrote: number twenty-nine – Mapmaker – 30+, tenant in first floor flat, video game entrepreneur.

Chapter Twelve
(Tallulah Towel)

Liz heard the dog-flap do its 'clatter-thunk' back into place. Moocher was right by her side as they descended from their attic kingdom into the lower domains of the house. He was doing his usual, I'll-push-you-down-the-stairs-if-you-don't-go-faster, thing.

So, she knew it wasn't him who had either entered or left the house via the dog-flap in the back door. It must have been the Smart Granny. Liz knew everyone else was out.

It seemed so strange to be sharing living space with someone and yet not to acknowledge her. Still, that was what she wanted.

The stakeout had been abandoned a few hours ago. Some people had to go to work, some to classes, and Liz was supposed to be doing some accounts, but had instead attempted to snatch an hour or two's slumber after a – mostly – wakeful night. That hadn't worked, however – she'd merely spent the time rolling around her bed hot with shame for deserting her post and allowing the window-smasher to do his – or her – thing. To make it worse, much worse, Philippe hadn't even shouted or complained – he'd merely pressed the chocolates on them and called up a glazier. Liz had been forced to scoff the lot for comfort (Laurel hadn't wanted any). If Liz had felt badly about it, Laurel had looked grey and ill.

Liz determined they would stake out the restaurants again tonight. She'd learned some lessons, though. This time – no expresso – in fact, nothing to drink at all.

She'd reached the bottom stair when the doorbell rang. She was just there so she opened the door without even thinking about it.

And there was Tallulah. Oh, no! She'd have to stop all this opening the door just because the bell rings thing!

Liz stared at her neighbour and wondered what on earth to say. She couldn't let her in. She knew that just a couple of days ago she would have let her in without a thought. But that was before she knew about Granny Smart. They say knowledge is power. Liz wasn't so sure. Sometimes it's disabling.

"Hello Liz," Tallulah Smart said. "How are you? I thought I'd pop over for a visit. Haven't seen you for yonks. Absolutely yonks."

Yonks??? Who says that anymore? "Um, how nice," Liz said, and automatically, even though she didn't want to, stood back to let her in. She must have called in before now while Granny Smart was in residence. Yes, sometimes ignorance is definitely bliss. Tallulah made a beeline for the breakfast room.

Liz hung back. "Oh, er, Tallulah, do come and sit in the front room." She beckoned invitingly.

"We always sit in the breakfast room," her neighbour said. Correctly.

"I know," Liz said, as confidently as possible. "But today it seems warmer in the front room."

Tallulah gave Liz a strange look, but obediently made her way into the front room, which was so cold, her goose pimples must have been jumping for their thermal underwear.

Moocher stuck his nose in the back of Liz's leg instead of greeting their visitor. Usually he showed massive enthusiasm for anything that moved. But not this time. This time he clattered off down the corridor and out into the garden. Presumably to warn Granny Smart that the enemy was in the house.

Tallulah settled herself on the sofa and Liz rushed out to the kitchen to get coffee. She was worried sick Granny Smart might come back in through the dog flap not knowing her daughter-in-law was here.

Even though Moocher had already gone out there, it seemed like a good idea to warn her.

Liz went to the windows, but they face the wrong way. The back door creaks and groans, except in August, so she couldn't open it without the whole street knowing. She took the only option left to her. She got on all fours on the floor and stuck her head out through the dog flap.

At that angle, though, she still couldn't see around the corner of the house to the shed. She had to put her hands out as well, flat on the ground, and putting her weight on them, she pulled herself forward a bit. Then she could see the shed, but she couldn't see any sign of life. Not in the shed anyway. Unfortunately, Danny, who lived next door, spotted her. He was outside minding his own business, having a quiet smoke and some deep thought, when he noticed her with her upper body leaning out of the dog flap. He looked surprised, threw his cigarette butt on the ground – she'd get him for that – and rushed over to the garden wall in between them.

"No, no," Liz whispered as loudly as she could, before he said anything and drew attention to her. But he still opened his mouth to say something. Liz flapped her hand at him in an attempt to stop him speaking, forgetting that she needed that hand on the ground for stability. Too late – she'd lost that corner support and fell, face first onto the concrete, putting her front teeth through her lip like she used to for a pastime when she was little. So, of course, when she looked up again, she could feel blood trickling down her chin from her shredded lip. Danny looked horrified and opened his mouth again. Liz gave up on subtle and simply hissed, "Shut up, Danny. Go away," and glared at him so hard her eyeballs felt as though they'd solidified.

Obediently he shut his mouth, looked furtive, and dived through his own back door. Liz knew he was still lurking just behind the window, watching, though.

All this had attracted Moocher's attention. Liz had forgotten he was out there. He thought this was a delightful new game. He bounded over and slobbered all over her face.

Liz shut her eyes in time, but nearly choked in her efforts not to yell at him. She rapidly backed through the dog-flap and, desperate to get his slimy drool off her skin, she rose from the floor, her eyes still shut to prevent dog spit getting in them, her hands outstretched, and fumbled for a towel.

She grabbed a handful of fabric that didn't feel right. It didn't feel like a towel. And it wasn't. It turned out to be Tallulah's blouse. That was a shock. For both of them. Opening one eye to a slit she spotted a dishcloth, grabbed it up and scrubbed Moocher's creepy leavings off her face, no doubt smearing blood around the place while she did so.

"What did you think you were doing?" Tallulah demanded. She brushed ineffectually at her silk, designer shirt.

Liz was afraid her muddy handprints wouldn't come off that in a hurry.

"Sorry about that," Liz said. "I was looking for a towel."

"I didn't mean that. I meant, what were you doing on your knees half out the dog-flap? Who were you talking to?"

"I was…" Liz's mouth locked up as her brain went into a frenzy. "I was looking to see if it was raining." Some useless frenzy that turned out to be.

"Why didn't you look out the window?"

"Too dirty." Oh, this was getting better and better.

Tallulah even checked.

"You're right," she said. "But even so – I've only just got here, so why did you want to know if it was raining? And who were you talking to?"

Before her stupid mouth could say, 'Because I have washing out,' which, of course, would make her visitor rush out and check, Liz said, "If you must know, I was having a private word with Moocher. I only said that about the rain because I didn't want you to think I was cracking up." There, that told her!

Tallulah gave her such a strange look! Then she busied herself in Liz's kitchen and put her kettle on. She looked for some biscuits. She'd been over often enough to know the drill.

They settled in the front room and made a few polite noises at each other.

"I was wondering, Liz," Tallulah said eventually. "I was wondering if you would baby-sit for me?"

Ohmigod. Baby-sit. The Spawn of Satan. No, no, not me. Please.

"I can't," Liz said. "I'm out. Sorry."

"I haven't told you when I want you," Tallulah said, a trifle tartly Liz thought.

"Well, whenever it is. I can't do it. I have a lot of work on at the moment. Sorry."

"Please, Liz. It's very important. It's tomorrow night. Only for a couple of hours. And the children asked for you especially."

Liz looked all around the front room, desperate for a plausible excuse to erupt from the aspidistra, or a flying brick to knock her unconscious so she'd be in hospital tomorrow night. But nothing showed.

"Now listen, Telly. Let's be brutal about this. You know I'm a hopeless babysitter. Last time was a disaster. No self-respecting mother would leave her kids with me." There – get out of that one! Liz barely restrained a smirk.

"Oh, it wasn't *that* bad. Marcus's hangover didn't last *that* long, and Sophie's bruises faded before anyone saw them. You're being too hard on yourself. Really. I'm prepared to give you the benefit of the doubt and let you have another go." Her smile could only be described as seraphic.

Tallulah thought she had Liz where she wanted her. She was right. Liz wanted to tell her unwelcome neighbour she would rather stab herself repeatedly in the eye with a rusty scalpel than baby-sit the Brats from Hell, but she didn't have the nerve.

She was also conscious that if it ever came out that Granny Smart, automatic child minder, was living in her garden shed at a time when Tallulah was desperate for a baby-sitter it could go badly for all concerned.

So she asked, "What time?"

"Seven o'clock," Tallulah said with an annoyingly satisfied little smile as though she'd known Liz's dilemma all along.

"I'll be there," Liz said.

That was all her neighbour needed. Abandoning half a mug of coffee she leapt out of her chair. "You're a darling. You're a star. See you then." And she was off so fast Liz didn't have time to see her out.

Chapter Thirteen
(Mapmaker)

Mapmaker was up earlier than he liked to be, but he'd been driven out of bed by the need to closely inspect his map and journal. He had to work out where he needed to make enquiries next.

He arranged them on his desk and then switched on his coffee machine to pre-heat it. He unscrewed the lid from his coffee jar and took a deep breath of the contents. Lovely – a lungful of coffee aroma. He pulled the filter from the machine's holder, emptied it of used grounds and filled it with fresh coffee, taking care not to spill any. Then he used his stainless-steel tamper to press the coffee down. It had a very satisfying weight about it, the tamper. He was pleased with it. He wiped it off and replaced it in its red velvet bag. It was part of the ritual.

He attached the filter to the machine, made sure the cup was under it and switched on. He was pleased with this machine, too. It made the kind of noises that would convince the person gasping for his caffeine fix to feel it was taking the making of it very seriously indeed.

He patted it. He patted his coffee machine. He was conscious while he was doing it that he was patting an inanimate object. He'd always done it. Ever since his mother told him to treat his video game machine more kindly. "If you treat things well, they'll treat you well," she'd said. She'd said it in passing as she moved through the sitting room in which he'd been battering his controller on the ground because he kept losing the game. She'd never said it again. But then, he'd taken to patting or stroking everything after that. And it seemed to work! He had many fewer printers break down on him than other people in the office. His car had never broken down on him while other people were always needing to be towed home or have them repaired by the side of the road. He often patted the dashboard and told it what a nice, good, reliable car it was.

He didn't do any of this cooing, patting or stroking of his

phone, computer, sound system or car when other people were around. He was fully aware what it might look like. But he'd got to the stage where he knew he had to do it or all his machines would malfunction. Worse than that, because it had started with his mother, if he stopped doing it, she would die. He just knew it.

Sitting at his desk, coffee at the ready, he started to record the inhabitants at number twelve. He couldn't believe he hadn't filled it in before. After all, the whole sorry story had been all over the papers and the television, on the radio, all over the online news streams for days at the time, some weeks ago.

The influential lawyer, Graham Smart (33), known not-so-affectionately by many as, 'Grabber', and his wife, the famous soap actress, Tallulah Smart (33), often known as 'Telly', lived there with two children, Marcus (11) and Sophie (12). The children were Grabber's but not Telly's.

Also, living at number twelve was another member of the Smart family – Grabber's mother, locally known as 'the Smart Granny'. She was 53 according to the newspapers. Everyone knew about this family because Granny Smart had gone missing and it had been splashed across all the tabloids. The odd thing was that the granny had gone missing a couple of weeks before the tearful appeals on the TV, almost as if they weren't going to bother until something had made them.

The actual timeline of events had been glossed over on the TV appearance, but every other factor for an appeal was present: they would start to say something, and then stop, apparently overcome with emotion. Mapmaker had watched the whole performance with deep cynicism.

Someone had seen her somewhere but when they got there she'd gone.

The grandchildren were crying themselves to sleep every night.

The dog was missing her. Dog? What dog? They didn't have a dog. He knew it, but checked his notes anyway. No. No dog.

The whole family was devastated. They didn't know where to look. All they could do was hope that, one day, she would walk back through the front door.

There had been no contact with her and they were

launching the appeal in the hope that someone had some information. If so, they were urged to come forward with it.

The last time they saw her was at Sophie's birthday party. The photo showed her at an earlier birthday party when Sophie was a lot smaller. Mapmaker wondered if they didn't have a more recent picture. She was happy with her grandchild on her lap, supervising a lovely tea for twelve children, having fun. They'd already made plans to go to the barn owl conservation place next week, and then to the open gardens cream tea day, so they knew she hadn't wanted to leave them.

There was a pause in the play-acting at this point for a few touching pictures of grandmother with grandchildren. No dog, though.

Now, if they actually had a dog and that had gone missing, Mapmaker fancied their desolation at its disappearance would be a great deal more genuine. He chided himself for his scepticism. Briefly.

Because of the perfectly happy family life Granny Smart had been living, Grabber and Telly couldn't believe she had willingly gone off and found a new life for herself somewhere else; they feared that some harm had come to her.

When last seen she was wearing a tweed skirt, and a silk blouse. She was not dressed for this inclement weather.

And finally, poor Granny Smart – she suffers from dementia and she may appear confused.

Enid, when asked her opinion, had given this statement short shrift: "Just the fact that she's disappeared proves that to be a lie. You'd have to be demented to stay there!" It was apparent that she had no good opinion of her near-neighbours.

So, she was missing for about a fortnight before Grabber and Telly bothered to do something. Mapmaker wondered why.

Not only that, but he knew where Granny Smart was – Enid had told him – but he knew a lot of stuff that wasn't his business. He also knew that she appeared to be absolutely fine where she was, possibly even enjoying life more than she had at her previous residence.

If she wasn't fine, he would feel compelled to do something about it, although didn't know what, but he didn't have to know what at the moment. So, he wouldn't be doing anything about it now. He was puzzled about that situation, though, no matter how hard he tried to be indifferent. He had the sort of mind that wanted to know how everything worked and why stuff happened – so he might enquire about some of it. Just to make sure that she was, indeed, absolutely fine.

Chapter Fourteen
(Ghost-lodger)

No sooner had Tallulah slammed the door behind her than it opened again.

"Liz," Danny said, appearing in the front room doorway. He eyed her split lip, but politely said nothing. "Why are you sitting in here? It's cold." He shivered, stuffed his hands in his pockets, and found the cigarette end he'd just stowed away. It obviously still smouldered. He yelped, pulled it out and pinched the end of it until it expired. He then replaced it where he could find it next time he wanted a few puffs.

The little incident reminded her so strongly of a lodger she used to have, Simon, that, for a moment, she was transported back to those heady days of chaos when he was around. The days of stalkers, part-time muggers, fingers in the fridge, bricks through the window – she missed them.

No, she didn't. It was him she missed. Not all the time, though, because she was pleased he no longer lived in her house – because he and his ex had got back together and they were living happily ever after!

She shook herself. This was Danny, not Simon.

In many ways, Danny was uncannily similar to Simon. He, too, was fiftyish, reasonably reliable, regularly set fire to his pocket, a bit absent-minded, but she was certain he was an all-round good chap. His only drawback was that he simply couldn't keep a secret. That was his main difference to Simon. Simon never told anyone anything.

It was all right Danny being a blabber-mouth – everyone knew it so no one told him anything they didn't want broadcast to all and sundry. Many was the time she'd gone up to the Post Office only to be asked if she'd ever got back the knickers stolen from the washing line, or had she managed to retrieve the earring from the loo where it fell when she was trying to fix the silly butterfly thing on the back while she was just sitting there not doing much else, and she was in a hurry – and, did she actually put her hand down the loo to get it?

It was always brought to her attention, one way or another, when Danny had been to the Post Office before her.

"It *is* cold," she agreed and struggled to her feet. Her joints had seized up. Or maybe it was all this extra weight holding her down.

"Let's go in the breakfast room," Danny said. "Having that wood-burning stove put in was sheer genius, if I may say so."

This was high excitement for Danny. He didn't usually get animated about anything much.

Once again, Liz noted, that he appeared to be spending more time in this house than in the house next door, his actual lodgings. But no one minded so no one ever said anything.

He stood as close as he could get to the stove without catching fire, a look of bliss on his face. Liz had found the biscuits and considered them and put them away and got them out again. She'd get around to putting such temptation behind her some other time soon. Although, it was already there behind her – on her butt. She thought this was so funny she fell about laughing until Moocher anxiously stuck his nose in her leg, and she realised Danny looked more than ordinarily nervous. With an effort she calmed herself and snatched up a biscuit. She'd get around to depriving herself of them some time, but not just yet. Not while she had grannies to worry about and mad sisters and brothers-in-law to tempt her.

That reminded her that she'd meant to get in touch with her ex, Hugh, about Granny, to see what he could find out about the position with regard to her possessions. She jumped up to phone him just as Danny spoke.

"Liz …" He hesitated. She sat down again. He continued: "Do you believe in, er, 'presences'?"

"Presences? What do you mean?"

"Oh, you know. When you know that there's someone or, perhaps, something, around you somewhere but it's not of this world." He looked at the floor, afraid to catch her eye, as if she'd make fun of him.

"Do you mean ghosts, Danny?"

He shifted from foot to foot. "I suppose I do," he said.

"Yes. Ghosts must be what I mean."

Liz wondered what to say. Her beliefs about ghosts and other worlds were somewhat hazy. And then, as though a door opened in her mind and lorry-loads of intuition spilled out, she realised that Danny definitely didn't know about Granny Smart.

She was as certain as she could be that he'd been noticing odd things and the only explanation he could come up with was not of this world. This was awkward.

"Tell you what, Danny – fancy a coffee?" She went into the kitchen and put the kettle on, feverishly pummelling her brain for what to say to him.

"Actually, Liz, I'll see you later," he called from the breakfast room, disrupting her lie-telling rehearsal. "You've got visitors."

When she looked up she saw Melanie standing there with some bloke.

Danny galloped off down the hallway. "See you, then," Liz yelled after him and turned to Melanie.

"Liz," Melanie said. "This is Ronnie. He wants to rent a room. I know you're busy so I thought I might show him Steve's old room next door."

If she had looked at her any more pointedly Liz's carcass would be skewered to the wall behind. Liz was completely at a loss. Her lodgers were definitely proving to be a challenge today.

Steve's old room next door was empty because he and a few of his pals had too good a time in there indulging in strange pursuits that brought the ceiling down, not to mention relieving the walls of most of the wallpaper. It wouldn't have been so bad, but they were accountants and so it was rather unexpected. Anyway, that room was about to be completely renovated. It couldn't be rented out as it was and Melanie knew that. So, what was going on?

Liz took refuge in avoiding the issue – and Melanie – altogether. "Hi," she said and stuck out her hand to Melanie's companion. "I'm Liz."

"Hello," he said, taking her hand in a very firm, almost menacingly tight grasp. "I'm Ronnie."

Moocher greeted Ronnie with no hesitation. Moocher being a good judge of character heartened Liz. Ronnie returned that greeting in a more restrained manner.

He was older than Melanie or Liz, maybe in Danny's age bracket. He was Liz's height, but slimmer. His hair had dark roots with bleached tips and it stuck up around his head in carefully arranged spikes. A few assorted earrings adorned one ear and a single pearl dangled from a chunky ear cuff on the other. A heavy chain hung from his neck and linked to his studded leather belt. Several layers of brown and black clothing made individual garments difficult to discern, except for his boots, which looked capable of climbing Everest in a storm. He looked very interesting, and yet somehow very familiar. Liz was struck with a feeling of déjà vu, but couldn't work it out.

"I hope you don't mind," Ronnie said. "But Melanie told me about this room and I know you want to do some work on it, but I would like to move in as soon as possible, if I could."

"Hang on a minute, Ronnie," Melanie said. "You haven't seen it yet." She turned to him and gave him a very meaningful look that Liz couldn't interpret at all. Well, whatever was going on between them she didn't want to know.

"No, that's true," Ronnie said. "But if the rent is as low as you say, then it sounds too good to miss. Especially as this is the part of town I want to be in."

'The rent is as low ...' as Melanie says? Liz looked at Melanie who stared at her as if daring her to object. Liz wasn't such a fool, however. She said nothing at all.

"I just thought," Melanie said. "That you can't rent it as it is, so any rent would be better than none." She did have the grace to glance at her feet at least once during this reasoning. "And the work," she continued, "could be done around Ronnie. He wouldn't mind. Would you, Ronnie?"

"No, no. Not at all," he said. "In fact, maybe I could do some of the work as part of the rent?"

"Oh! What a good idea!" Melanie exclaimed excitedly, as though they'd just discovered a cure for the common cold, and they weren't reciting lines obviously rehearsed between them, probably outside the front door before they came in.

Liz was completely lost by this time. And she did trust Melanie. So she gave up trying to work anything out and merely said, "Whatever, I have to rush. Gotta catch the Post Office before it shuts." She snatched up her phone from the table and headed towards the hall. "Nice to meet you, Ronnie," she called as she went.

She had to go. She didn't think she could keep up the charade any longer. Also, she had to get by herself and tease out the memory she knew she had of seeing Ronnie somewhere before. The feeling of familiarity was getting stronger all the time.

"Yep. See you then." Melanie followed her down the hall and shut the front door after her leaving Liz on the outside, supposedly on her way to the Post Office.

As soon as the cold air hit her, she had it!

The last time she'd seen Ronnie his hair had been silver, shorter, but softly curled. He'd been wearing a pink silk blouse with a tweed skirt and matching fluffy cardi, no doubt cashmere. He'd been sitting with two children leaning trustfully into him on a velvet sofa staring at her from the missing-granny page of the tabloids.

It looked like the Smart Granny was about to become one of her lodgers and, officially, Liz still wouldn't know it. But at least if that happened Danny would no longer be troubled by other-worldly incidents.

You win some, you lose some.

Chapter Fifteen
(Mapmaker)

Mapmaker realised he'd made a mistake. He fished out his map and journal again, removed the Smart granny from number twelve, and put her at number nine. In Liz's garden shed.

He paused. It was very cold today. Would she be warm enough in a garden shed? She wasn't elderly although Grabber and Telly had kept referring to her as such in their abysmal television charade of an appeal. She was only fifty-three. Even so, it was a cold day for anyone, whatever their age. He got up and walked through his flat to the back room which had been turned into a bathroom when the house was made into flats. He opened the little window in the back wall and peered around to his right.

He couldn't see Liz's garden shed from here. Of course, he couldn't. There was too much in the way – tall trees, scaffolding – there was always building work going on in Malvern Road – fences, trellis laden with honeysuckle and rambling roses, even a tall, thin pagoda complete with ginger cat snoozing on its roof. He couldn't work out how it didn't fall off.

Now he'd tried to see, though, and failed, he could feel anxiety growing about Granny Smart. He tried to shake it off. It wasn't any of his business!

The question was – *should* it be his business? He wished he didn't know about Granny Smart. Damn Enid for telling him!

No, he took that back. He was pleased to be told anything by Enid.

He wondered how she'd known where the granny was, though, and the more he wondered about that, the odder it seemed that she did know.

Chapter Sixteen
(The Smirking Philanderer)

Liz ambled up the road wondering when she could reasonably go home. She kept finding herself outside her own home when she would rather be in it. Circumstances had a habit of doing that, recently.

So now she had a definite granny to worry about. At least when she'd been in the shed it hadn't been quite so real. But now it was very real. Not only that but there was the whole Angela thing – the betrayal of her husband with some hammer-headed pillock. Just to crown it all she had to do the bratsitting thing for Telly tonight.

Why, oh, why hadn't she said no? Actually, she had, but why hadn't she insisted? She knew why – guilty conscience, that's why, because she was harbouring Telly's free babysitter. She wondered what Ronnie was up to now. Stripping the rest of the wallpaper from her room, probably, or varnishing the floor. Happy, innocent pastimes.

She sauntered along a bit more, wondering when she could return home when she spotted ahead of her the back of a well-built man, tall, full head of hair, wearing a dark suit. Her heart did a double-flip and her pulse revved up too far too fast until she was gulping in the air to keep up with it.

Robert! It was Robert. Eek! It was her fantasy-fancy-object! Oh, no! He couldn't be her fantasy-fancy any more. Not now he was actually available. That was no good for a fantasy-fancy. She stopped and had another look, and realised it wasn't Robert. It was her ex. It was Hugh. Good grief! Robert and Hugh had exactly the same build. Had she noticed this before?

She didn't want to analyse that too closely.

For a moment, sadness overwhelmed her as it hit her – again – that Hugh was indeed her ex. They had tried again, and failed again. They would always fail again. This time they had accepted that it wouldn't ever work. They were doomed to love each other but not to be able to stand each other in the same place for very long.

Yes, she was definitely free of Hugh. And she hoped he was free of her, too. This meant she was free for anyone, too. She hadn't thought of it that way before.

And, of course, it also meant Robert was free for any grasping woman because his traitorous wife was doing the dirty on him.

She had another look. It wasn't Hugh! It *was* Robert!

And Robert didn't yet know that he was free for any grabby woman to get her pointy talons in to him. She should tell him to be on his guard.

She hesitated. She could tell him now and start to get this whole sorry situation sorted out. She quickened her steps to catch up with him. She stretched out her hand to touch his arm and said: "Robert, I have to tell you that …"

Just as he turned towards her the phone in her hand rang and stopped the flow of her words.

She was shocked to see it wasn't Robert. Wow. That was close. She'd nearly told a complete stranger his wife was cheating on him. She mouthed "Sorry" at him and answered her call.

It was Angela. Liz almost dropped the phone when she realised who it was. She'd just this second nearly told her husband about her betrayal. Or, she would have done, if it had been her husband.

But, also, Liz hadn't got used to the idea of her perfect sister being adulterous. As Angela spoke, a feeling of monumental doom overcame Liz. For her sister to be having an affair must mean the world was in a much worse state than even she had imagined.

"Hello, Liz," Angela said. "I'm just up the road from you at that rather nice Italian coffee house. I've been seeing … Well, you know who I've been seeing. Anyway, he's just going so I thought I'd give you a ring and see if you fancied coming up here for a coffee. We didn't really have much of a discussion the other day, for one reason or another. I don't want to come to your house again with so many grubby lodgers about."

Liz wasn't going to rise to that particular jab from her stuck-up sister – not when time was a'wasting. "Okay. I'm on my way," she shouted, pocketing her phone and sprinting down the road to her car. She had more of a head start than Angela might imagine because she was already outside and she didn't have to do the somewhat lengthy leaving-the-house ritual required of a dog-owner.

She might be in time to catch sight of the lamebrain who was being such a bad influence on her sister.

Liz leapt in the car, raced it up the road and zoomed into the small, but conveniently placed, supermarket car park almost behind the coffee house. She was just in time to see a man get into his car. The unaccustomed haste had been worth it – it must be him! It must be the libertine. His car, which was large, black and masculine sat next to, and overshadowed, Angela's small, feminine, powder blue coupé. Every picture tells a story, and all that.

She was in time! She'd see who it was. Maybe she'd get a look at his face. Maybe she'd recognise him. She could at least take down his registration number. And work out what to do with it later. People are always taking down registration numbers, so there must be something they did with them, and she could do that too, once she found out what it was.

Then she looked around and realised there was nowhere to park except a narrowish space left due to bad parking. She'd wait for Angela's bit of muscle fluff to leave and go in his space. After all, he didn't know who she was.

But the mangy muppet made no move to drive off. He hadn't even put on his seat belt. Then Liz wondered if he knew Angela had rung her and maybe he was waiting to see what *she* looked like, although she couldn't think why he'd do that. In which case, she'd better just park and pretend she had no interest in him. Suddenly, she felt very self-conscious.

She edged her car forwards and had another look at the narrow space. In moving, the light reflections on his windscreen changed and she got a clear view of his face, although not much time to really note its features. The one thing she did notice was that he was smirking. Heat exploded through her and threatened to set her hair on fire. Why was he sitting there smirking at her? Poxie rakehell that he was. He was adding insult to injury by being a male chauvinist pig, too, because Liz knew why he was smirking as certainly as if he'd broadcast it on Radio Bristol.

He thought the space was too narrow for a mere female to get her car in it.

She'd show him. No dirty old man was going to sit there and have the satisfaction of seeing her chicken out. Oh, no! Just watch this! She stamped on the accelerator, streaked forward and pulled up with a bit of a screech beyond the space, threw the car into reverse while it was still rocking on its tyres, and just hurtled into that space. No hesitation, no dithering, no panic. Just roared into that space. She managed to stop in time to avoid slamming into the wall, yanked on the hand-brake, switched off the ignition, and then realised she couldn't get her door open.

There was no room for her door to open because she was too close to the car next to her. She immediately adopted the pose of someone who didn't want to get out of their car anyway. Liz bent over and, with a determined, I-know-what-I'm-doing air feverishly pretended to search through the glove compartment. She found a whole pile of biscuit wrappers, old crisp packets and a map. She pounced on the map and opened it up over the steering wheel. Then she studied it with minute attention, not seeing it at all, but fighting with herself not to look up to see if that stupid bloke was still sitting there watching her and smirking. She wanted him to think she hadn't even seen him, let alone had any interest in him.

While she was there, not looking at the map and not looking at the smirker and worrying about Angela wondering where she was by now, a little old lady came out of nowhere and stood right by her, staring at the driver's door on her own car. She couldn't get in it.

Liz didn't feel she could expect a little old lady to get in the passenger side and crawl over the gear stick into the driver's seat. Damn!

Ignoring Smirk-face even more, if that was possible, Liz started up her car and pulled out to clear the way to the next car's driver door. That car drove off and Liz reversed back into the space leaving herself enough room to get out and be about her business. But then she realised she couldn't because then old Smirker would *know* she'd wanted to get out of her car all along. So she stayed put until it occurred to her that to miss her appointment with Angela just because she didn't want to lose face with old Smirker was almost as stupid as sitting in a car park smirking.

Not only that, but who the hell used maps these days? Everyone had sat navs! She bundled it up and threw it on the floor.

So she got out of her car with the sort of flourish that surely must have said: 'I've just realised I'm a bigger person than you,' and went off to find Angela.

Who said: "You took your time," in a somewhat charmless greeting. (But who could blame her?)

"Sorry about that, but there was this man in the car park who was smirking."

"Oh never mind all that. You're here now and that's what counts."

Good grief! Angela voluntarily gave up a chance to be all superior over her. She must be in love.

"Yes, but this smirking guy – he was in a large, black car. Ring any bells?"

Angela stared at her as though she'd said he was in a large, black, racing chariot with blades sticking out of the wheels, and then her face cleared. She laughed. "You thought it was A… my lover, didn't you? That's why it's taken you so long. You've been messing about in the car park trying to find out who it was."

She knew her sister so well.

"No. No," Liz said. "I spent all that time trying to park, actually, Angela." Sort of.

"Well, bad luck," Angela said. "A… my lover left before I phoned you."

Oh. Anyway, now at least she knew his name began with A – Alan? Andrew? Augustus? Augustus! Liz looked at Angela with new eyes. Could she possibly be having it off with someone called Augustus?

"I got you a coffee," Angela said. "It's your fault it's cold." Oh, yes. It *was* her sister all right. Liz threw the coffee down her throat, reached for the plate of amoretti and waited for Angela to tell her why she'd wanted to see her.

"What I want you to do is baby-sit for me on Saturday afternoon. You will, won't you?"

"Baby-sit!" Oh, no! She was doing too much of that

already with Tallulah's two! "You swore you'd never ask me to baby-sit again after little Johnny fell down the loo." How she'd been supposed to know he used a different apparatus to the rest of the world she had no idea.

"Yes, well, he's using the loo now. He's bigger and more likely to survive your care. Also, if I got in someone who really was a babysitter then Robert, if he found out, would want to know where I was. Whereas if it's only you, you could easily have called in to see me and I would simply have taken the opportunity to pop in to see a neighbour or something."

"Angela. It doesn't seem right that I should do this. I don't want to condone your affair in any way, shape or form. I mean, if I refuse then you can't go off for a bit of nookie, can you?"

"Don't be silly. I would just take Johnny and drop him off in the nearest crèche facility I could find. If you don't baby-sit for me it won't stop me seeing my lover." Angela was defiant in the face of her sister's hindrance.

"My God, Angela! You really *are* besotted aren't you? I never thought I'd see the day when you'd abandon Johnny as well as Robert, for a bit on the side."

"Don't be so crude, Liz. I love him."

This all sounded so unlike her that Liz couldn't take it in. Even the language her sister was using was out of character. For a moment she did wonder if there might be something very seriously wrong.

"Angela," she said trying hard to sound neutral and reasonable. "Do you think you should see a relationship counsellor?"

"Don't be silly. Robert would know about my affair then, wouldn't he? And the whole point is to keep it secret. If you try very hard, you'll be able to understand that."

Suddenly Liz felt depressed and defeated. "Okay then. I'll do it," she said. She couldn't bear to think of little Johnny being dragged around to dodgy assignations if she didn't babysit him.

"I'll see you at two o' clock. Thank you, Liz. Now then, about your neighbour, Tallulah Smart. I'm getting up a bridge party and I want you to make sure she comes along."

Blimey. Her sister. How could she talk of adultery one minute and soap opera stars at bridge parties the next?

Chapter Seventeen
(Of course! It's Hugh!)

By the time Liz reached home she'd decided to try and introduce some sanity into the general situation. Where to start, though? Philippe's windows? Angela's lover? Granny Smart? It would have to be the last one. She wasn't sure she wanted to ask her ex about either of the other two items on her 'what-the-hell-am-I-going-to-do-about-this?' list.

Funny how when sanity was required it was her ex that first came to mind.

Yes, she'd call Hugh as soon as she got inside. As it happened, her phone started to ring as she entered the house. Glancing at the screen she saw it was in fact Hugh. Of course, it was! He had a sixth sense about when he was needed. He was a good ex.

He wanted to come over. It would appear he had news of his own.

Liz knew he didn't want to come over in order to try and get them back together again as a couple. They'd tried it too often and it just wouldn't work. She was too impulsive and he was too much the opposite. That was the most polite way of putting it that she could think of.

She still loved him, though. She wanted him to be happy. Hopefully, they could still know each other forever. Maybe he was coming over to tell her about a new girlfriend.

Her heart still did a tiny little jumpy thing when she opened the door to him. She expected that would die a natural death, that reaction. He was still a good-looking man, after all. And now she was thinking of it, he had many similarities to Robert. Maybe that was why she'd always pretend-fancied Robert, although Robert was around **before** Hugh came on the scene – he and Angela had been an item for a long time before Hugh pitched up. Ohmigod – did she marry Hugh because of **his** resemblance to Robert? What a terrifying thought. It made her feel she should be kinder to him.

"Hello Hunk," she said when she opened the door to him. She gave him a quick hug and stepped back to let him in the house.

"Hello Liz," he said, with a brief smile.

Liz's heart sank. He had 'the look' on his face. 'The look' that said she was in trouble. It was no wonder their relationship wouldn't work! Who the hell wanted to keep seeing 'the look'?

At least he was nice to Moocher when he scrabbled out from under the table to greet him, his entire hind-end wagging.

Liz put the kettle on and found some ginger snaps. She even found a plate to put them on. As if biscuits needed plates, but she was trying to be kind, which in Hugh's case, seemed to mean she had to try to be more 'conventional'. Whatever that was.

"I'm glad you came over," Liz said. "I wanted to ask you about Granny Smart."

"Oh, well, I wanted to tell you my news," he said. "Shall we do that first so that I do manage to tell you, and then talk about Granny Smart? Otherwise, I have a feeling we'll get bogged down with your topic and I won't get to mine."

Liz felt that was a bit of a back-handed criticism of her, but she didn't want to fall out with him. And he was probably right. He just could have said it differently. Her ears strained backwards on her head. She felt them do it. She had realised in recent years that they had this habit of doing that when she was trying not to get cross. Maybe they were trying to get away from the scene in front of them.

This wasn't a great start.

She sat down at the table and tried to arrange her face to look compassionately receptive.

Hugh gave her a suspicious glare, fiddled with his cuff button, undoing it, doing it up, undoing it.

Liz stopped herself from saying: "Well! Come on! What is it?" She waited as patiently as she was able.

He opened his mouth. Liz leaned forward a little so that she didn't miss any of the pearls that were about to pour forth.

And Melanie slammed the front door behind her, shouted a greeting from the end of the hall, and came bounding into the breakfast room, beaming all over her face at sight of Hugh.

"Hugh!" she cried. "How good to see you! We hoped we would see you soon, didn't we, Liz?"

Hugh stood up and exchanged a quick hug and pecks on cheeks with Melanie.

The look he gave Liz, though, was far from genial. He might as well have said out loud: 'There. I knew it! Now we'll never get onto *my* topic!'

Melanie burst into a torrent of words. "You'll be able to help us, Hugh. I just know you will! It's about the Smart Granny. She's been living in Liz's shed …"

Hugh shot Liz another look. This one said: 'She would be living in *your* shed, wouldn't she!'

Liz managed a feeble smile and just let Melanie get on with her flood of explanation about Grabber and Telly being awful and it's no wonder the Smart Granny had to get away from them, and …

Hugh headed straight for the back door, though, and Melanie's voice trailed off as she realised the helpful reaction she'd expected wasn't immediately forthcoming.

It looked like they'd caught Hugh on one of his convention-is-my-middle-name days, rather than one of his I-can-afford-to-be-more-mellow-than-usual days.

Thank Dog they'd realised in time.

"It's too damn cold for anyone to be living in a shed," Hugh said. "Let alone a granny!"

That's what she'd said, Liz thought, feeling vindicated for once. Fleetingly.

He was having some trouble getting the back door open. Liz didn't feel like helping him. The tone of voice he had used was his high-handed one, guaranteed to put her back up.

She noticed Moocher had retreated under the table. He hadn't actually put his paw protectively over his nose, but she imagined he would have if he'd been a more theatrical dog.

"We need to get to the bottom of this," he stated, still struggling with the door. The handle was going to come off in his hand at this rate. "We need the full story."

"We already have the full story," Melanie said in much dampened tones. It looked like her faith in the magical Hugh to sort things was eroding and he hadn't actually said anything concrete yet. It was his whole demeanour. He simply didn't look receptive to reason. Or sob-stories.

"And she can't know you know, either," Melanie said. "It would make her feel very insecure."

The look Hugh gave her was enough to make honey sour. Melanie even stepped back. She flashed a mystified look at Liz.

As if *she'd* know what was wrong with him this time!

To be fair, Hugh wasn't usually quite this bad-tempered. Liz could only assume it was something to do with what he'd wanted to tell her and hadn't.

He'd got the door open by now. For a moment they all looked at each other, frozen in a silent, timeless, tableau with a sub-zero blast of air streaming in.

Then Hugh stepped into the back garden.

Danny, having a quiet smoke next door, reared back, startled, and dived into that house. Melanie, Moocher and Liz slowly followed Hugh outside.

She could imagine how panicked she would now be feeling if the granny was still concealed in the shed. Liz was exceedingly thankful she wasn't. Even Hugh couldn't be blamed for being outraged if he'd discovered her stashing grandmothers in her garden shed.

Finding a punk rocker in her garden shed might be considered suspicious, let alone a granny! If she was really lucky, Ronnie would have completely established herself in Steve's old room by now and cleared all of her stuff out of the shed.

Liz was uneasily aware that she was seldom that lucky when it came to keeping things from Hugh.

Hugh gave her yet another one of his looks again. Liz stared defiantly back even though she had no idea at all what was going through his head.

Then he shot off down the garden and she wondered what he'd seen. When she realised he was about to leap over the garden wall she raced after him and got in his way. Whatever it was he thought he'd seen she didn't want him risking life and limb leaping over walls and generally behaving like a clod.

"Someone was in your garden, Liz," he said, staring over her shoulder, ready to give chase.

"It'll be one of the lodgers," she said. "They often while away the odd few moments out here."

"In January?"

Hmmm…

"Maybe it was a fox," Liz said. "We have lots of foxes, you know. They've started to come back after losing so many to the mange. It's good isn't it? Don't you think? I'm very glad the foxes have started to come back. Aren't you?"

"Not many foxes I know wear climbing boots and have metal through their ears," he said.

"You know a lot of foxes?" Liz asked in surprised tones.

Hugh turned away and marched to the shed. Flinging open the door he peered in to the cobweb-shrouded interior as if he expected to see a granny.

To Liz's relief there was no sign of recent occupation. The shed looked just as shed-like as it had before anyone's granny had moved in.

Hugh appeared to be coming to the boil so Liz jumped in and started trying to explain the assertion that a granny lived in her shed and how she *had* been but she wasn't any more and …

But he simply interrupted with a mournful shake of his head. "How do you do it, Liz?"

"Do what?"

"Get into these situations."

"I don't," Liz said. "They just happen, that's all. It's nothing to do with me. Anyway, that's not the point. We need your advice."

She was so bored with this conversation. They'd had it far too often.

"It's obvious," Hugh said. "You must tell Tallulah and Graham Smart immediately. You can't let an old woman live in your shed when she has a perfectly acceptable home across the road."

Liz registered Melanie's head suddenly come up from whiffling to Moocher. Her face showed her disappointment and Liz knew that Hugh had fallen off his pedestal as far as Melanie was concerned. She didn't look unduly worried, though, for the obvious reason that the granny didn't live in the shed any more.

Liz was puzzled. Hugh was a bit of a stickler for the standard norms of society, but he wasn't usually quite this dogmatic. She wondered again what he'd come round to say. It surely was that which had put him in this inflexible frame of mind.

"You don't seem to have listened to a word I've said," Liz said. "She doesn't have a 'perfectly acceptable' home to go to. If she did, she wouldn't have been living in my shed. That's pretty damn obvious, I'd have thought."

Hugh opened his mouth, but Liz rushed on: "But she's no longer living in my shed and I don't know where she's gone, so this is all a waste of time, anyway." She didn't actually add: "So you can go, now," but the words hung in the air between them.

Liz was very pleased that they hadn't got to the point in the story with Hugh where the granny had gone from living in her shed to apparently becoming a male granny, not to mention also becoming punkified. Punkified?

Thank heaven she hadn't given her away. Should Hugh decide to be totally foul, he didn't actually know where Granny Smart lived.

"Now, Liz ..."

"Don't 'Now, Liz ...' me," Liz snapped. "The woman needs help, not someone who thinks they know better than she does what's good for her. I'm sorry I asked you now."

"Now, Liz." Melanie said. "To be fair – you reacted the same way when you first heard that Granny Smart was living in your shed."

Liz reckoned Melanie was trying to heave Hugh back on that pedestal.

She'd have a hard job.

"An earring-wearing, bleach-haired fox!" Hugh slapped his thigh as realisation dawned. "She can't be that much of a granny the way she leapt those garden walls."

"She's not," Melanie said. "The word 'granny', used in this way, is really misleading in her case. What we need from you is some legal advice about her property and the position she's in with regard to it. Grabber Smart – he's not her son, you know – he's her stepson – got her to sign something or other when she was so ill after her husband died. It must have been awful – he died of a massive heart attack just when she was in the middle of a cancer scare and was having ops and chemo."

Liz hadn't known this – she immediately wanted to rush over to Steve's old room with hot water bottles, drams of whisky, chocolate, and lots of hugs.

Melanie continued: "She became very depressed and that's when Grabber moved in. She signed the authority, or whatever it is. This was a few years ago and ever since then she's been dependent on them. And, just by the way, she's also been a very convenient, free, housekeeper and babysitter while she's been recovering. Then he sold her house and everything else he could grab, and they all moved here."

"That doesn't explain how she came to be in Liz's garden shed," Hugh said.

Straight to the most irrelevant bit of it all!

"Although, she doesn't seem to be living in there anymore," he added.

"What does any of that matter?" Liz rushed in, staring meaningfully at Melanie. She didn't want her to relax so much with Hugh that she spilled the beans about the granny's current residence. Liz no longer trusted him. He was in too much of an awkward mood.

"We need to get back her property so she can live her own life again," Liz said. "What can you do to help?"

"I'll have to find out more about it first," Hugh said.

"But you must promise to keep secret our involvement in it," Melanie said, her hand on his arm. "Not that we know where she is now, but we don't need any hassle from the Smarts."

Melanie looked so shifty when she said that, it was obvious she was lying. She was the world's worst liar! Liz wondered if she could learn to be better.

Hugh sighed. "If you insist," he said. "Although I really think Graham and Tallulah would be civilised about this. I know the story is very sad, but I'm sure it's not quite what you think. There must be some other explanation and a solution that will suit everyone."

Melanie grinned. "As long you don't say anything to anyone, I'm not worried about what you think because you'll find out the truth as soon as you start making enquiries."

"I won't say anything," he said.

"So, what do you think about Angela? I'm sure Liz will have told you." Melanie said.

"Angela?" he queried.

"Yes," Melanie said. "She's having an affair."

"Mel!" Liz was outraged. Fancy her blurting it out like that to someone else. Even if it was Hugh. It was still someone else who hadn't needed to know. Liz was about to follow up on her annoyance with Melanie when she realised Hugh had blushed. Why was he blushing?

He was blushing so hotly she reckoned she could have fried an egg on his face.

She stared at him in utter amazement.

He dropped his gaze, made a studied point of getting his phone out of his pocket to check the time, and then started to stride away, saying: "I had no idea of the time. I must go. I have an appointment."

And he was gone so fast Liz felt much as she did if she stood too close to the edge of a train station platform when the high-speed locomotive skyrocketed through.

And, just like it would feel if the high-speed had driven straight into her, she suddenly realised why.

It was Hugh!

Of course, it was! He and Robert shared a lot of similarities. Liz had always fancied Robert. Angela had always fancied Hugh.

He'd come here to tell her something.

When Melanie had told him about Angela's affair he'd **blushed**!

Angela was having an affair with Hugh!

Chapter Eighteen
(Mapmaker)

Now he'd thought of it, he couldn't stop thinking of it. And the more he thought of it the more uncomfortable he became. He knew that a woman was living in a garden shed because of her family's skulduggery and yet he was doing nothing about it. What would his own mother think of that?

She wouldn't be impressed. Although she had a healthy respect for other people's business being *their* business, she wouldn't have ignored an old woman in distress.

Mapmaker shifted in his chair. He didn't want to get involved. He groaned and clutched his head as if to screw it off his neck and stop the thoughts from thrashing about in his brain. He had too much imagination, that was the trouble. It was good for his job, but awful for everyday life.

Abruptly he leapt up. His chair ground its feet into the floor. A lesser chair would have been overturned, but not his oak wainscot chair.

By habit he put everything away first – he'd had a special drawer made in his desk for the map – he placed it back in its secret compartment; the journal fitted nicely in the hidden ledge under the seat on his chair. He had no idea if it had been deliberately constructed to have a secret recess to hide things in, but he liked to think it had held someone's treasures, maybe their secrets, in an earlier time.

He needed to make sure that the Smart granny was safe. But first of all, he needed to know how Enid had known about her in case he was walking into something way over his head.

He left the flat and turned towards number twenty-two. As he approached, he became a little apprehensive. He hated people just turning up on his doorstep, hated it with a passion. He needed to be prepared for people. He needed the notice and the time in which to leave his own world and put himself in theirs. To have someone crash in on him out of the blue was like having his brain dislocated.

Undecided, he shifted from foot to foot until he realised he must look furtive. He got his phone out of his pocket and pretended to be engrossed in it while he tried to decide what to do. The universe smiled on him and out of the corner of his eye he noticed movement. It was Enid waving furiously at him from her bay window. Whitson lay across her shoulders, his tail hanging down one side and his head snuggled into her neck on the other side. Mapmaker smiled and waved back, but she made shooing motions with her hands before then making the generally accepted sign for a cup of tea. It seemed contradictory to him – she was offering him a cup of tea but telling him to go away?

But then she pointed her thumb back over her shoulder.

Oh! She would meet him in the café. For some reason she didn't want to be seen with him on the street. He smiled again, gave her a thumbs up and made off down the road. He was fine with that. He hastened away, turned the corner at the end of the road, advanced up Pikeland Avenue – and spotted a familiar face. It was a very familiar face. But he couldn't place it. It must be out of context. Mapmaker niggled at it, and niggled at it some more, all the way up the road, he turned left onto that small road that took him to the Gloucester Road, and then he turned right. He was still chewing away at it in his mind when he reached Greg's Grub. He got himself a mug of tea and ordered from the day's specials board – beef stew – and left his tab open at the counter. Greg knew the score. He would add whatever Enid wanted to it when she came in and they'd settle up later.

Why would he see a face he knew around here if it wasn't someone in his journal?

He fiddled with his teaspoon, pondering the strong sense of acquaintance he'd had when he saw that man. Looking around, wondering what was taking Enid so long he noted the other main course on the specials board was chili. And he had it!

Mapmaker was very fond of chili and on days when he couldn't be bothered to cook, he would amble around to the local pool table pub around the corner. The guy he'd seen was a regular in The Gamester. He was 'out of context' in his mind because Mapmaker's focus had narrowed down to Malvern Road and its inhabitants, but maybe he should make a note of him, having seen him in the local environs.

They did a decent chili in The Gamester; privately, Mapmaker thought The Gamester's chili just had the edge over Greg's. The Gamester also served up a decent pint, although he seldom imbibed, wanting to keep his wits about him at all times.

Even so, Mapmaker had been to The Gamester often enough that he considered the tiny round table in the corner to be his, and he could feel quite affronted if someone was already sitting there when he arrived. His preference was always for a corner; if he couldn't have the corner, he had to at least have his back to the wall. Circumstances had made him feel very insecure if his back was unprotected.

He had seen this man in there. He even knew his name because it was often being called in a jocular, playful manner. He was always in there with a crowd of other people, mainly men.

Mapmaker had spent some time trying to work out what held the group together as a group, apparently familiar with each other, although it appeared to be a bit of a shifting population. He'd thought maybe it was rugby, or football, or gambling. The pub was 'The Gamester', after all! They were mostly middle-aged, he thought, although he wasn't great at guessing ages.

But Mapmaker was always curious about people. It was largely what kept him ahead of trends in the world of video gaming. And, over a period of several months he finally had his curiosity satisfied. They were a bunch of scammers! They were like a club of scumbags who got together to discuss technique and compare results. Mapmaker was not surprised. Nothing about the depths to which humans could sink ever surprised him.

This one guy, Mitch, seemed to have a slightly different position in the group. He was younger than the rest by about fifteen years or so, and Mapmaker couldn't quite work it out.

He still viewed him with disdain – he knew people who'd been scammed – the woman who thought the younger man had fallen in love with her only for her to end up losing all her savings and her house and her self-respect; the elderly couple swindled out of everything they owned by a young woman who pretended to care for them. There were so many! And this Mitch was another such parasite.

Although he listened hard, whilst pretending to be absorbed

in his laptop, Mapmaker never heard any of the backslapping and congratulations going Mitch's way. In fact, he seemed to be constantly ribbed by the others, as if he were a callow young thing and not really an equal member of the group, which was why Mapmaker knew his name because Mitch nearly always turned up quite a lot later than most of them, and he would enter the pub to cries of: "Mitch! Here he is, shy guy, wimp, chicken, he who hesitates is lost, runt of the litter, hasn't made his mark yet," and other such heavy-handed but affectionate ribaldry, which he always seemed to take in good stead.

The sound of the café door opening and slamming alerted him to Enid's presence. Mapmaker shook off the thought of the man he'd seen and finally recognised. Successful at it, or not, Mitch was what was known as a 'sweetheart scammer'.

But now Mapmaker had to concentrate on Enid; he had to find out what was going on with the Smart Granny.

Chapter Nineteen
(Foxes in the garden)

Liz had been reeling from the realisation that her sister and her ex were having an affair. Why hadn't she seen it before? The awfulness of this recognition was so great that she'd dragged herself upstairs to her attic kingdom and tried to do some accounts. Doing accounts nearly always put her in a frame of mind more closely akin to stability than anything else. There was something soothing about the way the double entry system worked. The slightest inaccuracy and it didn't work. So, it all had to be right in order to work, and getting it to that state was very satisfying.

Shame her life didn't run along double entry lines.

The accounts helped a little, but not as much as she'd hoped. Eventually, she stood up and wandered into the dormer window to stare out at the world. Idly, she watched as the bloke from the flat a few doors down came out into Malvern Road. She looked away but then looked back when she saw that he was lurking suspiciously outside Enid's house.

She needed to keep an eye on him. Enid was vulnerable.

She watched as he fidgeted, moving about in small steps, getting his phone out of his pocket, pretending to look at it – she could even see from here that the screen was blank – then he looked up at Enid's house and waved. After which, he smiled, gave a thumbs up gesture, and strode off down the road.

Curious!

Even curiouser, Liz watched as he disappeared around the corner onto Pikeland Avenue, only to be followed by Enid shortly thereafter.

Almost as if they had an assignation!

Assignation! She'd been trying not to think of trysts and rendezvous and other such underhand get togethers. And here she'd just witnessed what looked distinctly like another.

Her thoughts were interrupted by the doorbell. She and Moocher stampeded downstairs, him trying to push her to go faster, her trying to keep her balance and not fall all the way.

It was Tallulah. She sashayed in saying, "I just wanted to check you were still game for tonight. Just in case you'd ended up in hospital or something." She grinned at Liz and winked as though they shared a secret.

Liz supposed in a way, they did. Unknown to Tallulah.

"By the way, I saw Hugh on your doorstep earlier."

She left the statement hanging in the air as if Liz would immediately burst into explanation. She didn't. She couldn't think what to say about Hugh that she was prepared to say. Especially not now she knew what she knew about him. And Angela.

While she stood there uselessly unable to think of any acceptable chit-chat to share with Telly, her visitor stepped past her and cantered off down the hall, through the kitchen and immediately tried to get the back door open. Almost as if she had some idea what she might find out in Liz's back garden.

Once again, freezing cold air blasted through the house. Tallulah stepped outside. Moocher and Liz followed.

Once again, Danny next door threw his half-smoked cigarette on the ground and fled indoors.

Liz felt considerably more nonchalant about this invasion of her garden than she had last time.

Telly ran around frantically, peering over the walls, down the side of the house, in the shed.

"What are you looking for?" Liz asked.

Telly ignored her.

"Do you have foxes in your garden, Tallulah?" Liz asked, trying for an entirely open and innocent expression on her face. "Is that what you're looking for in mine? It's good they've come back again after that awful mange business, isn't it?"

Telly gave her a look as sharp as a very sharp thing.

Ooh. Maybe she wasn't looking for foxes.

Moocher paid no attention. He nosed about in the thicket at the back of the garden, doing his flushing-out-the-villains-stalking thing.

"Come along, Telly," Liz said, taking her arm and leading her towards the house. "You're going to spoil your shoes if you keep running around like that."

Telly looked down and sure enough her lovely Jimmy

Choo erstwhile sparkly shoes were looking a bit dull and down in the dumps, and a bit muddy.

Liz led her uninvited guest down the hall towards the front of the house and its exit. She said: "And now you know I'm not in hospital, I'll be along later at seven, so don't worry." Liz managed to see her out without laughing.

Sometimes she impressed herself.

Chapter Twenty
(Mapmaker)

Mapmaker and Enid tucked into their plates of stew. It was good, and they gave it the respect it deserved by concentrating hard on tasting every mouthful.

Mapmaker waited for when Enid was ready to talk. He knew she was ready when she relaxed a bit more into her chair and gave him a quizzical look.

"How did you know about Granny Smart?" he asked.

"I was there. I was in the town centre with her when she was spotted by Liz's tenant, Laurel. By the time Laurel came along we'd already spent an interesting couple of hours discussing all kinds of things, including begging techniques, bin diving, soup kitchens etc. She's hopeless at it. She wouldn't have lasted at that game. Kudos to her, though, that she gave it a go. But it's not in her nature to beg for anything. Maybe she wasn't hungry enough."

"You were actually there? With the granny?"

"Yes. But no one saw me."

Mapmaker looked carefully at his companion. He wasn't sure what she meant but was sure that something important was forthcoming as long as he didn't say the wrong thing. So, he said nothing.

"People don't see me," Enid continued. "I'm old. And I'm female. I was sitting right next to her. We'd been talking for a long time. But when she was spotted, no one saw me. She was 'seen' because she 'belongs' to an influential family and they want her back. I wasn't 'seen' because I don't. But, the important thing to take home is that she was spotted because of the family, not because of her as an individual."

Vigorously, Enid wiped the rest of the gravy off her plate with the remains of her bread and butter and stuffed it in her mouth. She looked content. Her words had made her sound like she could well not be content. But she *sounded* very content.

Mapmaker kept himself on the alert for the possibility that

pudding was required. Greg made a mean treacle sponge! Enid was really the most satisfying person to have a meal with. No picking, no messing with the food or shifting it around the plate – no – just straight in with real enjoyment of every mouthful. He felt his own mouth quirk upwards at the corners. He was content just watching her.

She finished chewing, swallowed, and sat back with a gratified air. Maybe she didn't want pudding.

"The thing is," she said. "Felicity – yes, she actually has a name of her own – has been treated as a resource. She stopped being an individual when her husband died, and then she became ill. She became an object of pity. She became an object of virtue-signalling on her step-son's part. And his wife's. 'Look at us,' they were saying. 'Look at how wonderful we're being keeping this patient in our house.' By the way, Mapmaker – the house was hers. Felicity's. It was *her* house. After that she was wanted for her money, for her assets, for her housekeeping skills, for her babysitting patience. She was wanted as a grandmother, as a housekeeper, as a private bank, as a gardener, as a … She wasn't wanted for herself as her own person. This happens a lot, you know. I see it everywhere. Women who are wives, sisters, mothers, grandmothers, handy friends, wallpaper. Women who are not valued for themselves. I'm always amazed at how few of them break out like Felicity did."

Enid looked around the café as if searching for more fugitives who'd made a successful getaway.

Mapmaker wondered if his own mother had needed to break out like Felicity had? No! His mother had always been her own person. She'd also been his mother, but she'd always been someone in her own right first. He was sure of it. He couldn't ever think of taking her for granted and treating her like wallpaper. Anxiety gripped him. Had he? As soon as he thought it, he stopped thinking it. If he had treated her like that she would have told him.

"You don't have to worry about me not being 'seen'. It gives me freedom. I'm fine with it. I answer to no one and I do what I want. I get around and I see everything, simply because I'm not seen myself." Enid even leaned over the table to pat him reassuringly on the hand.

"Felicity was desperate. Her so-called family were taking

advantage of her situation. She wanted to get away from them at least to have a breather in which to decide what to do. They have taken all her assets – she doesn't mind that so much. I gather that Grabber needed it. He was in a bad position financially, and she was happy to have the children protected. What she couldn't deal with was the complete loss of her own independence and ability to decide what she wanted to do with her life. She didn't even mind all the housekeeping and babysitting. She's happy to be useful to her family. It was the expectation of her unquestioning compliance that she couldn't cope with once she'd come up for air from her pit of grief and despair after her husband's death and her own cancer ordeal. In her distress she just walked out one day."

"Couldn't she go back to her family and state her case?"

The sneer on Enid's face told him everything he needed to know about her opinion of Telly and Grabber. And, apparently, negotiation was no longer an option.

"Laurel, although she meant kindly, was a bit like that, too – she insisted Felicity couldn't carry on as she was. As if Felicity couldn't decide for herself. However, I'm afraid I did encourage it – I feel a bit badly because I did say she should go with Laurel. I mean, it should have been more her decision rather than us pressuring her. But, anyway, I'm glad she did go. Laurel and that bouncy person – Melanie, is it? – they installed her in Liz's shed. Without Liz knowing."

Of course, they did. Mapmaker's imagination had 'busy' as its default setting, but now it was in overdrive. Of course some tenants installed a granny in their landlord's shed without her knowing although across the road the granny's family were desperately looking for her! It was the obvious thing to do.

"Do you think I should do anything?" he asked.

"No! You don't want to get into that. It's all under control. And, if I'm not wrong, it is actually all under Felicity's control now, which is how it should be. And she can keep an eye on her grandchildren, too, from there."

He was happy to let it go if Enid said so. He felt his anxiety subside. Mapmaker smiled at his companion. His mother was going to like her when they met. He just knew it.

She smiled back, nodded towards Greg and said with a hopeful air: "Are we having pudding?"

Chapter Twenty-One
(The Spawn of Satan Revealed)

The yoblets were sitting at the table heavily engaged in something electronic. They had separate little machines that beeped and whined and so absorbed them they barely registered that Liz had come in and Telly had left. Maybe, if they took no notice of her at all, the evening wouldn't be the nightmare she feared.

She'd left Moocher getting some rest on her bed in preparation for his surveillance duties later on. When passing Telly in the doorway Liz had ascertained that she'd be back by ten at the latest so Liz knew she'd be in time for tonight's window-smasher stakeout.

Liz settled down on the sofa and opened the novel she'd optimistically brought with her. They stayed like that for a while, the peacefulness of the evening only interrupted by the rustling of her book pages, the squeaking of the chairs as the children settled more comfortably, and the occasional, reassuring human-noise – coughs, burps etc. Why had she been so negative about it all, so afraid?

It was a good book. Liz became totally drawn into its unfolding secrets.

The noise that alerted her was a repetition that gradually sank into her consciousness. She looked around to see the gizmos sitting on the table, beeping, but no sign of the children. Damn! Where had they gone? What were they up to? Her fears immediately rushed to the surface again. They must have agreed to a strategy, left their games running at the same point and snuck off. So, she snuck off as well. She slunk around the entire ground floor and found no one.

She crept upstairs and, hearing a low murmur, sidled along the landing and peered through the crack between the hinge end of a door and the door-frame. They were sitting cross-legged on what she took to be their parents' bed, watching television. The sense of relief that swamped Liz made her go all weak-legged. She had to lean against the wall. They were quietly watching television.

Perhaps the last time she baby-sat had been a figment of her fevered imagination and, in fact, they were nice, considerate children after all. They hadn't wanted to disturb her by watching television downstairs while she was so obviously involved in her book. She would make them her special hot chocolate, whipped cream and marshmallow treat.

Liz took another look through the crack and started to turn back towards the stairs when the hair all over her body shot out at right angles to her skin, lifting her clothes away from her and causing a draught. Imprinted on her mental retina was the image she had seen in that brief glance.

She had seen herself. And Hugh. Oh! Her and Hugh. The way they used to be. The way they weren't anymore. They were having a hug on her front doorstep and the image of that was playing out on the television in her neighbours' bedroom eagerly watched by two children for some reason totally beyond her comprehension. Why would anyone want to video them?

Liz took another look. This time she saw Philippe's face. It wasn't just his face she could see, however. It was all of him in startling clarity, his body skin a lot paler than she would have expected. And with him, pale all over too, was Laurel. They were clearly seen for a second or two before Philippe closed the curtains in his bedroom. The shot must have been taken from this house on a floor higher up than this one.

Her neighbours and tenants. Naked. Together.

Liz was unable to move, as if solidified in place, unable to process what she was seeing.

The view switched to a man on the scaffolding encasing the house a few doors down from hers. She didn't know him.

Then it zeroed in on two people in a car, their heads very close together as though one was whispering to the other. Liz could see that the woman was her sister, Angela. She couldn't see who the man was although she knew it wasn't Robert, Angela's husband. Ohmigod! It must be *him* – her beefcake.

It must be Hugh!

Liz stared even harder at the screen but nothing more was revealed to her.

Anyway, she should do something about this. She forced her limbs to wake up. Creakingly she walked into the room. The children ignored her until she stood between them and the screen. "What is all this?" she asked.

"We don't know," Marcus said. "We found it in the cabinet when we were looking for a film to watch. We don't even know who these people are." His little face shone with luminous innocence and Liz didn't believe a word of it.

Apart from anything else, even she knew they would have a hard job working out how to use a video machine. They would be used to calling up a film or box set on the telly, not finding an outside bit of kit 'in the cabinet' and inserting it into an antique machine.

Sophie tried to peer around her to see what was on show now. Liz turned and saw Philippe again. Again, he closed his bedroom curtains. She switched off the television at the power button, and then ejected the video from the player.

Sophie started to scream and Marcus to jump up and down on the bed so hard Liz thought she could hear its feet bounce off the floor in time with him. This was more like the satanic little blighters she remembered. But this time she was immune. She wasn't about to panic about whether she was doing the right thing with someone else's children any more when their parents were so insistent on her babysitting them when she was so obviously unfit for the job. She would simply use her common-sense although, given what she now knew about Telly and Grabber, it was hardly their fault they were so horrible.

Because, after all, what possible reason could they have for this type of recording, other than blackmail? Why else would someone have a tape like this? Who would have filmed it exactly? Liz wondered if the Satan Spawn could have done the whole thing. And why? She was more inclined to suspect the adults, especially Telly.

Liz, having checked there was nothing hard in range he could be damaged on, grabbed Marcus's ankle and he fell with a satisfying 'whumff' full length onto the bed. He raised his other foot to kick at her, but luckily for him checked out the expression on her face first. Sophie starting yelling, "Get your hands off him. You're going to be in deep shit now. We'll get you for abuse."

"Shut up Sophie," Marcus said.

"You deliberately set this up so I would see this video," Liz said. "Why did you want me to see it?"

They looked at each other, but said nothing.

"I'm waiting," Liz said. She said that because she couldn't think what else to say. Where do you go when you've got to this stage with a couple of bolshi children and then they do nothing? She was suddenly deeply thankful she and Hugh *had* split up. At this moment she couldn't imagine anything worse than having children. She'd rather have puppies.

And then she felt Marcus's ankle relax under her hand. He and Sophie exchanged glances again and he shrugged. It was like a miniature version of Philippe.

"Go on, then," Sophie said.

"Okay," Marcus said. "Liz, the video isn't ours."

"It isn't?"

"It's Telly's."

"Telly's?"

"She's the one who filmed it."

"She was?"

"She's trying to get leverage."

"Leverage?"

"Yeah. Lev. Er. Edge. It's American for having something on you so you do what she wants you to do. She thinks that's the way it works. You gotta feel sorry for her."

"You gotta?"

"Yeah. She's so pathetic."

"She is?"

"Yeah. She's got the hots for old Philippo there, that old guy that lives next to you."

"Old guy?"

"Yeah. She split up him and Laurel, that strange painter woman who lives in the house on the other side of you. Then she gets her way with him and then something happens, we don't know what, and they split up again, this time for good, we think. She doesn't take losing very well, though. I wouldn't want to be in his shoes."

By this time Liz had collapsed on the bed too. She'd never come across such world-weary children. Sophie merely nodded the whole time like a dog in the back of a car. Marcus lay there, one ankle resting on the other, staring at the ceiling, reciting his spiel as though well-rehearsed.

Liz could think of nothing to say. This was their mother they were talking about.

"She's not our mother," Sophie said, as though she'd been privy to Liz's thoughts. "She has tried as far as she's able, but she doesn't have what it takes. Gotta feel sorry for her. Dad's a useless husband, I reckon. When I'm old, and if I decide I want to marry, I shall make sure I don't get someone like him. That's if I decide I want to marry. There seems to be so much hassle and not much happy ever after."

Liz immediately thought of Angela. Liz had always thought of her when someone said they knew no-one who was happy in their marriage. She'd always thought Angela and Robert were the perfect couple. This was getting very depressing.

"You look so sad," Sophie said. "But, you know, children our age are a lot older than when very old people like you were our age." She poked her leg. "Do you understand?"

"I can just about make my aged brain cells grasp that notion," Liz replied. "And I had some idea that was the case, but I had no idea of how advanced that phenomenon had got. It's like you guys are ten, no, twenty, years ahead of my generation. Blimey, the rate you're going you'll be able to vote at ten, marry at eight and retire at thirty-five. Not to mention having a key to the door when you've barely left your pushchairs and, driving your granny, in your own car, to a residential home by the time you've left kindergarten."

An expectant silence fell. Marcus broke it.

"To be fair to the old man, he's okay with us," he said. Liz hoped he was speaking the truth. If that were the case, then maybe old Grabber might have some redeeming characteristics. On the other hand, it seemed to her that these children could pull the wool more easily than the most experienced solicitor. She couldn't tell if she was being scammed or not by them.

"It's other people he's useless with," Marcus continued. "Like Telly, and like Gran." He pulled a few metres of thread from the bed cover and studied it as though he was about to put it back. "Of course, we know where she is, you know. We didn't at first. Couldn't find her anywhere, but now we know."

Eek! Really?

Another expectant silence fell. Liz pulled a few threads herself before she realised what she was doing and discovered how impossible it was to put them back.

Sophie rolled over until her face was a breath from Liz's. "We know, you know," she said. "We know she's in your shed."

Liz rallied. "How can you know when she doesn't even know I know?"

"But she does know you know. The point is that you mustn't let her know you know, for the sake of her pride. After all, how can someone go on living in your shed if you let them know you know?"

Good question.

"But it's time you got her inside. It's too cold for her out there. And we can't do anything about it, because she'd be terrified if she knew we knew where she was."

"In fact," Liz said. "You're so far advanced compared to us that you'll be senile before you're born and then you'll seem like little children and the whole cycle will begin again with that wonderfully simple and yet complex perfection nature exhibits in us."

Sophie reared back like a startled cobra.

"I'm sure that Granny'd be delighted to know you know," Liz continued. She was guessing that, but Melanie had mentioned how fond Granny Smart was of the children, and they seemed to need some bolstering. "She might be feeling very alone and unloved. The fact that you know where she is and haven't told your parents, although that will make her sad, it will also make her happy. I believe she's very attached to you."

As she wasn't supposed to know about the granny, either, Liz didn't know how she'd pass on that message, but at the moment the practicalities were irrelevant.

Marcus and Sophie stared at her and she wasn't sure, in the uncertain light, but she thought they both looked a little pink. "She doesn't *have* to like us," Marcus said. "She's not really our granny. She's only Dad's step-mother. That's partly why he took all her property. She hadn't long married Grand-dad when he died and Dad was in trouble financially and he felt that his father's property should have been his. She'll never get it back. He's not stupid. He's done it all legally. So, she doesn't have to like us at all." He pulled out a few more metres of bed-spread. "Dad did take her in when she became ill. I know Telly saw her as a free housekeeper and babysitter, but they did sort-of look after her."

"So, we'd quite understand if she didn't like us at all," Sophie said. She was curling a lock of hair around her finger so energetically Liz could see the skin on her scalp pull out into little hillocks.

Liz gave in to the overwhelming urge that engulfed her and pounced on them. The hug didn't last long before they fought it off, but it existed for long enough. The Spawn of Satan had turned out to be just children after all.

"Don't worry," Liz said. "She's not outside any more. She's inside in the warm surrounded by friends. And Moocher, of course."

They took a moment to digest this news. Liz was pleased to see they looked a little less worried.

"You're not so bad after all," Sophie said. "You want to know what we've always called you?"

"No thanks," Liz said. "No, I don't."

"We've always called you Jellybutt, because when we see you, you're always rushing off somewhere and we just see this butt disappearing around a corner, and it's ..."

And they all heard the door go and the sound of Tallulah walking in and out of the rooms downstairs, and calling, and then her slow ascent of the stairs. They leapt off the bed, looked at each other and dived for the video player. After some fumbling the video was removed and replaced with another, the television switched back on. They re-assembled on the bed and were gazing in rapt fascination at the television screen when Tallulah found them. She stared at the television and back to them and back to the screen again. She seemed to have nothing to say.

Liz could understand it. When she finally focused on the screen it was to discover that they were watching, with apparent enthrallment, an instructional video on how to keep one's lawn in tip-top, shiny-green-grassed condition.

Chapter Twenty-Two
(Scammers R Us)

Mitch could see both ends of Malvern Road from his vantage point on the scaffolding covering number twenty-three. He saw Liz Houston head over to number twelve. He knew that was where the granny had lived before she took up residence in Liz's shed. He also knew the granny was no longer in the shed although he didn't know where she was now. He had no intention of finding out, either. He was pleased Granny Smart had got away from Tally, but she could always tell when he was lying so he didn't want to know anything he might inadvertently give away.

Tally – he gathered locals were calling her 'Telly' – for obvious reasons – might be his 'sister' but he wasn't wildly fond of her. She really was prepared to take advantage of anyone. Having said that, she seemed to change after she targeted, and hooked, the lonely heart that was Graham Smart at that time, almost as if she'd met her match. She ended up actually marrying him! Even though he had two children! And now she appeared to be playing the happy wifey for all she was worth.

Mitch fancied she might not be playing it. He thought she had found a man who couldn't be taken in by her. He felt a flicker of sympathy for her if it turned out that Graham was playing *her*, rather than the other way around.

In the meantime, it was annoying that their mentor, Troy, still held up Tally's example as something he should be aspiring to, and kept ribbing Mitch over his failure to score when his little sister had succeeded so well. What Troy never mentioned was that, since Tally's marriage to her lawyer husband, she hadn't visited him at all, and had certainly not been to the gatherings in The Gamester.

There were disadvantages to being the adopted offspring of one of the biggest con men around, and Tally wouldn't want Graham to find out that was who had brought her up. Mitch wondered what story she had concocted to explain to Graham why she had no family.

Probably something along the lines of the one he always used: parents both killed by a drunk driver, or maybe a driver high on marijuana. Being too young at that time to go it alone he'd been put in a home, fostered several times, each time to someone worse, until finally found someone who was everything a foster-child could possibly wish for, only for her/them to die from cancer just when it was time to be thrown out of the system.

Still, at least Tally was getting on with her life in a more constructive way than she'd ever done. Also, she was gaining success in television. He was pleased for her, although still didn't like her much.

He wondered what Liz Houston was doing over there. Surely not babysitting! He'd seen Tally leave, so it must be. He was only thankful it wasn't him.

Mitch saw a lot of what was going on whilst doing his job. People didn't think to look up so they didn't know there was someone above them. Someone who could see everything. Of course, they particularly didn't think to look up at scaffolding when it was dark like it was now. He liked prowling around in the dark. It made him less visible to the world.

He particularly enjoyed prowling around on his own house. It was his first house purchase and although the house needed a hell of a lot of work, just owning it made him feel more secure than he'd ever felt. As if he finally belonged somewhere.

He wouldn't be telling anyone of his purchase yet, though. This was his!

He'd always liked this area and recently he'd been supervising a lot of work here although he wasn't that keen on being in such close proximity to Tally and to The Gamester, but when, through being 'in the industry know' he had the chance to snap up this property, he jumped at it. And he already loved this house.

He also knew that Tally's disinterest in others would probably mean she didn't even realise he'd moved into the same road she lived on. That suited him just fine.

Business was good and he was in a solid position to buy now. His specialist knowledge on houses of this age was making him very popular. People were catching on that older houses require different treatment to newer houses if they wish to avoid problems later on.

Also, there were quite a few people who Troy would consider 'target-worthy' in the vicinity, not least, Liz Houston at number nine. Hmmm … Liz Houston. She owned her own house. She was single. Yes, Troy would tell him to get in there sharpish.

Chapter Twenty-Three
(The Second Staked Goat)

Telly was as good as her word and back by ten so there was plenty of time to prepare for their second stakeout.

Liz shared her car with Melanie, and with Moocher who dreamed, twitchingly, across the back seat. He'd got the hang of this business already.

They'd swapped companions for this session. Laurel was in Danny's car. Wayne and Jason were in Wayne's car. Philippe prowled between the sites, hoping to catch someone who may not be smashing windows because they were watching us watching for them.

"Strange it was that particular window done in last night," Melanie said out of the darkness. Liz flinched. She'd been deep in scandalised speculation about her sister and her ex getting it together. Even Moocher heaved himself upright.

"They had to be watching to do it exactly when you went for a pee," Melanie went on. "Ooh, spooky. You were being watched." Compulsively, Melanie looked over her shoulder and got a faceful of dog-spit as Moocher took advantage and showed her his affection. His tail thumped. As Melanie wiped his slimy kisses from her cheeks, Liz gave vent to a little shiver. Someone *must* have been watching her and Laurel.

Liz might have been even more spooked if her mind hadn't been on other things. She couldn't stop thinking about it and she couldn't stop kicking herself for not seeing it before.

Of course, Angela and Hugh would get together. They had always admired each other – no secret there. Hugh and Robert might as well be interchangeable, so no mystery there, either. As for her and Angela – Liz balked at the idea that she and her sister were similar in any way at all, but there must be some reason Hugh would start up shenanigans with his ex's sibling.

"I suppose the window-smasher might have come along," Liz said, trying to focus on present concerns, "but seen us staking out a goat."

"A goat?" Melanie queried.

"Oh, never mind. I mean he or she must have seen us. They must have had a good laugh – they'd have known we'd be out all night freezing to death and dying for a pee. All they had to do was wait until we left and then do it. Not tonight, though. Oh, no. It ain't gonna happen tonight. I haven't drunk anything all day today. My tongue feels like a lump of leather." She waggled it around expecting it to make wooden clonking sounds. It didn't.

"How could he do it?" Did Liz wail that out loud, or had she just thought it?

"I don't see how anyone could have spotted us, particularly amongst all the cars parked around the place." Melanie turned to Liz then and said, "Why shouldn't he do it? You've divorced him. You've turned him down every time he's tried to get back with you."

"But, just like that? With no warning whatsoever. He could have given me some warning." Liz stuffed a lump of pizza into her mouth before any more moans could escape it, and then she tried to talk without spitting. "Something might have given us away to the window-smasher, for all we know. We'll just have to hope we get him tonight, because two nights of staked goats, pizza and biscotti have already put me up a dress size. I'm trying so hard as well. 'Never eat more than you can carry' some film star once said, but boy, when someone else is carrying it and it's presented to me in a tasteful cardboard box it's soooo hard to refuse it."

Liz stopped to swallow. As if they'd waited for this chance, some prawns, making a bid for freedom, leapt off her pizza and landed somewhere near the clutch. She stared at the space on her seafood pizza where those shrimps had been. It was as if everything had slowed right down since *that* revelation, as though the world was about to stop spinning on its axis and they were all going to fall off the surface of the earth just like the prawns had fallen off her pizza.

"Hadn't you better pick them up, before you squash them underfoot," Melanie said, ever practical. "It was probably better that he didn't give you any warning, that it was already a done thing. So, you could take it in one go – yanking off the plaster rather than peeling it off slowly and agonisingly."

"Damn." Liz carefully replaced the slice of pizza on the dash and bent over to pick up the seafood before it became part of the carpet down there. Only the bending over was more in her mind than in actuality and that familiar feeling of breathlessness overcame her while her fingertips vainly strained to reach their target. Someone had draped a sandbag around her waist and it was getting in the way. "Well. Angela!" It was surprisingly difficult to talk in this position and it came out on a wheeze, but she persevered. "For God's sake. Angela. I *thought* he was a bit offhand when he turned up. That's because he was. He's already learning it from her." She straightened up, panting.

It took a while for her to realise Melanie was staring at her as if she had been talking nonsense, but she didn't want to say so.

"What? Why are you looking at me like that?" Liz demanded.

"You said, 'Angela'. Why did you say, 'Angela'?" Melanie asked in high-pitched tones of disbelief. "What are you talking about?"

"Hang on a minute – if that's not what *you're* talking about? What *are* you talking about? All that stuff about yanking off a plaster?"

"I'm sorry. I thought you must know by now," Melanie said. "Hugh was spotted in the centre of town canoodling with a woman – Laurel didn't know who it was – she only knew it wasn't you – she might have taken a closer look, but that was when she spotted the Smart Granny begging and knew we had to do something about it."

"You know – people are so deceptive! Laurel and I shared a car at the first stakeout and she didn't say a word! I wonder if that's why she was babbling so much."

"Well, she's not going to want to say anything about Hugh canoodling is she? Be fair. She doesn't know you that well, does she. Anyway, what's this about Angela?"

"It's Angela Hugh's having an affair with," Liz said.

"Don't be daft!"

"It is, though. I've seen him blush when she's mentioned and I've seen them in a video."

"Seriously? This is what you base this idea on – a blush, and a video? A video? Who would video such a thing?"

Well, when Melanie put it like that with such scorn in her voice it did seem a little unlikely. Even so, Hugh *had* blushed when she mentioned Angela, and then he'd rushed off, too; and he *had* been seen canoodling with *someone* in town. As far as Liz was aware, Laurel had never met Angela so she wouldn't know if it was her or not.

As for the video – come to think of it, she hadn't actually seen him. She'd only seen Angela with someone. And, she had no idea how old the video was. She couldn't imagine Hugh, for all his faults, canoodling with anyone that wasn't her on *her* doorstep. Maybe it had been her! She came over all hot. She needed to know how old that video was.

Not that she cared any more. She was exhausted with it all. She'd moved on and she really hoped he had, too. As long as he wasn't moving on with her sister. That would be an awful thing that only an awful person would even think of! Then she looked to check Melanie's reaction in case she'd said it out loud instead of thinking it.

"You know, Liz," Melanie said. "Line dancing is very good for getting fit and losing a few pounds."

Melanie had also moved on, apparently. Line dancing?

"Oh. Right," Liz said. She gave up looking for the runaway prawns. They would have got clean away by now and were probably sipping pina coladas on a beach in the Bahamas.

"Much better than just trying to work out or do exercises by yourself. You wouldn't get so bored and you'd be more likely to stick to it," she said. "You've got to move on. You've got to let Hugh move on, too."

It sounded like Melanie had an agenda. "Are you suggesting I go to line dancing lessons?" Liz asked.

"Yes. Except that, to save you going out I know someone who could give you lessons at home, if you like. Your front room has enough space in it. It could be a new thing to do in your new life that's starting now. It could be part of a whole new, moving-on you."

Liz turned to look at Melanie. Moocher lifted his head as though aware that a turning point might have arrived. "Are you suggesting I forget about Hugh and Angela and move on, perchance?"

"Don't be so dog-in-the-mangerish, Liz. You don't want him, so why can't Angela – not Angela – I don't mean Angela – it won't be Angela! Why can't someone else, whoever it is, have him? Do you want me to find out if my friend will teach you to line dance, or not?"

"Oh, all right, then." Liz knew when she was beaten. "Will you be doing it too?"

"I don't need to, thanks," she said.

Oh! Humphff.

Actually, it wasn't a bad idea. She didn't want to be less slim and lovely than the slim and lovely Angela!

Liz chewed with diminished enthusiasm on her cold Sea Tango pizza, and wondered what the woman in the centre of town, if it wasn't Angela, looked like. She'd dearly love to know. She bet that woman was all slim and lovely, too. Liz pushed the rest of her pizza back into the box and defiantly ignored the pack of biscotti. She resented the 'dog-in-the-manger' accusation. It wasn't that at all. It was that she couldn't imagine him being happy with her sister. She wanted Hugh to be happy.

"Anyway," Melanie said after a heavy silence. "I still think it's strange that particular window was done in last night at that particular time."

"Well, I hope we get whoever it is tonight," Liz said. "Because Philippe is beginning to make the sort of noises that mean he won't be beholden to us for any more effort on his behalf. Which is all jolly noble, but I want to know who's doing it now."

"I bet no windows get smashed tonight," Melanie said as though Liz hadn't said anything.

"Why are you so sure?"

"I think I know who's doing it."

Liz hastily swallowed a too-big lump of biscotti which had somehow sneaked into her mouth. "What? Who? Why didn't you say before?"

"Because I might be wrong. I might be."

"Who?"

"I could be wrong."

"Come on! Who do you reckon it is?"

"Laurel."

"Laurel. You're kidding! She wouldn't do a thing like that. She's far too high-minded." Good grief. Why hadn't that occurred to her? Of course, it was Laurel!

"The only thing to ruin that theory, however," Liz said, "is that she was with me the entire time last night, pee and all." Yeah. So how did she do it?

"Oh, poo." Melanie dismissed that trifling fact with a wave of beautifully manicured hands. "Last night she just got someone else to do it, having inveigled you away for long enough, to cover up for the fact that it's her doing it. In fact, that proves it's her."

"Duh. Inveigled? We were busting a gut for a pee. Even Moocher was." A snort from the back seat acknowledged the veracity of this statement.

"As for the high-minded bit," Melanie ploughed on. "She's not high-minded as far as Philippe is concerned. Absolutely the reverse, in fact."

"She isn't? What makes you say that?"

"She hates him," Melanie said.

"Does she? I had no idea. Why should she? If she hates him why is she doing a stint of goat-staking along with the rest of us?"

"To throw off suspicion, of course."

Absolutely. And she'd done it so well, too. Another biscotti had appeared. Liz bit into it and gave it a good chew. Things were adding up too well. "If I didn't know you better, I'd say you had it in for her," Liz said. Melanie turned so fast in her seat Liz flinched. "But I do know you quite well," she said quickly around a mouthful of crumbs and almonds. Melanie appeared to relax a bit.

"Okay, why should she hate Philippe?" Liz wanted to know.

"Because he dumped her."

"He dumped her?"

"Yes. Not many people knew about the affair."

But obviously many more than Laurel realised. "How come you knew?" Liz asked.

"I only knew after he dumped her. She was in a helluva state about it."

"Why did he dump her?"

"Another woman I think."

Liz wondered if the other woman had been Telly, or another woman altogether.

"At least he did that instead of stringing them both along at the same time." Liz really wasn't thinking of her sister. It was simply the first thing she thought.

"I think she would rather have been strung along."

"Oh. But what makes you think that she's breaking his windows? I don't think she's a petty person. Do you?" No, but she's a woman full of frustrated passion, Liz now realised.

"No, I don't think she is, but just think of what she gains," Melanie said, tacking on: "If it is her," a little belatedly, Liz thought.

"Go on then. What?"

"She gets him worried, because it has to be personal the way it's happening. And it's nice to worry people who've upset you. She's making him feel insecure like he did her. Also, she's getting a lot of business out of it and making a lot of money."

"Of course, yes. The signwriting. I suppose Philippe *is* giving her the jobs?" Of course, he is!

"Oh, yes. Definitely."

"There's something too tidy about it, though, Melanie."

"I know you can't stand things being too tidy," she said. Liz gazed at her in the gloom trying to work out exactly what she meant by that, but she should know better. Melanie always meant only the words she actually said. No less, no more.

"Although it does fit," Liz muttered, "I just can't see it. I just can't imagine Laurel doing something like this."

"I tell you what – if a window isn't done tonight then I reckon it has to be Laurel. What do you think?"

Unfortunately, Liz could follow the logic. No one would want to create a predictable pattern. "I suppose that would make it more likely that it was her."

"I bet a window isn't broken tonight. So, what shall we do then?"

"Let's wait and see," Liz said, a trifle snappily. And spent the rest of the night anxiously hoping that one of Philippe's windows *would* be broken, which wasn't quite the object of the exercise.

Chapter Twenty-Four
(Mapmaker)

That sweetheart scammer! Now he'd seen him he was seeing him everywhere – like buying a new car and only then realising how common it was. Worse – this person – this 'Mitch' was now living in the same road as him! And he was a purchaser, not a tenant, which suggested a permanence Mapmaker didn't like at all.

Scammer-Mitch had just bought number twenty-three.

Mapmaker tried very hard to *not* feel paranoid, but it was difficult. If he'd learned anything in his thirty-three years, it was that everything was worthy of suspicion. He patted his laptop, he ran his hand over the carving on his chair, he unscrewed the top of his pen and screwed it back on. He took a deep breath and reviewed his information. He knew the data was reliable.

The source for it was Logan and Daughter, the local letting agents. Terry Logan owed him – Mapmaker had got him out of a right mess involving an attack on his computer system by some malevolent software a few months ago, since when he had happily supplied information on the road he lived in. Terry lived in Malvern Road himself, at number thirty-two, virtually opposite.

He filled in the new information for number nine. There was a new lodger – an ageing punk. He'd fit right in. The only thing that had ever surprised him about number nine was learning that one of its residents – Wayne – was a tax specialist. Now *he* did seem out of place! Mapmaker went back and filled in that little nugget of information in his journal. On reflection, tax specialists could also be creative. On even more reflection, Liz was an accountant, apparently. Maybe she was so, so … volatile … colourful … he couldn't think how best to describe her – but whatever it was, maybe she was that colourful thing to counteract all the time she must spend on bookkeeping and spreadsheets and tax returns.

He was a little concerned that he had so many thoughts about Liz Houston, but anyone would worry about any female they knew if they also knew what that Mitch bloke was up to. No one was safe with scammers like him around the place.

Chapter Twenty-Five
(What a mess!)

Liz's wish wasn't granted. No windows were broken in any of Philippe's culinary establishments the previous night, and although he was very grateful for their efforts, he vehemently refused to have them spend any more of their time on further stakeouts.

Liz still couldn't quite imagine Laurel doing this dirty deed, but everyone else now looked upon her with deep suspicion. They'd realised how handy it was to have a job such as signwriting and then manufacturing the work for yourself.

At least no one else, other than Liz and Melanie, knew about Laurel being a woman scorned. If that had been common knowledge, it would have made any possible doubts anyone still had disappear like confetti in a fire.

Liz couldn't think what to do about it and when she staggered out of bed half way through the day she had more pressing matters on her mind. She didn't know why she'd bothered trying to get a few hours' sleep – she'd spent the time awake wondering about how miserable Hugh would be with Angela.

She just knew it *was* Angela, regardless of what Melanie had said.

She didn't mind him falling out of love with her, although she still had to get completely used to the idea of it. They had to move on in their lives and constantly hankering after the past wasn't the way to do it. But it was like she'd lost a protective coating.

Also, she couldn't believe Hugh would be happy with Angela. She couldn't see how they could possibly be good for each other. And then, of course, there was Robert and little Johnny to consider, too.

What a mess!

She couldn't immediately see what to do about any of that so, in a rush of enthusiasm she went in to see Philippe about her new idea.

He had taken some convincing, but he did tend to shyness. She persevered: "I've decided to start a new tradition," she said to him. "Every couple of months all the lodgers and tenants in these three houses – oh, and the kids from across the road – will meet at mine for supper. It'll be nice."

He'd been suspicious. "So, what's brought this on? You've never done this sort of thing before." Liz could only assume he was wary after their failed stakeout attempts. They hadn't solved anything, but they had consumed a lot of his supplies.

Talking of which: "It was so nice when we all pulled together for the stakeout. It made us seem like a team – like a community spirit brought us closer. And I think it would be great to foster that," Liz said.

He scowled even harder. Maybe he just wasn't in a very good mood.

"Admittedly," she went on, "we weren't very helpful and didn't catch your window-smasher, but we did all act together and we would have carried on staking out your restaurants if you'd let us …"

When she said that he suddenly couldn't meet her eyes any more, which was odd. She stowed that away in her mind for future examination. Something Was Going On.

"Also, you know – in this day and age of disaffection, lack of respect for one's elders, loss of a sense of identity, fly-tippers, the closing down of local shops, all this change and upheaval, don't you think it would be nice for us to have an anchor in this world of moving goalposts, this dark and uncertain environment we live in. Yes," she was getting into her stride after a faltering start. "We'll form a band of good-humoured, rough-justice sort of people, against a life grey and unjust. We'll stick together through all adversity and be there for each other when we whistle. We'll be …"

"Merry, and wear green," he said.

Liz decided he must have had a bad night. Maybe more of his windows lay in pieces on Bristol's pavements. She resolved to continue with her investigation into the window-smasher whether Philippe liked it or not. She just wouldn't tell him this time.

"And, anyway," he said. "Why the children from across the road? They're not your lodgers and given the way you've always described them I'm surprised you want to inflict them on us."

He had a point of course, and she couldn't explain that it was an opportunity for them to see their gran in her new guise and strike up an innocent-seeming acquaintanceship with her.

"I believe I was mistaken in them," she said loftily, and with a final: "See you tonight," she left in a hurry.

Chapter Twenty-Six
(Coals to Newcastle)

Mitch pushed through the door into the Post Office only to find the end of a long queue right in front of him. There was barely room for the door to shut behind him, and as soon as it did shut someone else came in and had to stand holding the door open because there was no room for him to actually come in. This funnelled a cold draught up Mitch's back.

He really didn't need it. His back was already dodgy. He'd jumped down from the last part of the scaffolding on one of his current projects, and landed on a half-buried dog's bone in the lawn, stumbled, and ricked his back. He had an appointment pending at the chiropractor to put it right. The cold draught wasn't going to make it feel better and he almost decided to go home because it was very painful. But he really wanted to get this letter off via special delivery. It was important. He gritted his teeth and decided he'd just have to put up with the discomfort.

Having resigned himself to the wait, he looked around at his fellow queue-captives. Most of them were staring at their phones. One was singing under her breath to a baby in a sling on her chest. Two were having an argument. And there was Tally.

Hurriedly, he switched his gaze back to the arguing couple. He listened a bit harder to them. The argument appeared to be about the current political situation. He switched off from it. He got enough of that down the pub. He stared at the cashiers – there were two of them at work today – not nearly enough. As usual.

He didn't think Tally had seen him and wondered whether to creep out, but he still wanted this letter to be posted so he stayed.

He concentrated on the cashiers. The expression on Bridget's face, his favourite cashier, or, rather, his favourite counter service consultant – she had put him right last time he'd called her a cashier – caught his attention. He could see she was biting the inside of her mouth, presumably so she didn't say something. He knew her as a forthright person prone to saying whatever was on her mind. But, apparently not this time.

He switched his attention to the customer in front of her. A young woman had plonked a large, distinctively patterned jumper on the counter. She had a loud voice. By now everyone knew that she wanted to send it to Fair Isle in Shetland. It looked to Mitch like she was sending coals to Newcastle, but, each to their own. Except she was asking what to send it in.

Bridget let go the inside of her mouth enough to say: "There are padded envelopes over there." She gestured in the relevant direction, while her eyebrows disappeared into her hairline.

Mrs Fair Isle ambled over to the shelf, apparently unaware there was a very long queue waiting for her to choose her envelope. She might as well have been aimlessly wandering along a woodland path sniffing out wild anemones and comparing them to a summer breeze. She riffled around on the shelf, pitching some of the stationery onto the floor. A helpful child, with his mother just ahead of Mitch in the queue, picked them up one by one and put them back only to repeat himself when Mrs Fair Isle knocked more off. Eventually a suitable envelope was chosen and taken back to the counter.

There was also a Mr Fair Isle. He was dead to the world, deep into his mobile phone. The only living thing about him was the chewing motion of his jaws and the smacking noise as the gum within stretched and snapped back together again as he generously shared the mastication sensation with the assembled crowd. His head looked as if he'd dipped it in motor oil, so close to his skull his hair cowered.

Bridget mumbled something. Mitch assumed she wasn't speaking with her usual clarity because she had hold of the inside of her mouth with her teeth.

"What did you say?" Mrs Fair Isle demanded.

Bridget mumbled again: "The envelope is one pound forty-five and ..." which was as far she got. Mrs Fair Isle took great exception to the cost of the envelope and chucked it back onto the shelf. "Where's the brown paper?" she demanded. "I can use your Sellotape."

Bridget, apparently incapable by now of anything civil leaving her lips, merely pointed a shaking finger at the wrapping materials shelf.

Mrs Fair Isle sauntered over and picked up the item required for her chosen packaging method. And then she sauntered back to the counter and proceeded to thrust the jumper into a carrier bag before trying to wrap it in brown paper.

The entire queue was transfixed by the spectacle of Mrs Fair Isle wrestling an enormous, woolly, seemingly-alive jumper into obedience in its paper prison. Silence, other than the rustling of the paper and the swearing of Mrs Fair Isle in between rapid open-mouthed chewing of gum, and the little snorty laughs of Mr Fair Isle as he continued to scroll down his phone screen.

Obviously, no one else had a life. They were all on this earth merely to observe this incredible display of complete indifference to everyone else in the world. Maybe they were all, rather like Mitch, somewhat envious of such utter nerve. He wished he had half of it! Then he wouldn't ever give a damn about anyone ever again. That would be handy.

And everyone present was letting her get away with it. He didn't have the energy or the inclination for the hassle of dealing with it; he had no doubt Bridget was hamstrung by some regulation or other from having a go at a customer, and no one else appeared ready for a fray. What was even more amazing was that Tally just stood quietly waiting. It was so unlike her – she always used to be up for a brawl – that he found himself glancing at her again, almost wishing it was the old Tally, and not this new, demure one.

Tally was looking directly at him, a smile twitching at one side of her mouth. His smile answered hers and she flicked her gaze away. So that was the way it would be. He felt a pang of sadness through the relief. It would be nice to have some family, but she'd never been a reliable 'sibling' so it was probably best not to think it would work now.

They'd always had the same sense of humour, though. It was the only thing that got them through childhood, that fleeting comradeship. But, yes, it looked like ignoring each other was the way to go.

As he turned back to observe an increasingly grim-faced Bridget, he spotted Liz Houston. She came in the door, looked around, and left again. Very sensible.

He resigned himself to waiting through the pantomime whilst trying to chill out so his blood pressure didn't suffer too much.

Mitch was deep into consideration of whether he could get away with second-hand double Roman tiles for his latest job on Malvern Road, or whether he'd have to have new. He wasn't prepared to consider a whole new roof – it had to be as close to the original as possible – both for him, and for his client – the double Roman with its gentle roll and subtle pans were the real deal and precisely what was wanted – it really depended on whether the colours matched – when raised voices brought him back to earth.

"No! This is exactly the jumper she wants!"

"It's costing too much to send. She can get her own."

"But we can send her this one!"

"You can give it to her next time you see her. You don't have to send it."

"I'm here now."

"That's not a good reason to spend all that dosh on sending her something she can pick up."

"Oh, jeez. Really? You think we should leave it til she comes down?"

And Mrs Fair Isle stopped packing the rebellious jumper and stared at her still-noisily-chewing-gum partner. The thought that maybe she didn't need to send the jumper was enough to stop her world turning.

And everyone else's as well, apparently.

Which proved too much for some who, with various levels of foul-mouthed exclamations of disgust, gave up on their mission in the Post Office, and left, no doubt swearing some more when they realised they couldn't slam the door behind them, it being on a soft-close mechanism.

Bridget, however, took the opportunity to silently shift the unruly package aside and gesture to the next in the queue to come forward with their requirements. So, the queue, unmoving for so long, took a leap forward.

Mitch moved up, feeling encouraged that he'd get out of the place this morning, rather than this afternoon as he'd feared when he first arrived.

Mr Fair Isle's sticky voice continued: "Why is she coming down, anyway? I mean, does she have to?"

A short pause followed this question.

Then Mrs Fair Isle's piercing voice answered: "What do you mean, why is she coming down? She's my sister!"

"That's not a good enough reason by itself."

"It is, too!"

"She eats everything and she drinks everything and she does nothing!"

"She's my sister!"

No one else said a word. They didn't want to draw the Fair Isles' attention back to life in the Post Office.

Mitch risked a glance at Tally only to find she was doing the same. They shared another fugitive smile.

"She hogs the remote!"

"She's my sister!"

Mitch was still surprised that no one out of all the people in the original queue had tackled the Fair Isles. No wonder such behaviour seemed to be spreading. Normally, he would have himself, but he didn't feel up to it. Thankfully, the queue was moving now, but this waiting hadn't done his back any good at all.

"She sleeps until the afternoon!"

"She's my sister!"

"The resemblance is only too obvious!"

Another pause before an enraged shriek: "You bastard!" Mrs Fair Isle picked up the jumper in its carrier bag and started beating Mr Fair Isle about his slicked-back hair with it. The bag burst, the jumper fell out, Mr Fair Isle ran for the door and Mrs Fair Isle raced after him screaming with every appearance of immense enjoyment.

The Post Office was suddenly engulfed in complete silence.

The queue moved forward.

The helpful child picked up the jumper and rubbed his face in it. His mother plucked it from him and tried to hold its bulk, somewhat unsuccessfully, by one finger and her thumb. Her lips formed the shape of a dying cod gasping for breath.

"I like that jumper, Mummy. Can I have it?"

"*May* I have it? Tristan."

"May I have it, Mummy?"

He looked expectant. He also looked as if he wouldn't know what 'no' meant if it bit him.

Mummy looked around her at the faces that mostly registered disgust. Heaven knew where this jumper had been – apart from around the Post Office floor and beating the head of a greasy-haired, gum-chewing individual.

"Uh. No."

Tristan's face fell. Mitch was happily surprised that his initial assumption was incorrect. Tristan was going to take the 'no' like a good boy.

However, in an entirely unexpected move, Tristan snatched the jumper from Mummy's grasp and raced for the door. Mummy followed at speed, mission to the Post Office forgotten.

The remaining members of the queue cheered. The Fair Isle had left the building.

Mitch was happy to finally reach Bridget. He handed over the letter. "Special Delivery, please." He smiled at her.

She smiled back. Her wordlessness said everything.

Chapter Twenty-Seven
(The Malvern Road Gang)

Liz couldn't be bothered with the Post Office when it had such a long queue in it. Whenever she tried to be patient and stick with it, she always ended up with some person getting too close to her behind, and quite often someone in front who smelled like they hadn't washed since birth.

She looked in and left, but not before she noted Telly in there exchanging glances with a man who looked familiar but she couldn't immediately place. Walking back down the road she wrestled with it until it came to her. That man had also featured in the video Sophie and Marcus had been watching at Telly's house.

What the hell *was* that video about?

If it wasn't for Angela and Hugh getting it together, and a load of window-smashing going on, she knew that video mystery would be occupying a lot more of her mental space than it actually was. She wondered if she should push it up the worry-priority list.

She might do that, but not until she'd got the first Malvern Road Gang dinner sorted out. It was coming together nicely and she was looking forward to it. All she had to do now was make sure the ground floor at number nine was accessible enough for ten people, and that she had enough chairs.

All of which was successfully achieved with the willing support of Melanie and Danny, and now it was all under way, Liz was very pleased with her idea.

Philippe had got over his bad temper and presented himself at the designated time clutching bottles of wine and boxes of Cantuccine biscuits, a suitably penitent expression on his face.

An over-excited Jason had launched himself into the breakfast room, tripping over a step that wasn't there and only saving himself from concussion by grabbing the table before he hit the floor. He'd go down a storm if he came to line dancing lessons.

Luckily, Melanie had grabbed the table before it had gone down, too, complete with all its crockery, cutlery and artfully arranged snacks.

They were a little cramped in the breakfast room. Maybe next time she'd clear out the front room and use that instead. In the meantime, everyone invited was there, supper had been served, and things were going well.

The breakfast room hummed with friendly chat accompanied by the harmonious clatter of spoons and forks on plates as Liz's Bolognese disappeared down receptive throats. She could also hear Moocher's claws on the floor boards as he shuffled around under the table emotionally blackmailing people to drop him the odd piece of garlic bread, but for once she pretended not to notice. She didn't want to spoil the mood by giving her: "You're not doing the dog any favours by giving him food" tirade. She would just give him less supper.

Marcus and Sophie, no longer masquerading as the Spawn of Satan, were involved in animated conversation with their gran and with Danny about some computer game. They appeared to be keeping up the pretence that Ronnie was Ronnie. Liz assumed everyone knew they knew the truth. She wondered if Granny knew she knew, but decided honour would be satisfied as long as she *pretended* she didn't.

Moocher had greeted everyone as they arrived and he'd been just the same with Ronnie as with the others. Of course, he would have known Ronnie before, when to Liz he was merely a spooky, steamed up mirror. Back then Liz had been blissfully unaware of grannies in sheds and such oddities. She wouldn't be surprised if Moocher hadn't whiled away a few hours visiting in the garden shed. She was glad.

Suddenly a chair screeched back, no doubt gouging tracks to rival the Grand Canyon in her original planking wooden floor. "And I suppose you think it's ME!" Laurel shouted. She towered over Philippe, shaking her fist in his face, which had paled. His dark eyes seemed fixed to her as if by invisible strings. He didn't move, not a quiver. She trembled in her fury like leaves in a high wind, but failed to bring out any more words even though her mouth opened and shut a few times.

It served her right for getting complacent over the success of her supper, Liz thought. It was asking for trouble, and trouble had answered.

"Think it's her what?" she whispered in what she fondly imagined to be undetectable decibels to Melanie, only to get the question echoing back to her from the suddenly silent cavern the breakfast room had become.

"Think it's her smashing windows," Danny obliged, smiling around him as though that would stop anyone from realising it was him who said it.

Laurel certainly looked like the wronged party. She looked all maligned and innocence personified. But Liz didn't think anyone fell for it. No, they just went back to stuffing their faces with spaghetti Bolognese and garlic bread. Laurel turned with a little, hiccupy sob, ignored Philippe's outstretched hand, and ran off down the hall. Liz sat there for a while and tried to nosh down more Bolognese, but it had quite lost its flavour, so she went after Laurel. Moocher came along to help.

She was in the front room. "Come back and join us, Laurel," Liz said. "We're the Malvern Road Gang and it's not the same without you."

"Everyone thinks I'm smashing Philippe's windows don't they?" she asked.

"Yes, they do."

Laurel spun around so fast Liz took a step back and found a dog to fall over. Not being one to miss heaven-sent opportunities he licked Bolognese sauce off her face while she was down. When she regained her feet it was to find Laurel in the same position with the same expression on her face. Liz wished she was still on the floor.

"But," Liz said slowly, hoping for inspiration to strike. "They'll think what they want whatever you say. In fact, the more you try to deny it, the more they'll think it's you. And the more you try to explain, the more suspicion will come your way. The only thing you can do is face it out." Liz didn't know if this was inspiration, but it felt right.

"But I don't *want* people to think I'm smashing Philippe's windows," she wailed. "I especially don't want Philippe to think I'm smashing his windows."

"Hasn't it occurred to you that maybe he doesn't think so? He hasn't reported you to the police. Or maybe he does think so – but if he does, the fact remains that he still hasn't reported you to the police. Why would that be, do you reckon?"

"Ooh, yeah," Laurel said, pursing her lips, a faraway look in her eyes. A smile bloomed, a first hesitantly, and then blindingly. It took over her face. She blushed and dropped her gaze. Liz wondered what she was thinking. "Ooh, yeah ..."

"Okay now?"

Laurel adjusted her bra strap, straightened her skirt that was so small Liz wondered if she had a butt at all, whipped out a mirror from some invisible pocket, checked herself over and marched out of the room. "Thanks, Liz." The words came whispering back to Liz as she watched Laurel take a seat next to Philippe again, a definite shimmy in the act of sitting down. Liz saw him notice it. Yes, things were far from dead in that quarter. On either side, it seemed.

Liz retrieved her plate and, making people shift around a place to mix things up a bit, she sat down between Ronnie and Jason.

"What's all this I hear about you line dancing, then?" Danny asked from across the table.

"I don't know," Liz said. "What *is* this you hear about it?"

"Oh, just that you're thinking of doing some exercise. You know, getting fit. And maybe, er ..."

"Maybe? Maybe what?"

"Well, you know ..."

"No. I don't know. Please, do tell." Liz flung her napkin down on the table like a gauntlet. A silence fell at their end of the room, people shifted uneasily in their chairs and Danny blanched. Liz waited, fondly expecting that her face looked like something made of granite, her expression forbidding, her air menacing. All of which was completely ruined by Melanie.

"Losing weight, he means," she said. "What else could he possibly mean?"

"I, er ..."

"Well. Please do tell. What else could he possibly mean?"

"I'll tell you what's mean. You are. You're mean. Mean to me." Maybe Liz pouted. A little.

"Only because we care," she said in a snake-in-the-grass kind of way so Liz couldn't be cross.

"Mean," Liz muttered. Moocher's nose pushed into her hand and she knew someone loved her just the way she was, fat and all. "All right then. Who's going to teach me line dancing?"

Everyone looked at Ronnie.

"You could teach me line dancing?" Liz asked, hoping she didn't sound too surprised.

"Yes, I could."

"And, would you be happy to teach me?" Liz wasn't sure what answer she wanted.

"I'd love to."

Crap. Now she'd have to do it!

"How do you know enough to teach me?"

"I've always been keen on line dancing, and I love the music, too."

Liz had never seen Ronnie so animated. She had to pretend not to notice when he gave a little start, looked down at his layers of ragged clothing, put his hand to the ear that bore the most ironware and Liz knew he must be visualising his hair as he'd last seen it in the mirror. He flushed, stuck his chin out and said, "Just make damn sure you don't tell any of my mates, or you'll be in deep shit."

Liz knew Granny Smart was trying to sound like a hard man who liked line dancing and anyone who thought that was odd could take a long run off a short pier.

It didn't quite come across, but Liz tried to react appropriately. "Okay, Ronnie," she said, wondering if she sounded sufficiently cowed. "I promise I won't give you away. As long as you don't tell any of *my* mates either."

"Too late! We already know!" chortled Danny. Liz ignored him.

"Oh! You want the lessons then?" Ronnie asked.

"Yes. That'd be great."

"We'll start tomorrow afternoon if that's okay with you?"

"Fabulous," Liz said, the word not quite suiting the tone of voice in which it was uttered.

And then Jason said, "Wasn't that amazing to find out Granny Smart had been living in your shed, Liz?"

Liz forced herself not to look at Ronnie. Surely all the people round this table knew what had happened to Granny Smart. Except Big-Mouth-Danny, of course. What was Jason playing at? Liz hoped someone would kick him soon.

"Yes. Awful," she said. "It's been so cold, too. I hope she's in the warm now, wherever she is."

"I wonder just where she is now," Jason said, his eyes wide.

"We can only hope she's found herself some better shelter and maybe even someone who's prepared to help her. People can be so mean," Liz ground out. And finally, someone kicked him. He leapt a foot in the air. Moocher jumped up too. He always expects a game around Jason. Jason is a postman.

Marcus made a big deal of offering Ronnie some cream to go with his chocolate mousse. He even wiped the spoon on his sleeve before he'd allow him to use it.

Danny, entirely unaware of the tensions down their end of the table, but as if to help the awkward moment pass, appeared to pick a topic out of the air. "Saw your sister in town today, Liz. Of course, we hid behind a litter bin, didn't we, Wayne?" He grinned at Liz as if she'd enjoy the joke about how all her lodgers avoided her sister like she tried to. Silly boy. It was all right for *her* to do it, but she had rights – it was *her* sister.

She glared at him, but left it at that, grateful the awkwardness with Ronnie had passed. She hoped Jason's shin would be sore for a week.

"Yeah," Danny persevered, maybe disappointed at the lack of reaction. "She was arm in arm with some chap." Liz glared at him again. "Thought you'd like to know is all," he added. Liz maintained a frigid silence, but couldn't keep it up for long.

"Well? Who was the bloke?" she demanded, afraid to have her Hugh-theory confirmed.

"Dunno. Neither of us had ever seen him before. But they did look, er, intimate." He paused as though wondering the wisdom of sharing any more, but continued as if compelled by some inner force. "We followed them."

"You followed them?" Liz was amazed. Almost as amazed at finding it wasn't Hugh canoodling with Angela. What a strange thing to do to your landlady's sister and some unknown bloke. "Why?"

"Thought you'd be interested."

She couldn't deny it, but didn't want to admit it, so she handed him the rest of the chocolate mousse in unspoken reward. He applied himself enthusiastically and she waited, impatience boiling her stomach contents to a gurgling irritation. She controlled herself with an iron will, and let him finish off the confection. When he started licking the bowl, however, having already scraped the glaze off it with his spoon, she snatched it from him and demanded to know what happened when he and Laurel followed Angela and the rat-turd lover.

Angela! Multiple lovers! Her sister was certainly turning out to be a surprise.

Danny looked sadly at the bowl in her hand, gave his spoon a final lick and said, "They got on a bus."

"And then?"

"The bus drove off."

"And you were on it – right?"

"No. Why would we be?"

She didn't know what her face looked like but suddenly he jumped up and ran down the hall and out of the house. He's not the sharpest needle in the cushion, ol' Danny, but sometimes he catches on quite fast. She stared at Wayne, but he merely turned away, saying nothing.

After that the evening was all quite uneventful, but pleasant. She was pleased. She reckoned it was a highly successful event. Next time, though, she would think more carefully about the menu and not present Bristol's premier Italian restaurateur with her version of spag bol – a thought that only came to her in the night whilst rolling around her bed trying to get away from visions of Angela with some family-busting ratfink *and* Hugh, and maybe even Hugh with Angela *and* with some woman with hair to her waist and always-clean, dead-white hands who'd use them to control his every breath until he had no more.

Chapter Twenty-Eight
(One Step Forward and Two Steps Back)

Too many biscuits and not enough exercise had made Liz a portly landlady. And although it might suit the vintage picture-postcard image, it didn't suit Liz. The problem was finding some sort of exercise that wouldn't bore her to tears because she'd just do it once or twice and then forget it. She knew a lot of people who'd paid out fortunes in gym membership, gone a couple of times, all kitted out in new athletic-looking gear, feeling highly virtuous, only to never go again and then look guiltily furtive when asked about it.

Even without paying for the privilege of working out, she couldn't imagine pounding the highways day after day, frightening all the paving slabs out of their cement, having to see people outside in daylight while she was suffering. And maybe someone speaking to her when she didn't want them to. It didn't bear thinking of.

So, it was Ronnie to the rescue. How very convenient her newest lodger had what it took to get her exercising. Liz knew she'd have difficulty committing herself to the same night every week to go to a class, so having her own teacher on the premises and a front room big enough for the purpose put paid to any excuses to get her out of it.

Liz rushed out that morning and bought a couple of CDs for her old player – there were loads in the charity shops and they all assured her on their Stetson-and-cowboy-boot-splattered covers that they were for line dancing purposes. Handily enough they had the steps to the tunes written in the insert. She couldn't make any sense out of them at all.

Of course, she checked there'd be no one in the house. Only Danny lurked in the garden next door and she threatened to lock him in the shed with no cigarettes for twenty-four hours if he opened the front room door while they were in there heeling and toeing and grapevining. The prospect so appalled him he turned white and scurried off clutching his smokes protectively to his chest.

Ronnie came round, they armed themselves with bottles of water and towels, and went into the front room. They closed the curtains and rolled back the rug, whereupon Liz found her driving licence, an old electricity bill, a fiver and a sock. This line dancing lark was proving to be a good idea already!

The CDs promised delights such as: 'Everything's Big in Texas' – Oh, what? (Is it really?) And then there was 'The Step Momma From Hell,' and 'Daddy's Dressing Up Again' – she glanced at Ronnie and hoped he wouldn't notice that one. But it did seem odd. Liz had another look at the front of the CD case and found that in her haste she'd picked up something calling itself, 'Hilariously Funny Lines'. Oh. Right.

Ronnie said, "Don't worry. The important thing is the beat. Just ignore the words. Right, we're a' gonna start with the 'Carolina Freeze'."

"The dances have their own names too?"

"Yessiree."

Liz didn't think it was her imagination, but Ronnie sounded as though he'd taken on the manner and the speech of an old cow poke. Did she have to do that to do line dancing? Liz tried standing with her weight on one leg and her hand ready at her holster with a John Wayne half-smile on her chiselled lips but was rudely interrupted by Ronnie:

"Pay attention, Liz!"

Ronnie seemed to have taken on a whole new authority. Gone was the skulking punk-type, gone the badly treated granny. He executed some rapid foot movements, travelling down towards the fireplace and then back again. "These steps are called the grapevine," he said.

He did it again, his feet flashing incomprehensibly back and forth. Thankfully, he then repeated it very slowly.

Liz tried it. She had to try it quite a few times before it started to sink in by which time her brain was getting tired too, but Ronnie was determined to keep her at it.

"And now, what we call a hitch," he said.

A hitch is like a little jumpy thingy bringing your knee up at the same time as jumping. Not both knees at the same time. No, no, no.

There was something about the hitch which affected Liz deeply. It started in the lowest levels of her stomach and quickly travelled up her body to erupt in gasping giggles over which she seemed to have no control. Moocher, who, up until then, had been entirely obedient and stayed where he was told, took this as the signal to join in. He leapt up and bounced on his back legs as if joining in the dance, woofing and wagging his tail so fast it was a blur. The giggles gained in enormity, her breath coming in short, strangled gasps between blasts of mirth.

It's actually extremely difficult to hitch your knee up and jump, simultaneously, whilst doubled over, gasping for breath and only able to emit the occasional little scream. It's incredibly difficult. But Liz was stubborn and determined.

Ronnie dragged Moocher off and made him lie down under the table, bribing him with a bone obviously brought for just such a purpose because it appeared, as if by magic, from the depths of his rucksack. He must have been a Girl Guide to be so well prepared. By this time, Liz was so hot she could have fried eggs on her skin, so she, naturally, tore off her jumper and shirt to enjoy any passing breezes. Ronnie looked startled. Liz immediately realised why and had to ignore it. She had forgotten he was being a bloke…

But, even so, they were really getting into it at this stage – putting some steps together and getting a rhythm going. Oh, yes, she could see herself doing this to lose weight. This was fun. The only thing was that it made her even more conscious of the abysmal state of her body, as if she didn't already know.

The bags under her eyes were so huge they leapt up when she did and temporarily blinded her. As for her boobs – well, they leapt up at the same time and blackened both her eyes in one fell swoop. And her bum – well, it was doing its own thing completely independently of the rest of her body – and, not only that, but it stopped doing its own thing a long time after the rest of her had stopped to grab a drink.

Ronnie was a brilliant teacher. He just kept on shouting out instructions and repeatedly correcting her as she repeatedly made the same mistakes. Things came to a head when the CD was going on about some Parisian cowboy who had cow horns on the front of his 2 CV. By this time, Liz was down to her bra and not much else, trying to do these hitchy thingies, shrieking with laughter, blinded and eye-blackened, bum going down as she was going up, and the door swung open to reveal a thoroughly worried-looking builder.

Liz had forgotten he was coming to complete the plastering in the kitchen. Danny must have let him in.

Jeez. Why *did* these embarrassing things keep happening to **her**?

Chapter Twenty-Nine
(Mapmaker)

Mapmaker had spent a more than ordinarily stressful day at work and now he was home he did what he often did to try and get back on an even balance with himself.

He sat in his dog-chair and imagined its original owner. He liked to think this man – he assumed it was a man rather than a woman – had made the chair himself. He couldn't imagine a woman had the time to be so fanciful in Scotland in the seventeenth century. He could imagine a man doing so and calling it 'work'. He smiled to himself as he traced over the carved words with his finger – there were definite echoes of his mother in that sentiment.

He didn't need to read the words. He knew them. He whispered them under his breath:

> *I made this chair for you*
> *because you constantly purloined mine.*
> *This is my chair now you're gone*
> *because in it you'll always live on.*
> *You were the best dog.*

He pictured Liz Houston's dog, Moocher, in his mind and wondered what it would actually be like to be so entirely responsible for another creature. He had no intention of finding out but there was no doubt there was a certain appeal about the dogs themselves.

He sipped his malt and leaned his head back against the chair.

Dreamily, he imagined the man who had created this piece of furniture with such care and such love for his dog. He imagined the laborious carving of the picture and the words. He imagined the world that chair was born in to.

He imagined the woman of the family – if there'd been one – she would have been baking the bannock cakes or stirring the gruel or sweeping out the old rushes with a besom.

Mapmaker laughed to himself. He could just imagine what his mother would have to say about that! She never tolerated any of that sexist stuff. She obviously knew it had been that way but that made it no more acceptable. There had never been any need for it to be that way.

He smiled fondly. He missed her rants. He missed many things about her but Camille's rants could be pretty spectacular. She had a line in rants which surpassed anything he'd ever be capable of, although he was hopeful of improving.

He refocused on the present as he heard the people upstairs. It always sounded much like he thought he must sound when he shifted his dog-chair around. He would move it about on the original heavy wood floorboards until it felt as if it was in the right place – like a dog will turn around and around before settling in his bed. And then he was there for the night in front of his laptop.

He thought by the odd sound that filtered down to him that the people upstairs were settling in front of the telly. It was usually at this time.

It was like he and them upstairs were synchronised tenants settling in for the evening. He knew the upstairs flat was also rented out and not owned by the current resident.

It was weird to think someone lived up above him and there were other people so close but he didn't know them. He reviewed what he knew about them.

Upstairs from him was the attic room. It wasn't like the attics he was used to – just a space beneath the roof with some kind of ladder affair that you'd have to be pretty agile to climb up – no, the houses on this side of Malvern Road had proper attics that were the depth of the house and had a staircase that actually went all the way up. So, he knew it was a very large space – plenty enough for living quarters – just the same size as his own. But he'd not been in one and didn't know how it was laid out. He'd seen from the outside that it had a large dormer window on the front of the house. Some of the houses had the same type of window on the back, but this house didn't – it just had a couple of those windows that lie flush with the roof to let light in. There was no window to stare out of, as such, on the back of the house.

He'd passed the upstairs tenant on the stairs – or, at least, one or other of them politely stood back on the nearest landing to let the other pass. And when they did the slightest nod of the head acknowledged each other as human. Neither of them wished to exchange trite chit-chat. So, they didn't. Fair enough.

Mapmaker stared at the name: Trevor Fairchild. There were no other notes alongside the name. did it matter? Should he expend time and energy finding out about this man? Instinctively, he thought not. He appeared to be just another man minding his own business trying to find his way through life. Mapmaker shrugged. While he was about it, there was a gap to be filled in for the ground floor flat, too. How had he missed that?

He couldn't think of seeing anyone, or of hearing anyone.

He puzzled over it for a minute. Maybe it was currently empty?

Chapter Thirty
(One foot in the gutter)

Liz and Ronnie stepped out into the day. It was bright and springy, slightly breezy, lovely and fresh. Just right to get the blood whizzing around the body and the mind to clear itself of dark thoughts, and winter doubts.

They'd decided to go down the road to the music shop and see what they could find for their line dancing lessons. Ronnie said he had a huge collection of suitable CDs, but they were in storage with the rest of his furniture, awaiting the time he got his own house again. Liz had made no comment on that. She assumed this was part of his cover story as, according to Melanie, Granny Smart had been done out of all her worldly goods.

Ronnie's 'background' concerned a business gone bust, a wife that left him when his money and influence ran out, him taking to the road until he regained his equilibrium, and now he intended working his way back into the life he wanted.

Liz knew it was a story and wasn't really concentrating. She couldn't get the picture of a loveless match out of her mind. Somehow, since realising Hugh and Angela were probably not having a torrid affair, although, maybe they were … she'd been worrying more about Hugh getting hurt again. She felt badly about hurting him herself. She didn't want other people doing it, too!

Unless Angela was having multiple affairs and Hugh was merely one of them?

No! Surely not!

This new thought brought her head up in shock. Just in time to spot, as if her thoughts had conjured them up, Hugh and Angela dodging the Saturday morning crowds.

Her first instinct was to bolt into the nearest shop, but she realised Hugh had seen her. By the way his face drained of colour she thought he might have preferred it if she *had* disappeared, so that settled that. No way was she running. She grabbed Ronnie's arm, as if donning armour. He looked a tad startled, but Liz was concentrating on Hugh.

The four of them stopped in the middle of the pavement and the crowds simply flowed around them, carrying on about their business, the affairs of four strangers of no moment to them. Then Liz realised Ronnie didn't know who Hugh was, or indeed, Hugh didn't know who Ronnie was, unless he remembered the fox in her back garden.

No one took the initiative, so she did.

"Ronnie," she exclaimed, her voice high, aiming for great pleasure at this accidental meeting. "I must introduce you to Hugh." She grinned in what she thought was Hugh's direction. She couldn't actually look at him. She didn't want to see his face. "Hugh," she said. "This is Ronnie. Ronnie – Hugh."

Liz waited while Hugh and Ronnie made all the right noises. She was trying very hard not to look at Angela. She was afraid of how she might react having actually caught her sister and her ex brazenly out in public.

"And, as Liz doesn't appear to be going to do it, Ronnie," Hugh said, "Let me introduce to you Liz's sister, Angela."

The admonitory tone was very irritating although Liz knew he was right. She should have introduced her as well. She'd forgotten. She was so wound up about the whole Angela with a stud-muffin thing, not to mention it turning out to be her ex as well as someone else at the same time that she'd quite lost her manners.

"But you do need to know if you're now a member of the family, too, Ronnie," Hugh added in what Liz thought he fondly imagined was a jocular tone but actually came out sounding like a threat to grind his fingers down to the knuckle.

Ooh. Liz nearly snorted. Hugh thought she and Ronnie were a thing!

"Oh, no!" Ronnie started to say, but Liz grabbed his arm and leaned into him whilst saying: "You are so right, Hugh. It's always best to know who's who, especially in this family. Ronnie – Angela's *husband* is called Robert. And her little child, a son, is called little Johnny."

She turned to Angela: "That's right, isn't it, sister dearest."

Angela gave her a look that could have frozen the ocean. "That's right," Angela said. "That's exactly right." She pushed her hand under Hugh's arm and, fluttering her lashes at him, she said:

"Come along Darling. If we dilly-dally exchanging social chit-chat too long, we'll be late for the intimate lunch for two you booked for us down by the harbour." She stared at Liz. "At the new place that no one can get in. Unless they're Someone Special. Have you been to it, Liz?"

"Dilly-dally!" Liz couldn't hold back the snort.

But she could think of nothing to say.

Ronnie tugged at her arm. Liz was conscious that it was much like the way she would tug at Moocher to get him away from a tasty bit of fox turd he wanted to roll in. He just loves that and then he jumps in the car and asphyxiates everyone all the way home and then refuses to get in the bath when he gets there. Liz knew what he felt like now. She didn't want to leave the scene until she had found a telling and squashing retort.

No wonder dogs want to roll in smelly stuff. It was an overwhelming compulsion. Liz determined to be more understanding of Mooch the Pooch in future.

Honestly, bright though he was, Hugh had fallen, gormlessly, for the first bit of skirt that had presented itself. And Liz knew so many who would have jumped at the chance of snagging him – so many who would make him happier than Angela ever could, even if she were free to do so. Liz wanted to cry with the frustration of it all. Maybe that's how parents feel when they see their children making mistakes.

Ronnie tugged at her arm again. Liz could still think of nothing to say.

So, they turned and marched away.

Liz bet to herself that Ronnie and Hugh had looked at each other before moving off, mute and mutual apology in their eyes.

Ronnie and Liz walked the rest of the way arm in arm as though supporting each other since tangling with a highly negative influence. Liz felt that Angela with her ex had taken something from her, some essential part that she needed for her self-respect.

"He looks nice, your ex," Ronnie said.

"He *is* nice. He's a very nice man."

"Why don't you take him back?"

"Because we really are better off apart. We have tried to make a go of it. More than once. He smothers me when we're together. I'm not organised enough for him – physically or mentally. So, he ends up irritated and frustrated all the time, and I end up feeling more than ordinarily claustrophobic. We don't do each other any good. But he's not going to be happy with her."

"Why not? Are you sure it's not just sour grapes?"

Ronnie had obviously forgotten his current disguise as an ageing but still forceful punk hardman. Liz wasn't about to remind him.

"She's already married, with a child. She's just playing with him, for some unimaginable reason. My sister never ceases to revolt me."

"Surely, he knows that."

"He does. That's yet another part of this whole thing I find extremely puzzling. And repellent. I had no idea he would do such a thing. I would expect him to behave better than that."

"Maybe it's not what you think."

"Maybe not," Liz said with a finality that changed the conversation back to line dancing matters, but still, an Angela-Hugh affair grew in her mind until it hovered over her world-view like a menacing black-fungus cloud.

Chapter Thirty-One
(Mapmaker)

Mapmaker idled in the hall, sometimes pacing up and down, sometimes staring at the door to the ground floor flat. The easiest way to find out if there was someone in there was to ring the bell. Except that, if no one answered, there was no way of knowing if there was no one in, or if there was someone in, but they simply hadn't answered.

He had heard Trevor Fairchild from upstairs going out or he wouldn't have taken the risk of being found lurking like this.

He felt very restless. More than usual.

He noticed a slip of paper protruding under the door. He pulled it out. It gave nothing away about a possible occupant – he had hoped it was something that had a name on it. It was a flyer for a local pub's movie night.

He snorted. Just the mention of 'movies' and he was transported back to the last time he'd watched a film with Camille. One of her most hated things was when there was no direct answer to a direct question – the most common one in films being when a character would answer a direct question with: "I hope so."

The last one he remembered was when the brother of the film's heroine was rushed into the operating theatre. Naturally, he was artfully prone on a trolley with a wispy but beautiful brunette sitting astride his chest pumping away at his heart; the heroine of the piece would be holding his hand, running alongside the gurney. They would disappear into the surgery suite.

Anxious relatives clustered outside, drinking machine-coffee and exchanging too-long-but-meaningful looks when, suddenly, from the theatre, would stride a blood-bespattered tall, dark and handsome surgeon. The heroine – breathy, busty and blonde, hands clasped to her magnificent bosom, asks him in a failing voice: "Is he going to be all right doctor?"

Handsome Physician considers this question with a lot of deep thought (and meaningful expressions flitting across his chiselled face) and, finally, into the suspenseful silence of the waiting room he says: "I hope so."

Whereupon everyone exchanges more meaningful looks full of relief for the outcome of the surgery, and of adoration for the modest but manful surgeon.

Then busty blonde heroine casts herself upon Handsome Physician's broad chest. His hands automatically come out to embrace her in return, but then he hesitates to be so familiar – finally, he realises comforting her is more important than his own issues with touching people, and he brings his hands to rest on her heaving back.

And Camille, hair sticking out at all angles, face creased with rage, would explode: "That is no answer! Why does anybody tolerate that kind of wishy-washy answer that is no answer? It doesn't answer the bloody question! Why are they treating that clack-headed clothes hanger like a hero when he hasn't even answered the question? The answer was either "Yes" or "No" or "I don't know" – there was no other bloody answer!"

It even became a joke between them – they would wait for it to arise in any program, because it always did. It was as if the world wanted people to believe that a non-answer was good enough. Well, it was not good enough for Camille! It was not good enough for his mother.

And it was no longer going to be good enough for her son. Mapmaker determined there and then that, in future, he would demand direct answers to direct questions. He was sure it would make him more business-like and efficient, and would stand him in good stead in so many ways. Oh, yes! He would become a new man forthwith! Camille *would* be pleased.

Chapter Thirty-Two
(Yummy!)

Conscious of nothing more than an intense desire to flee the country, Liz presented herself for yet another babysitting duty, this time at her sister's.

She hated that because she was babysitting her nephew, she was making it easy for Angela to meet up with her paramour.

She also hated babysitting in general. She didn't like the responsibility. It made her fearful. What if something happened on her watch? What if something awful happened and she didn't know what to do? If the something that happened was attempted kidnapping, she knew her rage would be such that she'd take the kidnappers down and they'd be sorry. But if it was illness and she couldn't get an ambulance in time, what then?

Angela barely greeted her, she was in such a hurry to get out of the house and meet up with her bit on the side. She did take the time, of course, to cast a look of repugnance at poor old Moocher. Liz knew what that was about. It was about Angela's immaculate house and Moocher's poorly attached fur which seemed to take great pleasure in clinging to anything clean.

Tough!

Creeping into little Johnny's room Liz confirmed that he was asleep. That was a relief! Something was going her way at last!

She stared down at his face. It was so smooth, the skin blemish-free and luminous. It was like looking at an otherworldly creature of such innocence it surely didn't really exist. She put her hand out to touch him, to make sure he was actually there, but then she pulled it back. 'Don't be silly, Liz,'" she admonished herself automatically looking over her shoulder to make sure no one had seen her be so soft.

Well – Moocher had seen her with his beady little eyes, but he was not judgmental. She smiled at him. He smiled back.

The next job was to investigate Angela's enormous fridge

for suitable babysitting snackaroonees. She played with the ice maker for a bit and then opened the door just so it could shut itself again with a subtle, but determined swoosh. She inventoried the contents – enough to feed an army. She wondered what Angela did with it all. Maybe she had loads of dinner parties all the time. She wasn't inviting Liz to them, if so.

Then she found the tray that had been left for her and immediately felt mean for thinking anything of Angela other than good-sisterly things.

There was home-made lasagne – one of Liz's favourites – with a salad that even Liz would eat given the tasty dressing on it. And – ooh – just look at that! It was one of Angela's world-famous bread and butter puddings that she made with brioche – not with just your bog-standard bread – and obviously it had cream in it. Even the custard was home made. Both the lasagne and the pudding were in their own individual stoneware dishes. Awww – fancy Angela going to the trouble to cook all this just for her. Not for *her* sister was it a slice of someone else's pie – no, she had her own pie!

Fancy her doing all that for her. Maybe it was Angela's guilty conscience at work. Yep. That'd be it. Angela was trying to get round Liz via her stomach. It was a successful ploy, at least for the moment.

She was sitting in a too-full stupor when Angela's landline phone rang. She had to get up to answer it. How inconvenient!

"Good afternoon," she said. She didn't believe in giving anything away to an unknown entity on the phone.

"Hi! Angela! It's me," a man said. "Why are you still at home when you should be here?"

Liz's bread and butter pudding-stunned brain started running about like a hyper toddler. It was Cupcake! It must be Cupcake! Although, why did he think she was Angela? Whatever – now was a good chance of finding out something useful.

"Oh. I, uh, where are we meeting again?"

The silence that followed wasn't encouraging.

She tried again. "Sorry, I'm not feeling one hundred percent and it's slipped my mind."

"You're not Angela, are you?" the voice said.

Damn!

"Why did you think I *was* Angela?" she asked. It was all she could think to say in the face of the not-unfounded accusation.

"Your voice is very similar to hers."

That was a downer considering she'd always thought Angela's voice sounded like a seagull on speed.

The speaker went on: "I'm guessing this is Liz, Angela's sister."

"It might be ..." she said. What the hell? Angela had been gabbing about her to Cupcake! Why on earth would she meet up with her bit of stuff and then prattle on about her sibling?

"No worries. I'll call back later." And he rang off before Liz could think what to say. So, she'd found out nothing about Cupcake. Nothing at all except he had a nice voice. Even in that short call it had sounded interested but yet somehow reassuring. Even when accusing her of masquerading as her sister.

But still, as a practised debaucher of women no doubt he'd trained his voice to sound all interested and caring.

And then the front door opened and Robert walked in. Liz felt immediately hugely guilty as if she'd been caught red-handed with a lover and Robert was her accusing husband suddenly appearing on the scene.

He looked as startled to see her as she was to see him.

And then there was the panging.

Robert was so ... so *comforting* in a stomach-panging (as against stomach-dives-out-of-body) and heart-thrumming (as against heart-leaping) kind of way. You knew he would supply all the romance you'd ever need just by being himself. He wouldn't give you a fiver on Valentine's Day and tell you to get yourself a card and some flowers. No, he would do all that stuff just perfectly without being reminded.

And yet, he was also so *solid*. You knew he would always be there for you. Always there in the dark hours. Always there when you needed him. Angela had been incredibly lucky to get him and Liz had never been able to understand how she'd managed it.

And here she was – throwing it away! It made no sense.

But now, if her sister was going to be so stupid, then it would serve her right if some sharp-taloned floozy happened by and snatched him up, making him feel wanted just when he would be at his lowest. He'd be devastated when he knew what Angela was up to – he would be far too easy prey for such a woman. Someone looking for a piece of gateau would know they'd come to the right cake shop if they found Robert at such a time.

After all, he would need the reassurance that he was still attractive. To find that one's wife was having it off with some sleazy geezer even after all that faithfulness must be extremely lowering.

Not that he knew about it yet.

But he soon would!

Liz was sure he looked at her with more than his usual warmth and felt a spark of alarm. She'd always known he liked her. He never condemned her like Angela did and often put himself between Angela and her when they were falling out.

But, surely it wasn't *that* sort of warmth ... *He* didn't fancy *her* did he?

Eek! Her stomach went into cringe-mode, and she dropped her gaze. For the first time in their acquaintance she felt awkward with him, almost self-conscious. Almost immediately, she admonished herself: for Dog's sake, Liz, stop finding unseemliness everywhere! Just because she'd found it in Angela, the most unexpected of people, didn't mean everyone was at it!

Then she realised he'd said something.

"Pardon?" she said.

"I was just saying how lucky it was that you decided to call in on Ange today. I should have been here but was held up by an accident in Church Street. But with you here at least Ange could still get to her appointment."

"You knew she was going out?"

"Of course. That's why I'm here. To cover Johnny while she's out." He looked puzzled.

Liz was puzzled too.

Did he already know about Cupcake? Was he babysitting his own son so his wife could get to her seedy assignation?

Surely not.

They stared at each other for what seemed a very long time but was probably only a couple of seconds.

Liz couldn't believe Robert knew about Cupcake. She had to tell him. But how could she possibly tell him of his wife's infidelity? She didn't want to be the bearer of such news, but who else would tell him with the consideration and sensitivity that she would show? Who else cared enough about him to worry about his reception of such news?

"So, it's good to see you, Liz," Robert continued, whilst moving kitchen-wards, "but if you want to shoot off now I'm here, don't stay out of politeness."

"There's something I need to tell you," Liz blurted.

"Also, I know that Ange has made me my favourite lasagne followed by her divine brioche and butter pudding. And I'm starving hungry because I saved myself for it." He looked at Liz, an eyebrow raised enquiringly, but she knew he was impatient to get to the fridge.

"Yes, I have to tell you ..." She stopped as two thoughts landed on her with all the shock of a bucket of iced water:

Angela had known Robert would be home. Angela had **asked** him to be home to look after Johnny. She had also asked Liz to be there. But she hadn't told Robert Liz would be there. Because why would Robert take time away from the office if Johnny already had a babysitter?

The first thought was that Angela **wanted** Liz to tell Robert about Cupcake!

The second was that Liz had eaten the meal especially prepared by his loving wife for Robert, and he was starving, having saved himself for it.

Aargh!

Her whole body cringed.

Liz wished she could instantly be teleported to Saturn. Unfortunately, such a transportation method hadn't yet been invented.

Moocher nudged her hand. Yep. He wanted to go to Saturn, too.

Robert didn't look at all ready to hear about his wife cavorting with some pustulant tub of rancid rodent droppings. He looked even less like a man who'd be happy to hear his sister-in-law had inadvertently necked his favourite meal – the one he'd starved himself for, the one he'd been dreaming about all day.

Liz was also finding, much to her annoyed surprise, that she didn't want to give Angela away, even though she deserved it.

Jostling for equal attention with that reaction was a gut instinct to not give her away because that had been Angela's plan all along, and Liz naturally didn't want to do what Angela wanted her to do.

But, most of all, she had to get out of there before Robert opened the fridge.

In what she hoped was a completely natural moment of recollection, Liz flinched as if suddenly hit with a thought of great urgency – "Ohmigod!" she yelled, "I have a client turning up. How could I have forgotten? I must go, Robert. I'm so sorry." She clipped Moocher's lead on, and grabbed her jacket.

"I thought you wanted to tell me something," he said, but she pretended not to hear, opened the door, gave him a cheery wave, and just before disappearing out of his line of sight, she added: "I'm so sorry. I ate your lasagne and your pudding. It was yummy." And she slammed the door and ran down the street hoping to outstrip the mental pictures she was now having of him in tears in front of the open fridge, or inspecting the empty stoneware dishes – maybe sorrowfully wiping his finger over a smear of creamy sauce in the bottom to experience the fleeting suggestion of his lost banquet, noshed down by his sister-in-law – who hadn't even washed the dishes, Liz realised.

She hadn't even washed the dishes!

She didn't think she could have felt worse.

She was wrong.

She was so embarrassed she felt as if her skin had turned itself inside out so that the whole world could see her for what she really was: nothing but a marriage-destroying, banquet-thieving slob. Aargh!

Still, although the intention had been there, at least only one of those things had she achieved today.

She hadn't told him about Cupcake, after all.

Now she needed to know why Angela was so desperate for her to tell Robert. With hindsight, Liz could see that everything Angela had done and said since the moment she'd parked her small, powder-blue coupé outside Liz's house just four days ago, had been designed to get Liz to tell Robert Angela was having an affair.

She was getting a stitch. She had to stop to wipe the sweat

of embarrassment – and unaccustomed exercise – from her brow.

Well – if Robert *had* fancied her for a fleeting second, there was no way he would now she'd eaten his brioche and butter pudding!

And, why the hell had she felt obliged to tell him it had been yummy!!!

Chapter Thirty-Three
(Mapmaker)

Mapmaker was chuffed to have new information. Having Enid on-side in his mission was brilliant. She could ask all kinds of intrusive questions and get away with it. If he tried the same thing he'd probably get thumped.

He retrieved his map and journal and uncapped his pen.

On the map he inscribed for number 8:
Tony Marchamp, late 20s.
In the journal:
Number eight: Tony Marchamp (owner/tenant?) – late 20s, lives alone? Known as Superpecs, also: Hedge Piddler; works out – (possibly on steroids?) – huge muscles – pees into his front garden hedge whilst whistling at the same time – when not grinning and waving to people (with his other hand…); puts on particular show for Liz Houston. Gardens – back – reported as 'regimented'; front – nothing but big hedge. House immaculate. Gym manager.

Number 10: Sylvana Wentrose, early 30s
Number ten: Sylvana Wentrose (owner), early 30s, lives alone? Takes photos of Superpecs while he's having a pee. (!) House and gardens – nothing to note (NTN). Face painter. Cats – 3?

He stopped, a sudden deluge of despair overtaking him. What the hell was he doing sitting at his desk on a lovely Sunday morning like this one recording details about his neighbours? Details like they peed in their hedge thinking no one knew what they doing; details like they were face painters who kept cats! What the hell?

He bent right over his desk until his head hit the keyboard of his laptop; darkness crowded his mind.

The radio was playing in the background. He hadn't been listening to it. Even so, a repeated phrase percolated through his concentration: "It'll be fine."

That's what the presenter was saying. Repeatedly. Mapmaker stopped to listen. What would be fine?

It was a call-in programme and a listener had rung up to say that his daughter had been in a bad road traffic accident and was currently in hospital. Things were touch-and-go. He was ringing up in the hope he could get in touch with his ex-wife. She'd left a couple of years ago and hadn't been in touch with anyone since, but he thought she should know about their daughter.

His voice kept breaking, but he persisted doggedly on to try and make an appeal for her, or anyone who knew her, to get touch.

The presenter kept saying: "It'll be fine. It'll be fine."

What would be fine?

What use was saying that to the man?

The presenter didn't know what was going to happen to the man's daughter. Nor did he know if the ex-wife would get in touch. What the hell was the use of him saying that over and over?

He should be helping as much as he could by broadcasting the appeal, not mouthing empty promises that were just bloody irritating in their hollowness and insincerity. What a dick!

At that moment, as his blood pressure skyrocketed, Mapmaker knew he was channelling Camille! It was working! He was becoming a more determined and decisive person already!

Carefully, he stowed his map and journal away and decided on which bit of work to concentrate on before making an appearance at the street party that afternoon – something else he would naturally shy away from, but in for a penny, in for a pound as they say. He might as well really go for the whole sociable thing, too, although he quivered at the thought.

What a great idea a street party was! To get neighbour knowing neighbour, especially in this era of isolationism of countries and of individuals, was a constructive and delightful thing.

Chapter Thirty-Four
(Safety glass, Pal?)

Mitch, hobbling a bit because of his recalcitrant back, but trying not to show it, walked out into the street enjoying the novelty of being in the road without looking because it was shut to traffic for the street party.

He really needed to make sure he got to his chiropractor appointment to get his back fixed. It was silly to keep on suffering like this although he fancied it was a little better. He also knew what wishful thinking could do.

Luckily for everyone concerned it was a really nice day for January – a bit brisk, but sunny. People were showing up dressed for the occasion in suitably warm outfits.

He nodded to a few people without engaging with them, found a chair and sat at a table in the middle of the road. He hesitated to help himself to a can of beer or glass of wine although he knew from the leaflet he'd received that he could, having paid his contribution to the event. He wasn't worried. He enjoyed simply being there in the middle of the buzz.

There were people trying to manage a glass and plate of cake, standing around chatting; children running around; a face painter over there with the resulting tigers and spiderman creations, some butterflies, not all on children he saw – some incredible designs on adults, too – must be a professional hired for the occasion. Music played – he was surprised to see it was live – a gazebo with all the gear under cover in case of showers, a man with a guitar, a woman singing.

As he looked around he was overcome with a feeling of surreality. No picture or environment could be further from his upbringing or his expectations than the one he was currently in.

So it came as a bit of a jolt when he saw Tally approaching. She said nothing. She had brought a chair with her; she placed it near him and sat on it.

After a few seconds she reached out and took his left hand. Then she waited as if she expected him to pull it away, but he didn't. They sat there holding hands.

To think that, after all these years, they would sit in the middle of a road and hold hands made Mitch feel even more unreal. It was almost like having family. Imagine having family!

He hardly dared look at her but eventually he did. He stared blindly in her direction and forced his face to look like it was smiling. She smiled back.

"Truce?" she whispered.

He nodded. She tightened her grip on his hand and they continued to sit there silently as if a new world order was settling into place.

Mitch had the strangest feeling that if he was really lucky he could gain that hitherto apparently impossible situation of strength where he could be whole and safe. The rest of the world carried on as it always did – fighting and striving and standing on the heads of others to get somewhere else, whereas he was now, for the first time in his life, in a place where he could be unassailable in the right place with the right people. He'd never consciously felt that before and it seemed to erupt in him in a terrible tinnitus experience. A whistling of such intensity that he could hear nothing else, emanated from the base of his skull and took over his head.

He knew what that was. It was his innate reaction to anything that looked good. It was the conviction that, if it looked good, it was going to go bad.

He was going to fight it with everything he had. This time, things were not going to go bad. Whatever happened, he was going to make the outcome good.

So, when the man who had approached spoke to him, he had to shake his head free from that world to bring it back to this one. "Pardon?" he said, awkwardly taking the hand held out to him. It felt weird with Tally still holding his other hand.

"I just wanted to check out the man holding my wife's hand in the middle of the road," the newcomer said.

Mitch resisted the impulse to pull away from Tally. This was his world now. No skulduggery. He had nothing to feel guilty about.

He still felt guilty and hoped he didn't look too much like a dog caught eating the Sunday roast as he stared at his sister's mark, now her husband.

"Graham, Sweetie – this is my brother, Mitch."

Mitch didn't say anything. He had no idea what Tally might have told her husband.

The handshake became more enthusiastic. "Good to meet you, Mitch." Graham said. "I gather I have to thank you for keeping Tally safe in the foster home."

Mitch bit his lip. What the hell **had** she told him!

"We don't really talk about it now, Love," Tally said. "We leave it in the past where it belongs."

"Sorry, Mitch. Just wanted you to know I'm grateful you protected Tally," Graham said. And, as if to make amends: "Let me get you a drink. Beer? Wine?"

"Beer," Mitch said. "Thanks."

Graham moved away and Tally moved closer again. In a low voice she said: "I know what you're thinking. And you're right. Graham **was** my target, my mark. But now he's my husband and I love him, genuinely love him." She stared at Mitch, her eyes pleading with him to believe her; to believe her and not give her away.

Mitch was conscious that it was a new start for him as well so he made himself smile at his sister and say: "Don't worry. I believe you, Tally. The past is the past and shall stay there."

"Is your past in your past, too, or are you here after a mark?"

Mitch wasn't about to tell Tally anything about his ambitions. "My past is my past," he said. It wasn't a lie. The past is always past.

She seemed to let go a held breath and she smiled at him with more affection than he thought he'd ever seen on another human's face. He nearly melted. But then he remembered all the betrayals. They might be in the past, but their repercussions would always be with him.

"Anyway," he said. "Here we are at a street party in a perfectly respectable neighbourhood. We never thought that would happen, did we? We should enjoy it."

Tally was rootling around in her bag. "I was going to ask you, Mitch," she said, before straightening up. She had a video in her hand. "If you'd be kind enough to keep this for me. I don't want it in my house but it won't do anyone any harm in yours."

Immediately he was suspicious. He looked at it and he looked at her, and was startled to see her blush. Tally was the original hard-faced bitch and yet here she was, blushing.

"I've come a long way, Mitch," she said, "a very long way. I might have made the odd unfortunate turn in the road, slept with the wrong men, broken the wrong windows, but I *have* come a very long way. It's all still new to me – the chance to live what one might call a 'straightforward' life and I can't shake the old life off completely. Or, rather, the insecurities of the old life. This video, pathetic though it is, happens to be the only insurance I have against a few people around here. I'll never use it, I'm sure of it. I've tried to destroy it but I haven't managed to make myself do that yet. One day I will. In the meantime, I can't take the risk of someone finding it in my house."

He sighed, but took it. "Does anyone even use videos anymore?" he asked.

"Well, there you are. You obviously don't so if anyone did happen to come across it in your house they'd have nothing to play it on. So, it won't harm you. There's not much exciting stuff on there anyway. That's the thing about leverage – you can never be certain what will become leverage and what not."

"Okay," he said, losing interest in Tally's schemings, and stowing it away in one of his capacious jacket pockets.

He'd spotted the restauranteur bloke, Philippe, and eyed him curiously.

He knew that anyone who had a big, commercial window smashed might replace it with the same glass simply because that was the glass in it when they bought the restaurant. They might even have a stock of it to keep up the authenticity.

Hang on, Tally had said something about 'breaking the wrong windows' – surely, she didn't mean ... Surely not ... He glanced at her and saw her looking in the opposite direction to the restauranteur bloke. Uh, oh! Maybe Restaurant Man had been the original mark but for some reason he fell through, and she moved on to Graham.

He wasn't going to ask. He didn't want to know.

He'd been in the Whiteladies Road restaurant. He'd enjoyed the meal, but he didn't think Philippe's restaurants required specialised glass. It depended sometimes on how it had been made, or how it had been individualised. Philippe's windows were all beautifully signwritten but that wasn't dependent on the type of glass in them.

But he was as certain as he could be that no one would keep on replacing broken glass with glass that went against building rules and regs. They might do it once, but no more. It made no sense. After the first go they would have had it replaced with safety glass, or with toughened glass of some kind. So, he was pretty sure that Philippe was neck-deep in some skulduggery. What it was, he couldn't begin to imagine, but it wasn't his business so he wasn't going to try and imagine it at all.

He had enough on his own plate without worrying about someone else's.

Which was also why he wasn't going to ask Tally what she had done with Granny Smart. For one thing it was her business and not his. For another, it was obvious to him that the ageing punk in Liz Houston's house was the missing elder and he didn't know whether Tally had realised, or not. In his experience she wasn't the most observant person. He wasn't going to give Granny away if he didn't have to.

Then he spotted a man with a very familiar face. Who was that? And where did he know him from? Immediately, it was as if the constant threat of his former life had popped up in front of him. Would it ever stay buried?

He relaxed when he realised that face wasn't from his far past. It was simply the face of a neighbour. A nerdy neighbour by the looks of him. He was standing so still in front of a painting it was like it had mesmerised him. Mitch couldn't think that guy was a threat.

Even so, Mitch was still conscious of everything going on around him. He was always on the alert. That was the only way he'd survived this long, and it wasn't something he would soon grow out of, he didn't think.

He and Tally sat there in companionable silence until Graham came back with drinks.

Chapter Thirty-Five
(Mapmaker)

Mapmaker had never been to a street party before. It was the kind of thing he'd expect to see on a TV series about idyllic country living in a Britain of the past. Home-made cakes, children running about, fancy dress competition, friendly dogs ambling around, lashings of ginger beer, a tug of war, a Morris dancing troupe. There was no brass band to round things off, but there was a musician and a singer.

Exactly the kind of thing he would have run away from before determining to come out of the chrysalis of his old self to become more of an optimistic, positive, sociable butterfly.

Seeing Mitch, the sweetheart scammer, brought him back to earth. Of course, that guy was a neighbour now.

He could approach him, pretend some kind of neighbourliness, but he already had him pegged, noted on his map and in his journal. He wanted to meet people he didn't already know. He wanted to make the most of this opportunity to fill in gaps on his map. He wanted to find out more about his neighbours.

He spotted Tallulah Smart. He saw Enid. He saw Liz Houston and Moocher.

He saw the Victoria sponge that had won the Best Cake award. He saw the cactus that had won the award for Looking Too Human. It actually looked remarkably like a brain in a pot. He certainly wouldn't keep *that* on his windowsill! He'd never get any sleep!

He saw the most amazing face painting of a colourful skull, or rather, half a skull, on a woman's face. Again, it was too realistic to be comfortable.

And he saw a painting that looked like it had been painted specifically for him, and no one else.

Trying not to look too interested, he ambled in its direction. It appeared to be an item on a stall raising money for a local charity for the homeless. He stopped in front of it.

He studied it. He studied the swirl with a big brush to suggest a distant forest; he studied the detail with a very small brush that would convince an onlooker that it was indeed a wood pigeon sitting in that tree three miles away. It was all visual trickery that appealed to the subconscious. And it worked every time. Some artists would have tried to paint in actual trees and an actual wood pigeon.

"It's good, isn't it," a voice said, right in his ear. Carefully, because he didn't want to cause offence, he edged away. The woman was too close to him. He didn't like people being too close to him.

"I like it," he said. "Do you know the artist? Does he or she live in Malvern Road?"

For one ecstatic moment he imagined this woman saying, 'Why yes, I do. She lives at number something or other. Let me introduce you.'

He turned in anticipation to the speaker. He didn't know her. "I'm so sorry," he said. "So rude of me. I live at number twenty-nine, first floor flat."

"That's okay. I'm Sunita. I'm at number thirty-six. As to your question. I do know the artist. He lives at number twenty-nine, too. Fancy you not already knowing him!"

This artist was the occupant of the ground floor flat in his own building! The one he'd been lurking outside only yesterday! And, before he could marshal his brain into some kind of functioning order, Sunita had grabbed his arm and marched him over to join a little circle of people who were hanging off the words of a man clutching a big glass of white wine in one hand, and a huge wedge of coffee and walnut cake in the other. He wore a cravat. Mapmaker couldn't remember ever seeing anyone wear a cravat in real life before. He was grey, this man, although his clothes said otherwise. His features were those of someone who would never be picked out in a crowd. He wore a Paisley design, glittery waistcoat and green shoes. Green shoes. And he was saying: "Yes, I have to wait until inspiration deigns to visit me.

145

This could be any time, night or day. But it's no good trying to force myself to paint. It doesn't work like that."

Oh, God. Mapmaker could feel a Camille-rant coming on: "For God's sake! If you need to earn a living and you choose to do it with an art or a craft, you can't afford to faff about *'waiting for inspiration'*. It has to be treated like any other business. It has to be the same as plumbing or driving a taxi or gardening. Set yourself the hours and stick to them and do it until you succeed. All this ridiculous swanning about wearing floaty scarves and smoking extremely long cigarettes waiting for riches to fall into your lap just ain't gonna pay the bills!" And she'd snort with contempt.

He'd always remembered that little rant when he was working so hard to get a foothold in the video game business. She'd been an inspiration to him in so many ways.

He could just imagine what she'd say if she witnessed Mr Grey coming out with this drivel to a crowd of adoring fans. And what she'd have to say about the cravat, he dread to think! He smiled warmly at Mr Grey and asked: "Do you have more paintings? Could I see them? I'd like to buy one."

Chapter Thirty-Six
(Some bread and butter puddings are unforgettable!)

If someone ate ***her*** brioche and butter and cream pudding, she would ***never*** forgive them. That was for certain. Not only that, but if she'd been the one to make it for the love of her life and some greedy gannet had scoffed it out of her fridge, she'd never forgive the scoffer, either. In one fell scoffing-swoop she had alienated anyone with any sense at all. Pudding was sacred!

Liz had been entirely unable to forget the bread and butter pudding business. Every time it arrived in her mind, which it did at frequent intervals, she went hot and sweaty, and then she went cold and shivery, and then she went hot and sweaty again. If only there was a way of rolling back time to wipe the incident clean out of world history. But, no, it would forever now be carved into the annals of time and she'd be forever infamous for noshing someone else's pudding. The shame of it!

She was drawn out into the street for the party earlier than she'd intended, trying to get away from her own squirmy thoughts. The street party was such a great idea!

Ambling down the road, Moocher alongside her, they returned greetings as they went. Everyone loved Moocher! Mmmm … Cake! Maybe if she ate some cake it would push out of her mind recent memories of another sugary confection.

Before she'd made it to the relevant table, though, she was side-tracked by Angela.

Of all people. Angela!

"What are you doing here?" Liz demanded. "This is the Malvern Road street party. You don't live on Malvern Road."

"You could have invited me if you'd wanted!" Angela said.

She was right. Liz could have invited her if she'd wanted.

Liz didn't know what to say. She wanted to say how yummy the lasagne and pudding was yesterday but it was too sensitive an issue.

She thought she might take the wind out of Angela's sails instead so she said: "Oh, Angela. I am so sorry. I would have invited you, but I've been so busy I simply didn't think of it."

There. That was syrupy enough to put anyone off the scent of anything untoward. And, sure enough, Angela's eyes glazed over with tears.

Tears!

That wasn't the reaction Liz had expected. And now she really didn't know what to say. Especially when Angela grabbed her and pulled her into a big hug. She gulped into Liz's ear: "Really? You would have invited me?"

Liz felt obliged to hug her sister back and say: "Yes, of course, I would." Knowing full well she wouldn't.

Could she feel any worse than she did right now?

Obviously, she could. She hadn't thought it possible to feel worse than she'd felt after the pudding incident. Now she felt really awful at the thought her sister was grateful for an invitation she hadn't even received.

What the hell was going on?

"Angela," she said. "Come and sit down. Let me get you a drink? Tea or wine? Would you like some cake? We have Victoria sponge, coffee and walnut, chocolate, cherry and coconut – you name it, we have it. All home-made."

She guided Angela to a chair but her sister wouldn't let her go so she lowered herself into another chair close by. "What is it?"

Liz wondered if she was going to get blasted for the noshing incident but instead Angela coughed as if having difficulty saying what she wanted to say. Eventually she came out with it: "How did Robert take it when you told him about my affair?"

Liz registered that this was the first time in her entire life her sister had asked her a direct question rather than beating about the bushes forever first. It must be very, very important. It was certainly very, very puzzling and, again, she wondered why Angela had set her up to tell Robert about Cupcake.

"I can't understand it," Angela went on, "he hasn't said anything to me about it at all. Wasn't he bothered when you told him? Didn't he care that I'm having an affair?"

Now she was looking more closely, Liz could see that Angela appeared quite strung out, distraught, even. On the other hand, that was understandable if your husband had been told you were having an affair and then didn't even give a monkey's!

So, she hastened to reassure her; she even patted her on the arm in soothing manner. "It's all right, Angela. I didn't tell him!"

If she thought that was going to help things she was mistaken.

"Well – *why* didn't you tell him? Why on earth wouldn't you tell him?"

Angela stared at her as if she'd really let her down. Liz was beginning to be extremely worried about her sister's manner and illogicality and general demeanour.

What the hell?

"Angela," she said, "I didn't tell him because I didn't want to drop you in it. Why would I want to get my sister in trouble?"

"You didn't want to get your sister in trouble," Angela repeated – before bursting into tears.

Even more alarmed, Liz pulled her into her arms and shushed her, rocking gently back and forth.

What the hell?

She might not like her sister very much but she hated to see her in such a state.

Noticing Melanie headed their way Liz infinitesimally shook her head and saw her veer off somewhere else.

Then she saw Robert coming for them. She'd never been more pleased to see anyone in her life before. He'd know what to do. He always knew what to do.

There was no sign that he was even thinking about his brioche and butter pudding.

His smile was as warm as ever. He looked at Liz and she knew he would take over now and Angela would be in the best hands. Angela let go her clasp on Liz, which had been quite a tight one as if she was hanging on in order not to drown. Liz could feel her blood beginning to circulate again. Clinging to her husband, Angela obediently followed his direction and, they left. Robert hadn't said a word.

Liz felt horribly unsettled. There was something wrong

with Angela, and she had no idea what it was. For once, it appeared to be a real something and not just some affectation to get what she wanted.

Liz stayed where she was for a while watching her neighbours moving around, chatting, eating and drinking, thinking how unreal it was to sit in the middle of the road on a sunny day early in the year, but she knew she couldn't do the sociable thing at the moment, so she slunk off when no one was looking.

She fidgeted about in her attic-office, looking out of the dormer window down onto the road with everyone in it being all neighbourly and she knew she wouldn't be able to relax so she took herself off to the Downs and walked herself and Moocher until she was shattered.

She didn't want to go home so they climbed into the back of her car and fell asleep.

It was dark when they woke but even so, she still couldn't bring herself to go home. Someone might try to talk to her and she didn't want to have to talk back. She'd go home later when hopefully everyone would be in bed. The whole thing with Angela had upset her more than she'd have thought possible. More even than the pudding thing.

So, she thought about doing her own stakeout. It would be nice to have a completely different problem to chew over.

And, it was no use Philippe suddenly deciding he wasn't interested in his own windows and the window-smasher and why the smasher smashed his windows. No use at all. Because Liz still needed to know what was going on. It's not that she was nosy or anything. It's just that she needed to know. Apart from anything else, it was very odd that someone who was having their windows smashed every night had suddenly become not interested in that fact. It was only a few days ago that Philippe *had* been worried about it. And then, suddenly, he wasn't worried about it. It made as much sense as Angela. That is – it made no sense at all.

So, Liz and Moocher decided to do an unofficial stakeout. Moocher was always up for a stakeout. They weren't going to ask anyone else and they weren't going to tell anyone else. Then no one need know what they were up to and maybe they'd discover something useful.

Liz decided she'd stake out the Westbury-on-Trym

restaurant for ease of parking. She had discovered a packet of custard creams in the glove box, too, which meant she could have a little biscuit-binge with no one around to yell at her and generally make her feel guilty. A little binge couldn't do her any harm, especially not with all this hurling herself around the front room to offset it. Surely?

So, there they were, Moocher and Liz, settling in for a night's surveillance – Liz with biscuit in hand, Moocher curled up on the front passenger seat – when she saw Philippe himself. She was surprised to see him. She'd have thought he'd still be at the street party.

She didn't want to get out of the car and say hello. She didn't want to speak to anyone yet. Too, she was being a bit of a vigilante, and he might not be very pleased. Also, the smasher might be close by – if so, then he or she would see Liz as well as Philippe. So, she didn't get out of the car.

She and Moocher carefully and slowly eased themselves below the level of the dashboard so he wouldn't see them. She wasn't worried about him recognising the car as it was dark and loads of people had similar shape cars and he'd never struck her as a car enthusiast.

Liz was still lowering herself down into the tiny little space in front of the driving seat whilst also trying to keep her eyes on a level so she could see – it would be so handy to have eyes on stalks at this point. She must look like a large frog with its eyes peering out from under a lily pad. A very large frog. Hmmm – maybe not. Anyway, Moocher ruined the picture by sticking his nose in her ear – after all, it was on a level with him – her ear being at his level wasn't a common occurrence. She jumped at the shock of his cold nose, and smacked her head on the steering wheel.

When she did lift herself up again to look out at what was happening it was to see probably the one sight she hadn't expected – she saw Philippe casually lean back against his own restaurant window and shove his heel through the glass. He did it so quickly Liz thought she'd been mistaken. But no, he strolled away and the whole window fell out of its frame and spread itself, tinklingly, over the pavement. Glass slivers glinted in the light from the moon.

Philippe!

Liz looked at Moocher and he looked at her. He couldn't work it out either. Still, it meant she could have a decent night's sleep after all now she knew who the smasher was.

Except that it made no sense at all.

Nothing in her world made any sense any more.

Even less so when she got back to the house and discovered that Philippe had, apparently, just been called away from playing poker with Ronnie and Melanie because the alarm was going off at his restaurant.

The alarm was already going off before he got to it?

He'd apparently been playing poker since the street party ended until his restaurant had been attacked and the window smashed. His alarm system had alerted him to the vandalism.

Liz looked at Moocher and he looked at her. Liz knew the same thought was going through Moocher's hairy head as through her own – did Philippe have a twin?

Chapter Thirty-Seven
(Hanging up his lighter)

In the meantime, Danny was behaving rather strangely.

He no longer set fire to his pocket which in some ways was a relief and yet in others was rather sad. It had been so much a part of him. The way he would half smoke a cigarette and then decide to save the other half for later. The way he would roll the smouldering end out between his fingers. Inefficiently. Before putting the stompie in his pocket. Then the sudden suspicion in his eyes, his nose wrinkling as the first faint tendrils of smoke arose to assail his nostrils.

The smell of burning pocket and leg hairs is unique. The frantic dancing on the spot as he thrashed his own leg in an attempt to put the fire out before it gained a real and devastating hold. On a still day if you stopped to listen long enough you would be almost bound to hear someone shouting, "Pocket! Danny! Pocket!"

But no longer. He no longer set fire to his pocket because Liz had given him a small, silver-plated, half-smoked-stompie case with a hinged lid. He could now stow the stompie away in that and put it in his pocket in perfect safety. Liz was glad Danny no longer suffered from pocket fires with all the attendant embarrassment and discomfort, and she thought he must be saving a lot of money on trousers now.

It had taken some of the colour out of their lives though, it had to be said.

Today, though, he really left them – Ronnie and her – gobsmacked. He came into the front room where teacher and pupil had just finished their line dancing session. They'd opened the curtains and replaced the rug. Liz was lying on the sofa, panting. Ronnie had made coffee and was sorting out the CDs. Moocher was serving as security detail and keeping a sharp eye on the packet of jammy dodgers.

Danny came in and stood for a while just watching as though he wanted to say something, but didn't know how to start. He shuffled up and down a bit as though rehearsing for a line dance routine, and fidgeted with his phone. Liz tried to ignore him. She knew he would get there in the end, left to himself. Finally, he coughed. That was the signal and Ronnie and Liz looked up and gave him their full attention.

"I would like to say," he said, "I would like to say that I'm packing in the smokes."

Ronnie and Liz stared at him. Liz's mouth fell open, and she didn't seem able to close it. Ronnie was so still it was as if she'd been turned to stone with the gravity of the pronouncement.

"On Monday," he said into the continuing silence of the front room. "I'm stopping on Monday."

Danny was hanging up his lighter. It was almost inconceivable. He would be unrecognisable. He would be a different person.

"I just thought I'd tell you," he said and started to shuffle backwards towards the door.

Liz could not seem to get it together to make an appropriate response. Thank heaven for Ronnie.

"Danny! Congratulations," he said. And running over to Danny he took his hand and shook it vigorously. "I'm so pleased to hear it. You're making a very wise move and it's very brave of you to do it after such a long time. I know how you enjoy your cigarettes."

Danny immediately turned the colour of an old, weathered telephone kiosk, muttered, "Thank you, Ronnie," and made off. He could be heard galloping down the hall.

"You could have told him how pleased you are, Liz," Ronnie said.

"I was too gobsmacked. I was incapable of saying anything. I can't imagine Danny without a smoke in his hand. How's he going to do it? It's not going to be easy, is it?"

"Even so ..."

"Yes. Right. You're right." Liz rushed off after Danny and found him outside furiously puffing away, no doubt smoking as much as he possibly could between now and Monday. "Danny," she said. "I'm so sorry I didn't react. I was surprised. But I do think it's a brilliant thing to do. How can I help? Is there anything I can do to help?"

"Best thing is not to mention it, if you don't mind, Liz. Don't keep reminding me by asking me all the time how I'm getting on. You know what I mean?"

"Okay. So just ignore it completely. I can do that."

"I was wondering," he said. "Could I join you and Ronnie in your line dancing sessions? I really don't want to get fat just because I've packed in the smokes." He wasn't looking at her when he asked this, but she could see the back of his neck was still old-telephone-kioskish, and a sudden suspicion took root in her mind.

"Of course you can. The more the merrier. After all, two in a line isn't really a line. Three will be almost a real line. And when we get really good we can go to some proper line dancing gigs. That'll be fun."

He shot her a glance of pure terror. "No, er, no, I just meant in the front room. And anyway, these *are* proper line dancing lessons."

"I didn't mean these weren't proper line dancing lessons. They are. I meant line dancing dances, with a live band. But anyway, don't worry. It'll be a long time before I can appear in public. Although Ronnie is very good. Anyway, I'm trying to do it at least twice a week, three times if possible. Next time is Monday as it happens. Two in the afternoon. Just turn up. Okay?"

"Thank you. I'll be there."

Liz went back inside and collected Moocher from the front room. He'd been doing his I'd-better-vacuum-up-all-these-biscuit-crumbs-or-we'll-get-mice bit and had dust all over his nose. Ronnie had gone back next door.

Liz and Moocher went up to the attic. She had some paperwork to see to, dealing with the building work she was having done next door. But before she could concentrate on it, she tried to imagine Danny with no smokes, no smell of smokes, no yellow fingers, no mushroom cloud as he got out of his car. And she failed miserably.

She had dearly wanted to ask him why he was packing in the smokes, but had felt that she shouldn't – there could be all kinds of reasons – some of them very personal – and maybe they would become clear. It wasn't her business.

She also spent some time trying to imagine Danny, with his immaculately creased trousers and his 60s safari tops with the epaulettes and his tie and brilliantly polished shoes and always-combed hair, line dancing. She failed with that visualisation exercise, too.

This was going to be interesting.

Chapter Thirty-Eight
(I'm gonna be a detective!)

"I know! I'll follow her. Why didn't I think of that before?"

Liz sat up in the night. She had no idea what time it was, but she'd been awake for hours.

This was a 'doh!' moment in her whirling thoughts. She even smacked her own forehead as if to wake up its contents. What was her brain thinking? Why hadn't it got this sorted before?

Moocher leapt on the bed looking for a game, but contented himself with settling down once he'd been hugged. It was the middle of the night, after all.

Liz stayed sitting up. Of course, she would follow her sister. It was what private detectives had done since the dawn of time. That is, follow errant wives, or husbands, but usually wives in all the private eye novels she'd read. Then she could track down Cupcake, catch him and her at it, confront them and get this unsavoury business sorted. Angela could then get on with her marriage and Liz could stop worrying that Robert was going to be swept up by some avaricious, dyed-in-the-hair temptress in maiden's clothing while Angela wasn't concentrating on him.

Angela needed Robert. He was her home, her security.

Why hadn't she thought of the whole detective thing before? Especially as it linked in with the whole stakeout and surveillance thing she was already doing. The obvious strategy had been staring her in the face all along and she'd failed to pick up on it. Until now.

First of all, she had to find out when Angela was seeing Cupcake again.

Frustratingly, she would have to wait until morning before she could find out, so she lay down hoping that sleep would come for her.

As early as she dared in the morning, sleep having been conspicuous by its absence in the preceding hours, she rang Angela: "Hello Angela. It's me. When are you seeing your lover again?"

"Why do you want to know?" Angela asked, suspicion plain in her voice.

"In case you need a babysitter," Liz said, airily.

A long silence followed, punctuated only by little Johnny's being a train in the background, including the bit where he ran over a cow on the line and was late so there were a lot of very cross commuters. So, when Angela finally replied, Liz was cackling to herself and had to choke it back in order to hear her sister.

"As it happens, I'm seeing him this afternoon, Liz. It's very kind of you to be so considerate …"

"Oh, dear," Liz said, laying on the contrition in her voice. "I am so sorry, Angela, I can't babysit this afternoon. Now, if it had been any other day …"

"You never meant it in the first place, did you?" Angela yelled before throwing down the phone.

Liz was well satisfied with herself although conscious of a feeling of unease. She couldn't imagine Angela ever actually shouting at her, or throwing down the phone, both things she'd just done. Even so, she had found out when her sister was seeing Cupcake again, and she'd done it in such a way that Angela had no suspicion of Liz's motive and was convinced she was only being nasty.

Unfortunately, Liz hadn't thought to check on the time, so she'd have to start following Angela earlier than she might have done, but she was new to this game. She'd pick up the techniques of it as she went along.

She debated long and hard about taking Moocher. It was a delicate operation she was embarking on and he wasn't the world's most devious dog. So, she left him at home for this phase of the operation, and scurried over to Angela's, parked a few streets away, walked to her house and hid in a bush in her front garden, waiting for her to leave, or for Cupcake to arrive.

She was there for two hours before anything happened, and then the babysitter turned up. She recognised the babysitter immediately.

It was Their Mother.

Bloody hell! Was she in on it as well? Why would she encourage her daughter to have an affair?

Liz had no time to contemplate this thorny problem because as soon as she turned up Angela left.

Liz had her first stroke of luck – Angela didn't get in her car. It hadn't occurred to Liz that she might until now, but of course she could have. This private eye gig had more about it than she'd imagined. Anyway, Angela didn't get in her car so Liz was able to trail her relatively easily.

In fact, it wasn't as easy as it is in the films. In the films the person being followed – would that be the 'followee'? – doesn't usually know the person who is doing the following – the 'follower'? So, Liz couldn't get away with pretending to tie a non-existent shoe lace whenever Angela turned around, or pretend to be engaging with her phone – no, she had to dive from hedge to hedge and throw herself behind parked cars whenever Angela stopped or turned her head.

A few householders out in their front gardens were a little surprised and even not very pleased, but it couldn't be helped. Liz was on a mission.

Then Angela got on a bus!

Aargh!

Liz had to sprint to catch it.

Safely on the bus she realised she had no money. And the bus driver had no sense of humour at all.

So, she was forced to reveal herself to Angela and get her to pay Liz's fare.

"Ooh, this is nice," Liz said, settling into the seat next to her sister. "Meeting you like this. Oh, and thank you for paying my fare."

"Yes, isn't it," Angela said. She didn't sound so pleased. And, Liz noted, she didn't say it was a pleasure to pay her fare, either.

Somehow Liz had to let her know she wasn't about to get in the way of her assignation without alerting her suspicions.

"What are you doing out here?" Angela asked.

"I suddenly found myself free after all and I came out to see if you still needed a babysitter. I saw Our Mother so I realised you were fixed up."

"Really? Have a nice chat with her, did you?"

"Certainly not! I looked through the window, saw her there and ran away as fast as my stubby little legs would carry me." She shuddered dramatically.

For some reason their eyes locked in that moment and they laughed. A lot. It felt weirdly wonderful to share a laugh with her sister. She couldn't ever remember doing that before. Maybe Cupcake had something in his favour then. It wouldn't have happened without him.

Suddenly, Angela sobered and her face hardened. "Are you trying to tell me you caught the bus to my place rather than driving? You never use the bus."

"I had to catch the bus," Liz said. "My car's in for an MOT." Pretty nifty lying footwork there, she thought. Angela appeared to accept that explanation.

Luckily for Liz's story Angela was going all the way to what would be Liz's bus stop, if she ever used it. What an amazing coincidence. Liz had begun to wonder what she'd do when Angela got off and Liz had no reason to get off at the same place. So that was extremely lucky.

They parted at the bus stop after Liz had offered her sister coffee and been refused.

Liz slunk along, peering back over her shoulder a few times until she thought she could get away with turning and following her sister again. At least this time they were headed down the Gloucester Road – that is, they were on *her* territory now so she knew where she could dive if Angela turned her head.

For someone on her way to meet her lover, Angela spent a surprising amount of time looking in shop windows. Maybe she was early.

Eventually, she turned off the Gloucester road, up a narrow, steep side street and then left again. A few houses along she stopped, looked all around and pressed the doorbell in front of her that was positioned centrally on a bright red door with a brass lion's head knocker on it, and a shiny brass letterbox. Liz could see it all quite clearly from behind someone's picket fence on the other side of the road.

She'd been ever so careful not to tread on any of their plants but she'd been taken by surprise when Angela suddenly stopped at that door so she'd had to leap in gazelle-like fashion over the fence. Hopefully no one was in and she wouldn't get caught.

Then she saw the door opposite start to open. Excitement clutched at her throat. She was about to get an eyeful of Cupcake. She peered intently across the road and nearly expired on the spot when a hand thudded down on her shoulder and a voice bellowed in her ear: "You're standing on my hostas. Why are you standing on my hostas?"

Liz whipped around to find a face bristling right in to hers. She lost her balance and fell backwards.

"And now you're lying in my penstemons. Why are you lying in my penstemons?"

"I ... I was just trying to ..."

"What? What? Speak up!"

Liz risked a glance at the opposite side of the street but she was too late. Angela had disappeared, presumably into the house and Liz had missed all the action and hadn't even laid eyes on her prey. She hauled herself to her feet and faced Bristler. "I'm so sorry if I've damaged anything." She looked around and could clearly see that she had – things were flattened and it was obvious someone had been hiding in his garden. She bent and tried to pull the stems back to the upright position but they didn't want to stay. They just flopped over again. As for the fat-leaved things, they were just mush. How dreadful. She felt awful. She'd had no idea this might be such a destructive operation.

"I am so very sorry. Can I pay for replacements? Or, what can I do?"

He cupped a hand behind his ear and bent even closer to her. "What?" His breath smelled of tinned mackerel.

He couldn't hear a thing she was saying and she had no idea how to deal with the situation. "I'll tell you what," she said. "I'll get some replacements and bring them back. Okay?"

"What?"

She made signs that, to her, were obviously saying that she'd go and buy some more of these, uh, what had he said? – hostas and penstemons – and she would bring them back and plant them in his garden.

But all the reaction she got was another: "What?"

Well, Liz had always believed that actions speak louder than words, so when she noticed, out of her peripheral vision, the bright red door opening she said to him, "I'll be back," and shot off across the road. She wasn't going to miss Cupcake again. She could hear Bristler still, though: "What? What?"

Liz had been brought up to say, 'Pardon?' Whatever happened to 'Pardon?' And they're always going on about the younger generation. Some of the older lot weren't too great, actually.

She belted across the street just as the most good-looking man she'd ever seen in her life appeared out of the house to join Angela who waited for him. Blimey! No wonder she was straying away from home. Who wouldn't? Hastily, Liz checked to make sure her mouth wasn't hanging open, drool falling to her chest.

Angela jumped back with a feminine little squeak when she saw Liz.

It occurred to Liz that maybe she looked surprised not so much at her sister pitching up, but at the sight of that sister covered in vegetation with the odd snail crawling up her leg. Liz flicked it off, heard it hit the road and immediately felt like a murderer. She hoped its shell wasn't cracked.

"Wait for me," she yelled after Angela and Cupcake. They were rapidly disappearing down the road, almost at a trot. Liz ran after the snail. She found him, and checked his shell. It looked okay. She immediately felt better. She placed him carefully in Bristler's garden. "I'll be back," she shouted at him, and raced after the rapidly fleeing couple with "What? What?" echoing in her ears.

Falling in beside Angela and Cupcake, Liz asked breezily: "Where are we going, then?"

"We're not going anywhere," Angela said in tones fit to freeze oil. "*We* are going somewhere. You are not."

"Oh, yes I am. I have a duty to protect you from yourself. I'm not leaving your side now until you go home to your *husband*." Liz emphasised the word whilst staring at Cupcake. "And your *child* – poor little almost-motherless Johnny." There, that told Cupcake a thing or two in case he didn't already know his lover had attachments. Legal and moral ones.

"Don't be ridiculous, Liz. You can't stay with us all night."

Liz was surprised to see Cupcake visibly wince and his face, previously lightly-tanned in its chiselled perfection, reddened to the hue of his own front door.

"I *can* stay with you all night. Of course, I can. And I *will* stay with you for however long it takes until you go home. Is Our Mother in on this as well? How do you know she'll stay babysitting all night?"

"You're impossible," Angela snorted and strode off. Liz fell into step with Cupcake who was doing his best to look as though he wasn't really there, but not succeeding, not by a long chalk. Every person they passed, regardless of age or companion, ogled him. Liz knew how they felt. She couldn't take her eyes off him. Maybe that was the answer. Maybe *she* should seduce him away from Angela, save their little family unit and have him for herself.

She couldn't quite believe she was thinking of another human being as if he was a package to go to the highest bidder. But still – it *was* Cupcake! Served him right.

They arrived at a café. Liz was sure they hadn't intended going to a café, but she was willing. Cupcake bought her a hot chocolate and a double choc chip muffin. She'd line dance it off later. Oh, yes she would! They sat there not making conversation for a while. Their drinks went cold. Until Angela exclaimed: "This is ridiculous. Let's go to the pictures. In *your* car." She gave Cupcake a most telling look which Liz couldn't work out.

"By the way, what *is* your name?" Liz demanded of Cupcake. "Ethelred, Edmundo, Edgerton, Emiliano, Entwistle? Just what is it?"

He looked frightened. Poor thing. She didn't blame him – he had two sisters staring at him meaningfully. These two particular sisters. He was only lucky Their Mother wasn't there as well. He looked at Angela. "Okay," he said in a strangely stifled voice.

He looked at Liz and said: "John" in a puzzled voice.

Liz was puzzled too. His name should have started with an 'e' – or was it an 'a'? Either way, a vowel, not a 'j'. She noticed Angela looking pleased with herself and wondered if she'd deliberately misled her.

They left the café and walked back up the street until they stopped by a little car with two perfectly good front seats but only a little shelf thing where the back seats should have been. Angela's look of triumph was explained.

"What sort of car is this, then?" Liz demanded. "That it hasn't got a proper back seat in it?"

"A coupé," John muttered. Liz couldn't keep calling him Cupcake. He simply didn't look like someone's cupcake at all. Cupcakes have beer bellies and stubble long past designer length. Or, at the very least, they have sneery faces. John had none of these attributes.

But Angela should have known better than to underestimate her sister. Liz barrelled past her, pulled the door open, yanked the seat forward and, turning sideways and lengthways she stuffed herself onto that little back shelf. Her knees scrunched up against her chin, she couldn't breathe very well and, when the front seats were put back into their upright position, she was hemmed in on all sides, but she would put up with that and worse if she had to. She was on a mission.

Her companions said nothing.

At the cinema they had yummy ice-cream and popcorn. Angela and John seemed unable to finish theirs, so Liz helped them out. She noticed that John kept throwing Angela haunted, despairing looks and that Angela gave him back stony glares. They certainly didn't seem very loverlike. Maybe they'd had a tiff.

The film was good. It was a sci-fi and quite violent, but did have a story to it. Liz had no idea Angela was into sci-fi and rather fancied she wasn't. They came out of there and Liz did her shoving-a-large-human-peg-into-a-small-inhuman-crevice thing in the car and they all went back to John's house, Angela trying to get rid of Liz along the way, to no avail. Liz was on a mission. Liz even had to ring Danny and tell him what to do about Moocher as she was on a mission. Thank heaven she hadn't brought Moocher with her. He'd never have been comfortable on that back shelf.

Back at John's house, he and Angela shared a small sofa. Every now and then Angela would edge up to John and put her hand on his arm or his knee. And every time he would freeze and deliberately not look at this hand that had appeared on his person as if his lack of acknowledgement would make it disappear. Angela would occasionally address him as: 'darling' or 'lover' or 'honey-bunch', and he would mumble something undistinguishable in reply, a tidal wave of the blood under his skin churning up his face to disappear into his hairline.

Liz watched all this in some bewilderment. What the hell?

They stayed up all night eating pizza and playing rummy, and three-handed crib, and snap. Playing snap was the only time Liz saw John relax at all – he really seemed to enjoy himself, which was quite endearing. Other than that, he was on edge the whole time. At one point he whined, "Angela. I want to go to bed."

She gave him such a look, flicked a glance at Liz, stared back at him, and said: "John, really! While Liz is here?"

He went such a horrible shade of puce Liz was afraid he was about to keel over, all the blood vessels in his body broken. "I didn't mean ... I didn't mean ..." but he never managed to say what he didn't mean. Angela made sure he didn't.

By this time Liz had ascertained that Robert was away on business so he wouldn't even know Angela hadn't been home all night. Their Mother had obviously been organised to babysit all night if need be.

At six in the morning Angela finally cracked and decided they should go home. She tried to get Liz out of the car at Malvern Road but Liz was conscious that her own car was parked near Angela's so she insisted she had to stay with Angela all the way to make sure she really did go home. Angela gave her a filthy look but Liz ignored it, too busy trying to fold herself like some fleshy origami puzzle into the back bit of John's car.

At their destination, having disgorged his passengers, John, with an extremely brief, "Bye, then," zoomed off as if he couldn't get away fast enough.

Of course, at Angela's house Liz didn't want to go in no matter how much Angela tried to make her. She didn't want to court any interaction with Their Mother in there so the sisters parted company on the doorstep.

"I hope you're satisfied now," Angela snapped. She did look tired, but at least Liz knew it was from a night of board games and not a night of unremitting adulterous passion.

"Yeah, I am," Liz said. "I'm very satisfied. Thank you for a most revealing night. The pizza was yum too." And she walked off to find her car and go home to flop in bed with an ecstatic Moocher.

At which point it suddenly became obvious to her exhausted mind that John wasn't Angela's lover at all. He wasn't Cupcake.

The unreality of the whole idea of Angela having a bit on the side struck her anew. Maybe she didn't – maybe she didn't have a lover at all.

In which case why was Angela telling her she did?

Chapter Thirty-Nine
(Danny's Achy Breaky Heart)

The knock that came at her attic door was tentative. This was not surprising. The attic was her domain and she didn't appreciate being disturbed in it. People had to have a damn good reason for approaching her in her lair.

Moocher heaved himself up, with great creakings, from his new favourite spot. He'd taken to leaping into the washing basket, doing his turning in three magic circles bit and then throwing himself down onto the washing with a great 'oomph' and then sighing mightily before falling instantly asleep to snore with wild abandon. This was okay as long as it wasn't damp, clean washing. Liz had learned her lesson – these days she made sure she only kept dry, dirty washing in it. She didn't want Moocher developing arthritis from lying on soggy clothes.

He shuffled over to the door and sniffed noisily all along the bottom of it. Then he looked at her as if to say, "It's only Danny. Oh, go on. Let him in."

"Come in," she shouted.

The door slowly opened and, sure enough, it was Danny, who appeared a bit at a time as though something was holding him back.

Moocher greeted him enthusiastically and Danny scratched him behind his ears and briefly laid his face on the top of Moocher's head. They were old friends.

"Have a seat," Liz said.

Danny retrieved the director's chair Liz kept in a cubby-hole at the back of the room, unfolded it and sat down almost opposite where she sat at her desk in a swingy executive chair.

She waited to see what had brought him up here to risk her ire.

He did his usual fiddling-with-things ritual. He pulled his phone out of his pocket, turned it around in his hands, polished the blank screen, put it back in his pocket. He took out his cufflinks and put them back in again, rolled up his tie and let it down to hang limply with a little curl in the end. Finally, he opened his mouth: "Do you think Ronnie likes me?"

There was one thing Liz could guarantee about Danny and that was that she never knew what he was going to say next.

However, the suspicion that had poked a little tendril of an idea into the air when Danny had originally said he was packing in the smokes and wanted to take up line dancing, grew a metre and shot out a whole bunch of leaves and branches! This **was** going to be interesting.

"Yes," she said. She was sure that Ronnie **did** like Danny. She had seen the care he took showing Danny how to do the steps when they had their line dancing sessions in the front room and the way he would make sure there was always a drink for Danny to have when he was gasping with effort.

"Really? Do you really?"

"Danny. It's not that difficult to like you, you know. You're a very likeable chap."

The expression on his face was so amazed Liz could have cried. Why should he ever have thought that he might not be likeable? And yet he looked at her as though she was a regular lie factory. Eventually he turned away and stared at the ceiling so meaningfully that she looked too. But all she could see was a few cracks and a whole city of cobwebs.

"I like Ronnie," he said.

"Oh, good. I'm glad. Ronnie is also very likeable."

"Yes, but …"

"Yes, but what?"

"Ronnie's a man."

Without hesitation Liz said, "He can't help that, Danny. He's still very likeable. You're a man and you're very likeable." She thought she'd try a bit of reinforcement here. Not that that would patch up his ragged self-esteem in a hurry.

"Yes, but you're a woman and you like him. *I'm* a man and

like him. Like him a lot." By now his tie resembled nothing more than a whippet's tail.

Liz was feeling a little lost about where they were going with this. It must have showed because he became quite snappy.

"For God's sake, Liz. I'm a *man*. Ronnie's a *man*. I like him *a lot*! Too damn much!" He was almost panting with his vehemence. It was unusual for Danny to get snappy. It must have been the lack of smokes. Liz had heard that people often got bad-tempered when they stopped smoking.

"Oh!" she said. "You mean you *fancy* him? You don't just like him, you *fancy* him."

Danny's face pinkened and he looked all around the room as though expecting a horde of policemen to leap out and arrest him any minute.

"Sexually," Liz added, helpfully.

His face now had so much blood rushing around it, Liz thought the rest of his body must be empty. He was incapable of answering, so she assumed that he *was* sexually attracted to Ronnie.

This was a dilemma. She could tell him that he wasn't undergoing a radical change in sexual orientation. She could put him out of his undoubted torment and tell him that he wasn't really thinking of playing for the other side. She didn't hold it against him that he was perturbed. He was in his late fifties and had always been attracted to the opposite sex so it was not surprising that he might be unsettled about suddenly discovering he was attracted to his own sex. It would just take a little adjustment.

Except that … Ronnie …

She wanted to tell him that he didn't actually need to make that little adjustment.

The trouble was that it wasn't right to tell Danny that Ronnie was actually the Smart Granny in disguise because the Smart Granny didn't want people to know that.

She might be perfectly happy for Danny to know that she was who she was, but Liz couldn't even ask her if it was all right for her to give Danny this information because she wasn't supposed to know who she was either.

Her original suspicion had been correct, though. Danny had developed a liking for Ronnie. A serious liking. "Danny, did you give up smoking because Ronnie hates it so much?" she asked.

He bunched his lips, but nodded slowly and repeatedly. Each time he nodded, his chin went down lower and lower until in the end it was bouncing off his chest. His fair hair hung down in lank, miserable defeat.

"Well, it seems to me that if a confirmed smoker can pack in the smokes to gain favour with someone then that person can keep a secret." Oh, God – surely she wasn't going to say what she thought she might be going to say. Of all people, Danny could not keep a secret! He looked so miserable, though!

His head came up, but he said nothing.

"Especially as it's you, Danny, my most reliable and trusted lodger."

A tiny smile flickered and went out.

"I do have to say, though, that this is a deathly secret. You are a bit of a flap-mouthed git sometimes."

His face took on a blank expression as if it couldn't possibly be him who'd told the queue in the Post Office that her knickers had been nicked that time.

"You have to promise me that what I'm going to tell you will remain a secret."

He still said nothing. He nodded his head.

"Let me tell you this. If you tell anyone what I'm about to tell you I shall have you thrown out of your room."

"You can't do that!"

"Yes, I can." She was sure she couldn't. "I'll get Hugh on to it," she said. She knew that would finish the argument.

"Oh. Hugh. Okay. I wouldn't tell anyone anyway, Liz, now that I know how important it is to you that I don't. The knickers thing was just a funny story. You didn't really mind that, did you?"

She gave him a stern look and then she said it: "Ronnie's a woman."

He stared at her. She seemed to have caught his attention. He removed his glasses from his top pocket, huffed on them and polished them vigorously with a blindingly white handkerchief.

"Now, don't forget – you mustn't tell anyone and you mustn't let her know you know, because I'm not supposed to know either."

She expected shock, or questions, or something, but he

merely finished with his glasses, stowed the handkerchief away again, got up, folded up the director's chair, put it back in its cubby-hole, stood in front of her for a moment and then leaned over and kissed her on the cheek.

Well! You could have knocked her down with a blade of grass. Liz thought her mouth was open. Again.

"Thank you, Liz. Thank you so much," he said and left the attic looking twenty years younger than when he entered it.

Ah, if only all life's problems were so easily solved.

Chapter Forty
(Upping her detective game)

Buoyed up by the possible happy-ever-after occurring on the
Danny and Ronnie front, but even more mystified by the whole
Angela-thing, and even more determined to get to the bottom of it,
Liz went back to her sister's house the following day.

She sat in the car watching the house for a while. Again,
she had left Moocher at home despite his pleas to come with her.
She'd been worried about what would happen to him if, for
example, she was out of the car and suddenly had to follow
someone on foot. She never left Moocher in the car for all kinds of
reasons – the heat, someone breaking in to nick him, someone
breaking in and letting him loose, a lorry running amok and
crashing into her car with Moocher in it. The reasons were
numberless. She couldn't take the risk.

Gosh, this surveillance lark was incredibly boring. She got
out of the car and lurked in some bushes.

Then it occurred to her that, instead of merely hanging
around in a shrubbery, she could check out her sister's bins. All the
best detectives checked out people's bins, didn't they? Yes.

Enthusiasm for something to do encouraged her to follow
this course of action. She might find something incriminating that
would tell her something useful. She pulled her collar up as far as
it would go, wished she had some dark glasses with her to
complete the look, and crawled around the side of the house.

She discovered that Angela kept her bins in a specially built
enclosure of red brick, tastefully lidded with a fitted wooden roof
modelled after the roof of her house. Of course, she did! It did look
like a little house alongside the garage, which looked like a
medium sized house, alongside the main house that the people
actually lived in. The three structures looked like three siblings
arranged small-to-big or like baby house, mother house and daddy

house. And Liz was the wolf creeping around waiting to pounce. Or should she be a bear?

Liz cautiously opened the door of baby house, but she needn't have worried about rusty squealings alerting anyone to her furtive activities – nothing would dare squeak around Angela – everything was well oiled. But she nearly spoiled the quiet by screaming in agony when she put her hand out to the big, black wheelie bin in order to pull it out so she could open its lid – and it shot towards her – it was obviously *too* well oiled – and attempted to run her over.

Liz tried to leap out of its way but it bashed into her knee and took off down the drive like a Formula One car from the start line. Liz could see it zooming out into the road, squishing a pedestrian on its way, before causing a major multiple pile up in sleepy old, leafy old Coombe Dingle. She couldn't let it happen!

Trust Angela to have her rubbish bins on their own, wheeled platforms!

Liz chased after the bin, but it ran along on its little wheels like it was being chased by a rabid bin-crusher. The noise it made telling the world of its escape, was like a giant roller-skate in full trundle. Liz ran alongside it trying to get ahead a bit so she stood a chance of bringing it to a halt without getting crushed herself. She managed to grab its handle and, arms fully extended with the weight of it, swung it around. She nearly lost her footing but just managed to hang on and they ran together like two people in a three-legged race, back up the drive and straight into its little bin-house.

It must have looked choreographed to an onlooker. Despite the perfection of her bin-dance, Liz hoped no one had seen her or that was her cover blown.

This time she knew what she was dealing with, and when she pulled the bin out for the second time, she kneed it against its little house and wedged her foot under its outer edge so it couldn't run away from her. She drew in a deep breath and held it, then she opened the lid, and found herself peering down into a whole microcosm of perfect order. She let her breath go. Of course, Angela's bin wouldn't smell so bad! She should have known. No, Angela's bin smelled of summer gardens. Of course, it did.

Liz could identify wafts of lavender, maybe some rose, possibly a hint of honeysuckle. To look at its contents, too, was like inspecting a model of organisational genius; everything tied up neatly in different coloured bags. There would be nothing insecure about any of Angela's rubbish – it would all know where it belonged.

Nothing could have been further from the state of her own bin which had to be approached with caution depending on which way the wind blew.

She poked amongst the bags. She could see roughly what the contents were. And here was one labelled 'fabric'. Why would Angela put fabric in the bin? Liz could clearly hear Angela saying in that unbearably virtuous voice she had sometimes that all her clothing went to charity shops because none of it was ever so worn or torn that it had to be thrown away.

And yet here she clearly had some clothes in her bin.

A sudden disturbance in her stomach warned Liz that her sister's uncharacteristic behaviour was indeed abnormal for her and there might be something very wrong. They might not get on terribly well, but she didn't want there to be anything seriously wrong with Angela.

The reluctance she felt to further investigate the 'fabric' bag forced her to do it. She knew she was close to finding something of significance.

She pulled it free of the other bags and studied it.

Then she opened it and pulled out a very pale lemon-coloured set of baby clothes. There were those all-in-one things she'd seen babies wearing, complete with feet; dear little cardigans, vests, even a darling little cap; and an incredibly soft, delightfully embroidered blanket, or maybe it was a shawl.

Liz felt sick. She felt as if she'd invaded Angela's most private business. Which she had. It should have remained hidden. But it was too late – she could never not-know about this now; and, more than that, she was overwhelmed with a desperate sense that there was something very, very wrong with her sister.

Although the mystery had deepened and Liz wanted to know more than she did, she was also conscious of a strange feeling of worry and concern and love for her sister. The thought that Angela, who had everything and always has had, including

Their Mother's whole approval all her life, had suffered something and had worked so hard to keep it to herself and throw people off the scent, was almost unbearable for Liz. The uprush of fiercely protective feelings for her sister shocked her.

She felt like slinking home and minding her own business for ever and ever, but she was too worried about Angela to leave now she'd come this far.

Wishing she was as far away as possible, but knowing she had to see this through, Liz marched up to the front door and rang the bell.

Angela opened it straight away as if she'd been waiting for her. "Liz," she said. "I'm so glad you're here." She stepped out of the house and pushed Liz in. Lowering her voice to a hoarse whisper she said: "Robert's in. You can tell him all about Cupcake now, can't you. I know you're dying to. I'm off to see him now, as it happens."

"Ange …" Liz said, but her sister had run down the drive and disappeared around the hedge.

"Liz? Were they your dulcet tones I heard?"

"Coming, Robert," Liz replied, shutting the door and bracing herself for she didn't know what. Just the knowledge that her sister was out seeing her lover – if she had one – was enough to make her quail. She didn't want to give her away now although it was becoming increasingly obvious to her that, for some obscure reason, Angela *wanted* Liz to 'tell' on her.

She approached the living room doorway to be greeted by Robert, the lovely, calm, Robert. She nearly cast herself on his chest but managed to stop herself.

"Hello Liz." He stooped to kiss her cheek. "What a delight to see you. I seem to be seeing a lot more of you these days." She was certain he didn't mean there was more of her to see … He wouldn't be that mean. "Long may it last," he said, and beamed at her. Then she did nearly burst into tears and throw herself onto his big, comforting, charcoal-grey-clad shoulder, but somehow she still managed to restrain herself. Thankfully, because she could not have explained herself to him if the world had depended on it.

"Hello Robert. I wasn't expecting to see you home today, but I agree – it is lovely to see you."

She wasn't going to think about bread and butter pudding. She wasn't going to think about bread and butter pudding … She wasn't. No.

He dropped his jacket onto the back of an armchair and loosened his tie. When he rubbed his face with both hands and sighed before turning to the drinks cabinet, Liz realised how tired he looked. He didn't normally. Normally he looked like a clean-living chap, full of health and verve. Whatever was going on was wearing on him, too, it would seem.

"Drink, Liz?" he asked waving a cut-glass decanter in her general direction.

"No, thanks, Robert. I'll make a coffee, I think."

But she didn't move from where she was and he joined her. They smiled slightly at each other and both collapsed into an armchair. A silence fell, but Liz couldn't relax.

She wondered if he'd ask her if she knew where Angela was, and she wondered what she would say. Her mind had gone on holiday and left a vacancy in its place.

But he didn't ask.

She began to feel quite strained, more than she did already. Why didn't he ask?

Her racing brain decided he must know something. Or he would ask. Surely.

"Um. Maybe I will have that drink after all," she said, and levered herself out of her chair to get it before he could offer. She helped herself to a serious dollop of orange liqueur she knew her sister had brought back from Cyprus last year. She topped it up with dry ginger. She fancied something exotic.

Settling in to her chair again, she noticed Robert's eyes were shut. She stared at his face and wondered how such a man came to have such a wife. He caught her at it, suddenly opening his eyes and holding her look with his grey one. She couldn't tear her gaze from his and took a big gulp of her drink.

"Out with her lover, is she?" he said and half a pint of sticky, alcoholic liquid shot from her mouth and spattered all across Angela's hand-carved, hand-knotted, super-washed Chinese rug.

"Aargh!" she yelled and, leaping from her chair, she raced out to the kitchen to scrabble about for a suitable cloth and bowl of water. She dropped to her knees in the living room and starting scrubbing the rug. Angela would kill her for this.

"Liz," Robert said. "Don't worry about it. I'll get it cleaned! Liz! You're making it worse. Leave it alone." She sat back on her heels and realised he was right; the bits she'd scrubbed looked a lot worse than the bits she hadn't, so she took the cleaning stuff back out to the kitchen and slowly made her way back into the sitting room wondering what to say.

As she passed him in his chair Robert let out a whoop of laughter. "Your face!" he gasped, suddenly doubling up with hilarity. "Priceless!" He could barely get the words out he was so convulsed with mirth. "I was joking," he said when he could get breath. "Angela hasn't got a lover."

She looked at him pityingly. Much he knew.

"No, seriously, Liz. She hasn't got a lover. I know she's told you she has. But she hasn't. You're supposed to have told me she had one. Why haven't you?"

Liz was beginning to feel as though life was sprinting ahead and leaving her miles behind. "If you know so much, why don't you tell me?" she invited him, getting up for a refill. To hell with it. She'd have to stay the night now but she didn't care. Except for Moocher. She left the refill on the side. She wanted to get home to Moocher more than anything.

"Wait a minute – if I'm supposed to have told you, then how do you already know?"

"Because Your Mother told me."

Their Mother? What the hell! "Oh," she said. "Well, if Our Mother has already told you, why did Angela tell me?"

"It's my fault. I should have reacted properly when Your Mother told me, but I couldn't swallow it from her and didn't react properly. Silly of me."

"You know," Liz said. "I haven't the faintest idea what you're talking about."

His face softened. His eyes, capable of being as cold as a frozen pork chop, gazed on her so warmly she felt enveloped in a winter duvet. She also felt confused, a feeling becoming ever more familiar to her.

"Liz. Nothing could please me more than the sisterly loyalty I see in you this evening. It doesn't surprise me although I know Angela wouldn't believe it. Otherwise she wouldn't have bothered telling you she was having an affair. She really believed you would jump at the chance of dropping her in it.

Her face must have spelt out to him that her brain had taken a leave of absence.

"She really expected you to tell me she was having an affair," he added slowly. "That is why she told you. For that one reason. For you to tell me. I think you've probably put a spanner in the works by not telling me."

Liz got up and headed for the drinks cabinet to snatch up her refill. He joined her and refreshed his whisky and water.

"But I'm very pleased. And Angela will be too, when she comes back to herself. She feels very alone at the moment. It'll be nice for her to have a sister after all, a sister who cares enough for her not to give her away."

Someone must have nobbled Liz's drink and made it way too strong. Her head felt as though the hamsters that usually ran her brain had stopped to have a fight.

There was silence for some time then.

Robert must have realised she was struggling. He heaved himself up from his chair and coming over to her he knelt on the floor and grabbed one of her hands. He looked her full in the face and spoke slowly and carefully in his lovely, soothing voice.

"Angela is suffering a lot at the moment. She's been told she's unlikely to be able to carry a baby to full term again. This is where I could happily wring Your Mother's neck having brought you two up to believe that having herds of children is a woman's destiny in life and if you don't, you're less than nothing."

Her hand must have attempted to clench at this point because his grasp became firmer and his voice even gentler.

"Because of the way Angela thinks, as a direct result of her upbringing I would suggest, she feels less than useless. She feels she is utterly worthless and how could anyone love her now she's unlikely to have any more children?"

Yes, this all figured. This made perfect sense to Liz, being so familiar with Their Mother and with the effect she'd always had on her sister.

"I didn't know you wanted any more children."

"I'm happy either way. I love Angela and I love Johnny and they're enough for me. But Angela feels she's letting me and Johnny down by not producing another child." He sighed heavily. "She's been and had all the tests done by herself. She told me none of this at the time."

"This makes no sense," Liz said.

"What no one else knows, other than Your Mother, is that we've had two miscarriages since Johnny. That's why Angela went for the tests. So, of course Your Mother tells me her daughter is having an affair. Think of her logic. If you can't have another child then you are failing your husband. What can you do if you fail in such a monumental way? Nothing. It's the most complete failure isn't it?"

Liz nodded, unable to speak. She could hear Their Mother coming out with this garbage.

"So, your husband is going to cast you aside if you fail the most important task of all as a wife. He couldn't be blamed for throwing you out, could he?" His face whitened and Liz saw his tiredness again. He was right. That was how Their Mother would think. Liz had often wondered what idiot-sexist-cave she'd crawled out of. Their Mother had at one point advised Hugh to 'sort Liz out'. He'd been appalled. Liz had been furious, of course. Like women need other women to put the boot in, as well as the rest of the world.

"So, Your Mother persuaded my wife," Robert continued, voice grim, "to come up with a cock and bull story about her having an affair. To throw me off the scent of my wife's barrenness." He almost spat the word out, his contempt for it apparent. "I would be so jealous and macho about it I'd spend all my time searching for the lover and dealing with him and treasuring my wife even more and keeping her under lock and key so no one else could have her, and I would be so possessive, because real men are supposed to be so possessive – that's all they're really interested in – their possessions – that when it eventually came out that she couldn't have any more children it wouldn't be the prime importance to me that it would have done if I hadn't nearly lost my wife to another man. Are you with me now?"

"Yes. With those two. To anyone else it would be a recipe for straitjackets and sedation. But for those two ..."

Sadly, Liz could envisage it all only too well.

They both headed for the drinks cabinet in silence. What could anyone say? It was ridiculous. But they were talking Angela and Their Mother here. It made perfect sense.

"Angela is a little unbalanced at the moment from the grief of it all. She wouldn't normally be this daft." He threw back his whiskey.

"Do you mean she is really not having an affair?" Liz wanted to be clear on this point.

"No, she's really not."

"What about John wotsit?"

"Poor John," Robert laughed. "Don't tell me she's dragged him into her machinations?"

"Who is he?"

"A friend she met at counselling. I can imagine her persuading him into pretending something. He's very amenable. Yes," he said in answer to Liz's surprised look. "She's finally going to counselling sessions. Not nearly as soon as I'd hoped, but at least she is now going. We haven't told Your Mother."

"Don't worry. I won't tell her either," Liz agreed. "Now I know what you meant by not reacting properly. You mean, if you'd reacted properly to Our Mother telling you Angela was having an affair, you'd have lost your temper, shouted a bit, maybe slapped her about a bit, and it would have been settled then and there."

"Yes. But I just couldn't play up to your mother's twisted ideas of what a man or a marriage should be. But maybe I should have. Maybe I've made things worse." He rubbed his face again as though cleaning the whole mess away.

"Don't be daft. What do we do now?"

"Somehow I have to get Angela to believe that I love her as she is for always and I'm completely happy with our life as it is. But I don't think I can do the whole jealous husband thing. It's too stupid and it goes against too many things I believe."

"How else though?"

"We'll just have to think of something. After all, you've already let the side down by not behaving like the jealous sister you're supposed to be. You didn't give her away. Your mother won't understand that either. We're simply not playing the game, you and I."

"Which is why we're in this mess," Liz said, swigging back the dregs and looking yearningly towards the drinks cabinet.

"Yep. That's right. It's all our fault. Another?"

Liz handed him her glass and sank back in her chair, trying hard to think the way she'd always been taught to, but she couldn't do it. She'd never been able to think the way Their Mother had wanted her to think. The rows they'd had! She'd left home as soon as she could and tried to avoid Their Mother ever since.

Now she wondered if all this was partly her fault. Leaving Angela alone to deal with Their Mother. Maybe she, Liz, should have stuck around to take some of the flak so Angela didn't get the full force of the machinations and emotional blackmail.

"What we should do is what they want," she said reluctantly.

"I don't think I can do what Your Mother wants."

"Not even for Angela?"

"I would do anything for Angela. But not stuff that I think isn't going to help her in the long run. I don't want to do anything that bolsters Your Mother's idea that marriages, and particularly men, should be managed with a series of manipulations. Angela and I need to sort it out. If I go along with this, we'll never be able to break through all that conditioning. We'll never really be able to talk. And we weren't doing too badly until all this other baby stuff started. It started when you thought you were pregnant, you know."

Liz winced. She *had* thought she was pregnant at the time. Their Mother had even insisted on visiting Liz – something they both tended to avoid as a rule. While there, she'd had something to say about it all. Of course.

"Now you're pregnant, you must get rid of that filthy animal, for a start," she'd said, gesturing towards Moocher. Who, at that precise moment, just happened to be seeing to some delicate and private grooming.

He'd looked up, consternation clear upon his furry face, and then gone back to his task.

It was the casual tone Their Mother used that infuriated Liz as much as anything. The assumption that it would come to pass, without question, that she would throw her dog out into the street just because she was pregnant.

She'd thrown Their Mother out instead.

That in itself didn't go down too well, but when, not long after, she'd realised she'd been mistaken about her condition, that seemed to add fuel to Their Mother's fire, who became even more vitriolic than she'd always been before.

All of which made no impression on Liz. She was appalled to think that the woman had genuinely expected her to get rid of her dog.

Liz had spent ages playing with Moocher after that, trying to help him get over the insult.

Their Mother seemed to take it personally that Liz wasn't pregnant. That had bothered her even more than being thrown out of the house.

Liz fervently hoped that mother-ejection hadn't made her double down on Angela instead.

"That's really when Your Mother got on her high horse about how a man needs a brood of children to spoil, and a child needs a sibling, and, of course, a grandmother needs a litter of toddlers around her knees. Blah blah blah. I can't endorse this rubbish. I have to regain my wife and we have to work it out together without interference from anyone. And you just have to carry on being the caring sister you have shown yourself to be."

"I know you're right, Robert. You really are right. It's just falling in with them would be much easier."

He just looked at Liz. "Like you ever have!" he snorted. He refilled their glasses and they relapsed into silence.

They stayed like that for what seemed a long time. And then Angela came home.

When she saw them slumped into the sofa together, she stopped and stared, her handbag dropping to the floor.

"We're having a fair," Liz said surprised that her mouth wasn't working very well. "A fair. An fair. You know what I mean. No! Wait! Not me. You."

Angela paled and swayed, and even through the mists of what must by now amount to alcohol poisoning Liz could see the strain on Angela's face, especially around the eyes.

Why hadn't she seen that before? Liz supposed she hadn't really looked because it was Angela, her tedious sister. Shame engulfed her. She attempted to stand and fell on her face at Angela's feet. Luckily Robert made it up and didn't fall on his face.

"Silly Billy," he said to Liz in passing.

"Darling," he said to his wife, and grabbed her. She disappeared into the depths of his hug. From where she lay, entirely unable to move, Liz saw her sister push her hands around her husband's back and she held on as though he was the only thing that stopped her falling through cracks in the earth into the molten centre of the planet. Perhaps he was.

Chapter Forty-One
(Orange liqueur? Seriously???)

Liz lay as still as she could because her skull had broken and her brains had fallen out. They had probably slid off the bed and fallen on the floor and would be covered with dust. Or they would if she was at home – oh, yes – at home her brains would be covered with dust and dog hair. But she was in Angela's spare room, so probably her brain was just as clean where it must be on the floor as it was when it first fell out of her broken head.

Orange liqueur was the worse to over-indulge on, she knew that. What had she been playing at? Life was getting too confusing for her – that was the best excuse she could come up with.

A cold, wet snout pushed into her cheek. Moocher! She knew it! She was dying and someone had brought Moocher to say his farewells to her.

Tears of self-pity rolled down her cheeks. They were very loud tears.

She was too young to die. It wasn't fair.

"Don't worry," a voice said. "You don't have to move. I'll look after Moocher – Danny brought him over. He was getting anxious."

Liz forced an eye open. It was Angela sitting on a chair by the bed. This really wasn't how she wanted to see her sister to try and build a whole new relationship. She couldn't ever remember feeling this bad just from a few drinks.

Angela's smile was tentative. Liz was desperate to connect with her and, despite the world whirling around her head, she levered herself almost upright as her sister piled pillows behind her. Gratefully, Liz leaned back against them.

"I'm really sorry, Ange," she said, the old name she'd used for her sister when they were small and still friends. "I'm really sorry I wasn't there for you. I'm really sorry I didn't throw Our Mother out of your life, too."

"You couldn't have done that," Angela said. "I do love Our Mother. Although, she has been a bit of a trial. I think she *thought* she was helpful." Absently, she chewed the corner of a nail. "After the second miscarriage she said I shouldn't have eaten the soft cheese; I shouldn't have gone to yoga classes. She told me 'it wasn't really a baby'. Then she told me to just not think about it because no one wants to hear or think about dead babies."

"Vile," Liz said. It was all she could manage for the fury blocking her throat.

"Not really – she just has, uh, limited thinking."

"Vile," Liz said again.

"What about you? How did you feel when you found you weren't pregnant?"

"I'd made a mistake, Ange – I'd lost the *idea* of being pregnant – I hadn't lost a baby – I didn't think about it, really, past that fleeting disappointment. I thought that we would move on and another chance would arise. I didn't have time to be upset, anyway. It was shortly after that Our Mother intimated to Hugh that I'd been lying all along about being pregnant to keep him in tow."

The pain of him querying that with her had been more sharp, but she couldn't bring herself to say that even on this day of unprecedented openness with her sister. It had to be enough that this was the first time she'd even told anyone that her husband had believed Their Mother over her. She still couldn't quite grasp that he had. For even one second. How could he have thought her capable of such a thing? Pretending to be pregnant might have been an accepted strategy for marriage in Their Mother's circle, but it wasn't Liz's style at all. And he should have known that.

Angela's sharp intake of breath was very satisfying and vindicated Liz's own anger. She was starting to feel better and reached out for the glass of water on the bedside table. Angela handed it to her so she didn't have to move too far. What a thoughtful sister!

185

"The fact that Hugh hesitated over that means we were never meant for each other," she concluded. Liz checked Angela's face. She looked sad. "We can still be friends – and you can still be friends with him, too – but he and I are not cut out to live together. We've tried too often now and that episode underlined it."

"I'm sorry I thought the worst of you, too," Angela mumbled. She kept her head down and pleated the bed cover. "Our mother told me you would do anything to get back at me. But her strategy does sound a bit nuts now I'm saying it out loud."

"It *was* nuts! It was lunatic! Although my initial reaction was to tell Robert, it was only so he could sort it out – it wasn't to get you in trouble. And when it came to it, I couldn't tell him just in case it *did* get you in trouble!"

Tears shimmered in her eyes. "I didn't know you cared."

"Of course I care! The difficulty is that Our Mother has always come between us. And you seemed to be welded to her apron strings and it's not somewhere I'm comfortable."

"My counsellor has explained to me that, from what I've said, it does sound as though I have an unhealthy dependency on Our Mother, and that it sounds as if she pitted us against each other since the day you were born. Apparently, it's quite common that parents do this. I can't understand why. Why would she do that?"

Liz let the mention of the counsellor go. If Ange wanted to tell her more about that then she would at some point. She did wonder if that was the man who had telephoned that time when she thought he was Cupcake. Yes, she'd keep that to herself, too!

"It's the whole divide and rule thing," Liz said. "Feigning victimhood. Loving the drama. I think she's a bit narcissistic. But we don't have to keep putting ourselves in that picture of hers. We can find ways of being detached from it if you don't want to lose track of her altogether."

"I really don't. She's Our Mother."

"Okay. I'll make more of an effort, too," Liz said, determined to be more of a buffer for her sister. It was dawning on her that Angela was a lot more fragile than she was, even though she was the elder.

"So ..." Liz said casually. "You didn't believe Robert and I were having an affair, then?"

Angela laughed. It was nice to hear her laugh, but, really, would it be so unbelievable that her and Robert might get it on? Yes, she supposed it was.

"You two have a really nice friendship. I can't see you messing it up with sex," Angela said. "It's only Our Mother who can't imagine a man and a woman being friends without sex involved. You're better than that."

Why, yes, yes, I am! Liz thought, relieved.

"It's the same with me and Hugh, you know," Angela said. "He's been a great shoulder to cry on. I'm sorry things didn't work out for you two."

"That's okay. At least we found out in time." Liz fidgeted. To think, she had actually thought Angela was having an affair with her ex. She'd keep that to herself as well.

Chapter Forty-Two
(Mother from hell)

They had cleaned and tidied Liz's house. Liz hadn't wanted to, but Angela was on edge and did want to, so Liz had gone along with it.

Wayne and Laurel were out. Liz had persuaded them to go to the pictures for their own benefit as Their Mother had always treated any lodgers and tenants that came her way as inferior creatures.

When Their Mother turned up, Liz found herself noticing that Moocher didn't greet her. He didn't bare his teeth, cringe back and then run off and hide, which was what Liz always wanted to do, but he didn't greet her. He merely stayed put in his basket. Watching.

Thinking about it now, Liz realised Moocher had always been all right with Angela even though she sometimes screamed at him for being smelly and hairy. He always treated that like a joke. After all, what else would any self-respecting dog be, other than smelly and hairy? Liz reminded herself to pay more attention to the people he said 'hello' to, and, more importantly, those he did not.

Their Mother had barely got through the door before she started on Liz: "Why didn't you tell Robert Angela was having an affair, you stupid girl? You never get anything right, do you? Not even a simple thing like this."

"For heaven's sake, M… Deirdre," Angela said. "Leave her alone. She didn't tell him because of her loyalty to me."

Their Mother gave her eldest daughter a very odd look. Liz thought it must be because her children had never addressed her in any way other than by her title of 'Mother'. Which was why the sisters had decided to call her by name in future. A definite little detachment there, a drawing of a line, a tiny little bulwark against her power.

At the same time Angela looked at Liz, a strange expression on her face. This was something else they all had to get used to – she'd been loyal to her sister. Why would she be? They'd never really been sisters – just two people born into the same family and turned against each other.

Liz felt tearful. She kept it to herself, though.

"And, anyway, my Robert is not for manipulating. He is not just a stereotype whose strings need pulling, M... Deirdre."

"Oh? And what's brought on this sudden turnabout? You were happy enough to follow my advice before."

"I was out of my mind before. Literally out of my mind."

Deirdre stared at her eldest and then at her youngest. Her face darkened. "This is you, isn't?" she said to Liz.

"What's me?" Liz asked, knowing that Deirdre couldn't cope with any signs of rebellion, especially from Angela who had never been the slightest bit rebellious.

"It's you that's making her ..." Their Mother started, but Liz interrupted her: "I'm not making Angela do anything. She's a perfectly functioning adult in her own right."

"At least your sister doesn't lie."

"Really? What about telling me she was having an affair?"

"That was strategy. That's not the same as lying."

Deirdre, having made this pronouncement, settled herself on the edge of her chair, carefully avoiding the table in case anything about it tainted her immaculate silk and linen mix suit. Moocher snuffled up to her from under the table and she let out a little shriek glancing all around for a man to rescue her before remembering where she was.

"Of course, it's the same as lying." Liz knew there was little point in having this conversation, but she couldn't let that pass.

"And, anyway – yes, I do lie," Angela insisted.

"Don't be silly, Angela!" Their Mother snapped. "*You* lie, Liz. For a pastime. But not Angela."

"I do not lie!" Why she always rose to the bait she knew not. It must be the strange power mothers have over their children forever and ever.

"You're lying now." She said it so casually, more interested in making sure Moocher kept his distance from her legs. She didn't even look at Liz. It didn't matter to her that she believed Liz lied. If Liz had a daughter it would damn well matter to her if her child lied. Was she a really strange daughter or was her mother as unnatural as she thought she was?

"And I do so lie!"

Liz wasn't sure quite where Angela was going with her insistence, but she'd play along if she could. "She lies all the time," Liz said loyally. "She's known as Angela-the-saintly-liar. Oh, yes!"

Liz was leaning against the mantelpiece, hoping she looked nonchalant, although her blood pumped so noisily through her head, she could barely hear what people were saying. Angela leaned against the sideboard. She might have been trying to do the same nonchalant thing by the looks of it, given that she checked her nails, checked her bracelet still undid and did up again, got her mobile out – checked that, stopped leaning, leaned again.

There were three adult women in that room and the only one sitting was Deirdre. She wasn't infirm or anything. Why didn't they sit at the table with her?

It was going to take quite a while to get used to the whole idea about changing the way they reacted to her, about changing the patterns of power within the trio. Liz forced herself to sit at the table.

"Anyway. So. Yeah. Angela *does* lie. She lied about having an affair." She stared meaningfully at Angela, who hesitated but then took a chair at the table, too.

"But that was perfectly understandable," Deirdre said wearily as if speaking to an idiot.

Liz knew this was a waste of time. They should stick to the plan, which was to invite Deirdre round and show her that they were now a united front and that she had not the control over them that she had previously.

She wondered if they'd done enough of that already or if they had to continue with this painful interlude.

Maybe they should do a duet – burst into song, clasp hands and skip down the garden path together, pigtails flying.

She snorted at the picture in her head and then had to ignore the enquiring looks from Angela and the disgusted ones from Deirdre. Their Mother had tried to break her of the habit of snorting years ago, which is probably why Liz would snort for the rest of her life.

She had to put an end to this, Liz decided.

"Right then," she said, levering herself to her feet. "Time to go, I think." She stared at Deirdre.

"I've only just got here," Deirdre said.

"Maybe you have. I could argue and say you'd been here for ages. But, as you've said to me many times, a little goes a long way."

"You haven't even offered me a drink!"

"There's no point. You've never accepted a drink under my roof. I don't need to keep offering only to have it thrown back at me. I've got the message."

"So," Liz said starting towards the hall and the front door. "Come along."

"You're not going to let her treat Your Mother like that, are you?" Deirdre appealed to Angela. Liz listened hard for her reply.

There was a pause and then a definite: "Yes, I am. We're sisters. We have each other's best interests at heart." Liz could have cheered, but she maintained a dignified silence. Moocher nudged her in the leg. He knew how restrained she was being. He was proud of her.

Deirdre stalked down the hall. Liz hurried to get the front door open.

Their Mother stood on the doorstep staring at them in turn, her face an unhealthy mottled claret mask.

Angela and Liz linked arms. They'd start skipping together any minute!

"I hope you're satisfied now!" Deirdre spat at Liz. "You were always the troublemaker!" Turning to Angela she said: "And just wait until you find out how you're going to get on without me."

"We don't want to be without you," Angela said.

Liz said nothing. She couldn't possibly agree with her sister's statement but she wasn't going to argue with it.

"Well, too bad. You've made your choice." With that final volley Deirdre stomped off down the path. The two sisters and the dog stood in the doorway and watched until she was out of sight.

They turned to each and hugged. Liz found she had tears rolling down her face. Angela was sobbing hard.

"You haven't lost her," Liz said when she managed to find her voice. "It's just that she has to come to you now on your terms, rather than hers."

Angela couldn't speak but nodded her head into Liz's shoulder. Moocher stuck his nose in her leg.

Although Liz felt triumphant about finally 'overcoming' her mother; she also felt sad – why had she ever had to? But still, even if she had lost a mother, she had gained a sister. She'd always wanted a sister.

Chapter Forty-Three
(Sisters: shoulder to shoulder)

"Right," Liz said. "We have a lot of catching up to do. We have to do a lot of sister-type things to make up for lost time."

"Ooh," Ange said. "Like what?" Her eyes were wide, a lop-sided smile had appeared on her face. And she looked nine again.

"Well – we have to have midnight feasts and tea parties with Moocher and Johnny, maybe get a tattoo, and we have to break some windows – ooh, break some windows ..."

Where had that idea come from?

As it happened, she had the perfect window to break! Angela was looking slightly dubious now. "Do sisters really do that sort of thing?" she enquired.

"Why, yes. Yes, they do," Liz assured her. "But first we have to buy some plants and take them to one of John's neighbours because I squashed his when I was hiding in his garden.

It was quite nice the way Ange merely accepted this at face value. She didn't feel the need to query any of it. So off they went to the garden centre down by the river and purchased a load of hostas and a load of penstemons.

Then they went back to the scene of the crime.

Liz banged on the door a few times but Bristler didn't answer.

The garden did look bad so she planted them herself while Angela went to see John to make sure he was okay after being used so badly by the sisters.

She came back smiling so he must have put her mind at rest.

"There's so much we don't know about each other," Liz said. They'd got back to her attic kingdom by now. "I mean, for example – do you think the best way to eat peanuts is one at a time and crunch them, or loads stuffed in and chewed to a smooth paste?"

"I don't eat peanuts," Ange said. "I do eat the occasional macadamia nut, maybe the odd natural pistachio."

"Of course, you do!" Liz laughed. Ange looked puzzled.

Liz passed her a bowl of really unhealthy goodies.

"Is it really over with Hugh?" Ange asked, stuffing a chocolate and marshmallow confection in her mouth, smearing her face with stickiness.

Liz nodded, marvelling at this newly-found sister of hers who previously would have run screaming from the idea of such monstrosities getting anywhere near her. And frequently had when Liz chased her with them until Deirdre would intervene and send her to her room. Her own mouth was full of peanut brittle. Yum.

She knew it was over with Hugh. Well and truly over. She hadn't quite got used to the idea, though. It did seem a shame.

"He's such a lovely man," Ange said, her voice slightly muffled.

"Yes, he is a lovely man and I'm glad he's your friend. He's a good friend to have. But, in the end, we realised. Or, to be entirely accurate – *I* – realised that it wouldn't do."

"I don't mean to be a pain ..." Ange said.

"But you're going to be, I'm guessing." Liz said.

Ange nodded her head vigorously. "I want to be one hundred percent certain that you're doing the right thing before it's too late."

"Our problems have always stemmed from me being too scatty and independent and him being too possessive and tidy, and a bit too materialistic. It's not things that leave you, it's people," Liz said. "Hugh didn't turn out to be my knight on a white charger. I can look at him and see that he could have been and I thought he was for a few years, but the moment he entertained the tiniest thought Deirdre inserted into his brain about me blackmailing him with a pretend pregnancy I knew we were finished."

"Are you entirely sure that's what happened?"

"I was there," Liz said. She gave Ange the look she

reserved for Moocher when he'd been told to 'stay' but she could see him inching towards the bread and butter pudding she'd just dropped on the floor. It was a hard look!

Bread and butter pudding! Arrghh!

"Oh, I'm sorry, Sis," Angela said and threw her arms around her, rocking her back and forth and crooning into her hair, probably blessing it with stickiness, too. "I just wanted to be absolutely sure before we moved on."

"Moved on to what?" Liz was suspicious. "We?"

"Well, we need to find you a new man."

Liz pulled herself away from the embrace. "Don't be ridiculous. We don't need to do anything of the sort! Rid yourself of that notion immediately! That's a Deirdre thought. I'm perfectly capable of living my life without 'a new man' in it! I don't have time for 'a new man' anyway. I have a new sister and she's taking up all my time."

"What about Hugh?"

"What – he needs 'a new man' in his life?"

"No – well, at least I don't think so – I think he needs 'a new woman'."

"Ooh, well, we'll have to keep our eyes open for a suitable contender."

"So, it's all right for him, but not for you?"

"Absolutely! He can't cope as well as I can. He needs someone. He needs someone who likes his overly possessive manner and his general air of knowing better than they do. Some people like that!"

"Is there anyone in Malvern Road that would be a good match?"

"I can't think of anyone off-hand but will keep my eyes open. We also need to check that his future women are above board. He's a bit easily taken advantage of, a bit too easily influenced."

Like by Deirdre.

"In the meantime," Liz continued, "we do actually need to see Hugh about Granny Smart. I can't quite believe that there's no way of getting back what is rightfully hers."

There were very few things Liz hadn't told Ange now. It was such a relief to have a sister she could trust so implicitly.

There were the occasional moments of Deirdre-inspired thinking to be seen, but Liz was on the watch for them and neutralised them the moment they appeared.

She'd even told Ange about the video she'd seen in Telly's place. Neither of them could work out what it could possibly be for. Liz had suggested blackmail but none of what she'd seen was that bad. Maybe there'd been more and worse on it that she hadn't seen.

Ange had practised with the dog flap in case she ever forgot the key Liz had now given her. She could limbo through the dog flap at amazing speed. She was a different creature to the one who'd previously climbed through it, cursing and falling and stressed, and making a mess of her clothes.

The very idea that Angela Rowbottom, mother of little Johnny, wife of Robert Rowbottom would join in a line dancing class was so outlandish that it made Liz laugh just to think of it. But that was exactly what had happened.

Liz had always thought the idea of line dancing in a line of two was hilarious, but now their sessions in the front room had grown well beyond two, the hilarity had grown exponentially.

It was no longer just Liz who clicked her heels and saluted the boss, Ronnie. There was also Danny and Ange. The Spawn of Satan had joined in, too. There was an unspoken acknowledgement that they knew fine well who Ronnie was. The clothes and ironware hadn't confused them at all, and they were there because they enjoyed his company.

However, Liz no longer took her shirt off no matter how hot her exertions made her.

Chapter Forty-Four
(Wicked sister)

"What on earth is this?" Ange squeaked, and pounced on something out of Liz's sight. "I keep finding such odd things in your place. It's like being inside an enormous lucky dip!"

Liz smiled. She was trying to pay the electricity bill online before they were cut off, but having Ange around was like having a boisterous puppy forever getting into trouble. It was endearing in a way she hadn't expected.

And, only last night, she'd had a text from Robert that said: "Thank you for being such a great sister! xx" So, it would seem that Ange's change of outlook was benefiting more than just her.

She clicked the final clicky thing and her bill was paid. Just like that! She loved all this online stuff. So handy!

Then she turned to see her sister standing staring at a gadget in her hand that looked like a very large, metal spider with a long, narrow, cylindrical metal handle. Moocher was watching her as she was watching it, as if he expected it to suddenly explode into a game.

"I wondered where that had gone," Liz said. "That's a head massager. It's quite good, actually, for something so cheap and easy to use. Try it."

Ange's forehead crinkled as she tried to see it in the guise of a de-stresser. Hesitantly, she lifted it above her head and then watched it as it descended towards her face.

"Ange! Turn your head down," Liz said hastily. "Before you poke your eyes out with it."

Ange turned her head down. The legs of the massager spread out as they met her scalp and crept along under her hair. She pushed it right down until it would go no more.

"Now pull it up by the handle and then push it back down a bit and then up ..." Liz said.

Ange did so. Liz watched as the expression on her face changed to delight; her own mirrored her sister's. It didn't take much these days to make Ange happy. Liz ignored the sudden uprush of tears as she thought that only a short while ago Ange had been living in utter misery. She was sure they were nowhere near out of the dark and shadowy woods of grief just yet, but things did seem better.

They were better for her, too. She had a sister now and it was great. Ange was here a lot and Liz didn't even mind her messing about in her attic room, the very hub of her business empire.

"It's pretty good for lessening stress, or a tension headache, or just tight muscles around your head or neck."

Ange squeaked. She'd tried to pull it off and it had got tangled in her hair.

"Why take it off?" Liz asked.

"My arm's aching from holding it above my head."

"Just leave it on your head," Liz suggested. "And then it's still in place when you want to use it again, and then your arm won't ache. It doesn't weigh anything. You'll just need a hairbrush when you're done."

"Good idea." Ange settled the massager in place again and went back to perusing the somewhat diverse contents of Liz's bookcase. She pulled out a book on origami and started looking through it. Liz went back to her online banking. She'd just remembered she needed to pay her credit card.

"We could do this," Ange said. Liz looked up to see a picture of an origami frog sitting on a lily pad. Ange's face was alight with enthusiasm as she pointed at it.

"We could indeed! And I think we should," Liz agreed. "We could even marble our own paper to make it with."

She smiled. Ange had obviously forgotten the massager. From the front it looked like someone had sunk a knife into the back of her head leaving just the handle protruding.

"Why are you smiling?"

"I'm just thinking what a great idea. Let's do some origami frogs. We can do marbling another time. All the materials for frogs are in the front room and we have a couple of big tables in there, too, that we can use." Liz jumped up, Ange jumped up, Moocher jumped up, and all three ran down the stairs. Liz thought it probably sounded like a stampeding herd of goats. She was sure the house liked it, too – that feeling of being properly lived in.

Engrossed in their respective frogs in the front room, Liz was at a particularly crucial stage when the door-bell rang. Moocher leapt around barking, wondering why neither of his play-mates had jumped up to answer it. "Could you get it, Ange, please? I don't want to let this go at the moment."

"Sure." Ange pushed back her chair and ran out, closely supervised by Moocher.

Liz tussled with a particularly recalcitrant frog leg but dropped the whole thing when a piercing scream rang out, followed by another. Her chair fell over she was in such a rush to get to Ange.

When she did, she saw her sister leaning back against the door, her hand to her chest – was she having a heart attack? Would she waste breath screaming if she was having a heart attack? Liz wanted to rush to her side but felt as if she was trying to run through mud.

The visitor was Deirdre. No wonder Ange was screaming as if she'd seen hell itself.

But another scream shivered the air and Liz realised it wasn't Angela from whom the unearthly sounds emanated – it was Deirdre! It was a terrifying noise. Liz didn't think she'd ever heard her mother scream in her entire life. It was such an unladylike thing to do! She couldn't remember they'd ever been encouraged to do it. Little, feminine, breathy squeaks, yes; out-and-out bring-the-house-down screams, no.

What was Deirdre doing here? She hadn't shown up uninvited at Liz's doorway since she'd been thrown out when Liz thought she was pregnant. Deirdre, who was Their Mother back then, had declared that Moocher had to go because he'd infect the baby, he'd infect Liz, he'd sour the milk by his very presence, he would fly around the moon on his broom and kidnap the baby leaving a troll in its place, or he would at the very least savage it when it turned up.

Finally, the shrieks stopped. Angela looked as if turned to stone, all colour and life had fled from her face. Seeing her so suddenly revert to her former, stricken self, Liz experienced a rage the like of which she couldn't remember feeling before.

She grabbed Angela and pulled her into her arms. Over her

shoulder she hissed at Deirdre: "Go away. Wait until you're invited before calling again."

But there was no denting Deirdre. "Look at what you've done to me!" she declared, holding out her hands and making them shake. Liz didn't believe for one second the tremblings were real. "It's amazing I haven't had a seizure, the fright you've given me. It's *you*, isn't it – you're a wicked girl, Elizabeth! Only you would do a thing like that. My death will be on your conscience!"

"My conscience can take it," Liz said, having no clue what she was going on about, and not caring. She pulled her sister inside and slammed the door. She helped Ange back into the front room and sat her down in an armchair. It was only when she stepped back to assess the damage done, that she realised: Ange looked just like someone had sunk a knife into the back of her head. Only the handle showed.

Oh!

Oh, God.

Liz snorted.

Deirdre had cause to have been shocked. Liz knew she should feel awful. She should feel badly that she'd maligned Deirdre. She should feel guilty. She should feel like she had, once again, let her mother down.

But the hilarity rising up her body was too much and couldn't be held back. She opened her mouth to explain to Ange who now looked quite worried, but Liz couldn't speak for the tide of laughter that swept from her throat. Snatching a mirror off the wall she held it in front of her sister so she could see for herself.

Some time later, Ange wiped the tears from her face and managed to gasp: "I nearly wet myself."

"Is that a first?" Liz asked.

"Absolutely. It'll be my last, too. Pelvic floor exercises are in order if I'm to carry on being a proper sister."

"Worth it, though."

"Oh, yes!"

That evening she had another text from Robert saying: "Thank you for being such a great sister! I will never tire of saying it. I am so glad you ate my specially made lasagne, and my brioche and butter pudding! Xx"

Chapter Forty-Five
(Smashing times with one's sister)

She did actually feel a bit mean about Deirdre and the case of the knife sticking out of her elder daughter's head. But she couldn't decide what to do about it. Angela wasn't nearly as worried about it as Liz had expected. In fact, she merely burst out laughing every time Liz mentioned it.

That must be healthy. Mustn't it?

Every now and then Liz would wake in the night and worry about Angela's mental health. She had no idea if they were doing what was best for her. But Ange was going to her counsellor regularly – she refused to see anyone else at all about anything so Liz and Robert had to be content with that, at least for the time being. Most of all, she was having fun-times with her family, now including her sister. These things must surely be helping to take her mind off dwelling too much on sad things. Surely …

And Liz could always think of distractions. She was too good at it, in fact, as her recent work record showed …

"I want you to break someone's window," she said.

"You want me to do what?" Ange was shocked.

"You heard me." Liz said. "And you owe me."

Angela tried the old mother-inspired heaving bosom thing of outrage.

"You need bigger boobs than you've got to do that successfully," Liz said, unimpressed.

Angela gave up on it and threw herself into a chair like a sulky teenager. That was better!

"Why should it be *me* that does it?" she demanded but she couldn't meet Liz's eyes.

"Let me count the ways you've set me up," Liz said. She threw herself into a chair, too. "You tried to stitch me up with Robert. And with little Johnny. You conned me over that friend of

yours you pretended was your lover. You made me make a fool of myself in front of a smirking philanderer in the car park up the road and a little old lady couldn't get in her car until I moved ..."
She noticed Angela's eyebrows disappearing into her hair, and hurried on: "I feel you used me as bait!"

"Bait?" Ange queried.

"Goats get staked out as bait. They get tied to a stake to entice in the bigger prey – they get sacrificed, Angela. You were happy enough to sacrifice me for your *game*. So now I'm going to blackmail you into doing something for *me* to just get a teensy-weensy little bit of my own back on someone else who used me as a goat. Mind you, I can't think of *anyone* just now who *didn't* use me as a goat." Liz's mood swayed dangerously close to bitter and twisted.

"Who was that?" Angela demanded, sitting up straighter in her chair, and leaning towards Liz. "Who else used you as a goat?"

"You're not denying you did, then?"

"Certainly not. Of course, I did."

"Oh. Right. Um. The other one was Philippe. He was trying to protect his lover but he used me as a goat to do it."

Liz was puzzled to see Angela's normally pale and perfect complexion change to a startling mottled effect, not at all attractive.

"What do you want me to do?" she demanded. "Nothing's too bad for him. Fancy him using you like that. I thought better of him. After all, he does own a few restaurants. But, really, who does he think he is? You don't need to blackmail me. Whatever it is, I'll do it."

She sounded really, really cross.

Liz felt a strange, warmth encase her, such that she'd never known before in relation to Ange. At that moment she was like the older sister Liz had never had. She could have cried with the joyful pain of it.

"It's all right, Sis. You don't need to do it. I don't want you getting in trouble."

"Don't be silly. Tell me where and when."

Liz probably looked at her sister properly then for the first time in her life and found her lovely grey-greeny eyes looking directly into her own. And she giggled. Angela giggled! Liz grabbed her hands and they both made their stomach muscles ache laughing too much, although quite what at, Liz wasn't too sure.

When she recovered, she said: "Actually, it's not all bad – we'll be doing Laurel a favour. Laurel is a signwriter, but a traditional one. She did years of apprenticeship to her own father, but it was all getting out of date already because now it's all digital print and cut vinyl lettering and no one is prepared to pay what a traditional signwriter is worth. It's such a shame. She does beautiful work."

"So, what has that got to do with this – oh, you mean she will get the job of painting the window when it's replaced?"

"That's right."

"What makes you so sure she will get the job and Philippe doesn't give it to a computer to do it?"

"Because Philippe is in love with her and she is broke."

"Ahhh – that's so sweet!"

"Yes. It's such a pity that so many traditional signwriters have lost their work. Laurel paints pictures as well. They're really good, but she hasn't got anywhere to sell them and is hopeless at marketing herself so the ones she does sell she lets go way too cheaply. I think she should do something more constructive with her pictures, and I know Philippe would be happier if she wasn't prancing up and down ladders as much."

"Well, at least we can do this for her," Angela said.

"Yes, we can. So, anyway, the odd thing is that the windows of two of the restaurants have stopped being targeted. It's only the one in Westbury now, which does seem weird."

"Let's even things up a bit – let's go and break one of the windows that haven't been broken recently, then."

"Seriously?" Liz was taken aback at how easy it had been to corrupt her always rule-following, law-abiding, hitherto goody-goody-two-shoes sister. She wondered what Robert would have to say about it. She knew only too well what Hugh would say, but she wasn't going to think about that. She wasn't actually going to let Angela do it. If she got in trouble, she wouldn't be able to handle it nearly as well as Liz could.

"Yes. Let's go!"

And they went.

They pulled up and parked in position near their chosen target. They got out of the car and moseyed around, their collars up, looking very, very casual, trying not to laugh too much. Not always successfully.

The moment arrived. Liz and Angela and Moocher all looked at each other. Yes, now was the time.

Liz pulled a brick she'd prepared earlier out of her bag, and instead of handing it to Angela, as agreed, she hurled it at the window.

It bounced off and flew straight back at her. It didn't miss.

Everything went black.

Chapter Forty-Six
(The only good woman is a mark)

Mitch had been minding his own business slouching around the area looking for opportunities. If there was one thing Troy had taught him that had always proved useful, it was that if he didn't look for opportunity it wasn't about to come calling at his door. So he always looked. And it had worked for him.

He now owned his own home in a sought-after area of Bristol, his business was going well; and on top of that he and his sister might be able to have a reasonable, trusting relationship. It was all good. He hardly dared think it to himself in case life was waiting in the wings to sweep it all away from him.

He'd considered Westbury-on-Trym as an area that was likely to see a boom for a while, and now he was spending a few nights just walking the streets trying to get a feel for it. It was so much better at night because of the lack of people. Also, it was near the cemetery, which he knew how to get in to, although it was shut during the night-time. He liked to visit various people in there. They all inspired him. Some he had known in life; some he'd got to know through their headstones.

Mitch had seen the car pull up and two women and a hairy dog get out. He'd stopped his ambling and edged back into deeper shadows as he watched them. Initially, he thought they were drunk the way they were laughing and joshing each other, but he decided they were soberly merry. He recognised the dog and wondered for a second if it had been stolen from Malvern Road. But then he realised one of the women was Liz Houston. What on earth was she up to? He edged even further back but kept them in view.

He saw them pull up their collars. He saw the way they looked at each other as if they were about to pull off some fabulous heist of the century, and he couldn't help smiling. They were behaving like mischievous children.

But then he saw Liz Houston pull a brick – a house brick – from her bag and hurl it at the restaurant window.

What the hell?

The brick bounced off the window, and shot back. Liz Houston fell to the ground like a sack of rocks.

It all happened so fast Mitch was stunned into immobility for a second, but when the wailings of the other woman hit his ear drums, he catapulted out of hiding and raced over to the recumbent body before the wailer could do it any damage.

"Get back! We need to be certain there's no harm done if you move her."

A few more wails of: "It should have been me. It should have been me," and the wailer stopped wailing and pulled a phone from her pocket.

Mitch dropped to his knees beside Liz Houston. She didn't appear to be lying in an awkward manner so he said to her: "Are you okay?" and when there was no answer, he patted the side of her face a few times. Nothing. He could see no blood. She was breathing just fine and her pulse was steady. Her friend was calling the ambulance, *and* the police he realised. Bloody hell – maybe she'd called the fire brigade, too!

He wasn't going to hang around for the police, but first he checked Liz's wrists and neck to see if she wore a medical tag of any kind. No. She whimpered. He was in a hurry now so he rolled her into the recovery position, snatched up the delinquent brick, and ran off. He heard the other woman calling him, but, instinctively, he wanted to avoid any interaction with the police.

Once more he hid in the shadows to make sure things turned out the way they should.

He was pleased to see that the restauranteur had finally got around to using safety glass, although he hadn't expected this particular outcome.

He couldn't shake off the leaden feeling that had landed in his stomach when he'd first seen Liz Houston lying there, possibly lifeless. The minute he got home he'd have a strong drink to drive that sensation away. He didn't need any of that kind of complication in his life and he wasn't going to allow it to mess up his current good fortune.

Because, in his experience, women always did mess everything up! Women he fell in love with, that was. The only good woman was a mark, Troy had always said. All the women Mitch had ever known had messed things up so maybe Troy was right.

Chapter Forty-Seven
(Hero brick-stealer)

"But, what did he look like?" Liz asked Angela again.

Liz was sitting up in bed at home in her attic. Ange was running up and down three flights of stairs with glasses of very dilute elderflower cordial, and hot water bottles.

"Ange! Come and sit down. Stop worrying. I'm fine."

The police hadn't come out, to Liz's huge relief. She still couldn't fathom why Ange had called them considering she was inviting them to a crime scene created by her sister. Thankfully, the brick had disappeared, apparently taken by this hero-type bloke who had appeared out of nowhere and taken charge of both her and the brick.

Liz felt a bit weird knowing some strange man had laid his hands on her and moved her body, but at least he had made Angela feel less alone in a crisis and more reassured that Liz wasn't dead.

The hospital had been great, although stretched to the limit given shortages of staff and resources, and she was glad to become one less concern of theirs when she'd been allowed home with warnings to look out for headaches, change of mood, feelings of nausea, dizziness and all those things. Ange had insisted she go straight to bed.

Liz said: "Someone must have replaced that glass with proper safety glass! Damn nerve! When I saw Philippe do it, all he needed was his heel – and possibly he'd prepared it a bit before hand – as in cut it with a glass cutter so all it needed was a nudge with his heel – but when he did it the whole lot fell out and smashed, dramatically, across the pavement."

"Are you sure you don't feel dizzy or headachy?" Angela handed Liz another glass of cordial – on a little tray. Of course. Apparently, she wasn't allowed coffee yet or something awful would happen to something or other. Liz was humouring Ange for the time being but she would need caffeine the second she got out of bed, or she'd go into withdrawal and that wouldn't be nice!

"I'm fine. I can imagine what it looked like when I chucked the brick at it. It must have looked totally bonkers. Like the window was getting its own back on me." Liz laughed, visualising it. "Let's hope there's no CCTV or it'll end up online, I'll become a laughing stock and will have to leave the country."

Moocher snorted from the depths of the duvet. He took up half the bed. He'd been worried for a while but had been reassured enough to fall into a deep, snore-infested sleep to make up for disruptions during the night. Liz had insisted Ange had gone home for a break from sisterly doings.

Now she was back she produced a hamper as if by magic and started to spread plates and napkins around the small space of bed left. It was a picnic! There was home-made lemonade, and little egg mayonnaise sandwiches, and smoked salmon and cream cheese sandwiches; there were little butterfly cakes with yummy butter icing and flapjacks dipped in chocolate. It was almost worth getting hit by a brick.

"He looked like a hero," Ange said dreamily, sandwich poised halfway to her mouth as she looked back on her mental vision of the night before. "He looked a bit like Robert, actually. And Hugh, of course."

"Oh. I think I've had my fill of tall, dark and handsome. They don't work out for me." Liz knew her sister was having romantic imaginings on her behalf over this hero and she wanted to put a lid on it before it got out of hand.

"Oh, no! You no longer have a crush on my husband?"

"I'll always have a crush on your husband! But I know I don't stand an earthly in that direction so you can keep him."

"Phew!" Ange cried dramatically and stuffed the rest of her sandwich in her mouth in a most unladylike manner.

It was so nice to see her complete confidence in Robert. She'd never had any need to doubt him, but such were the depths to which she'd been lowered.

Chapter Forty-Eight
(The New Malvern Road Gang)

It was the New Malvern Road Gang supper. Their number had increased to include people who didn't live there but were honorary members, which, of course, included Ange and Robert and Johnny.

Also, Hugh. And he was bringing his new girlfriend, Ange informed her.

"Really? He has a new girlfriend?" Liz had been startled.

"Will you be all right?" Ange had been worried.

"I'll be fine. I don't know why I'm surprised. I think it's great. He's moving on. It's time." She really did mean that. It would just take a little adjusting to, that was all. "Have you met her?" Liz knew Ange saw Hugh more than she did.

"No, not yet. This will be the first time."

"Are you sure this is a good idea? What if she can't take the Malvern Road Gang en masse? What if she can't take the joshing, the dog hairs, the noise?"

"Well, she needs testing," Ange said. "We have to make sure she's suitable for our Hugh!"

Eek! Liz had seen definite shades of their controlling mother when she'd said that. She would be watching out for that, ready to squash it before it blossomed, that was for sure!

They'd cleared the front room and set up the table in there. The breakfast room wasn't nearly big enough for this event. Liz loved using all the rooms in her house. She always felt the house appreciated it.

And then Telly, who was now asking people to call her Tally, had phoned to say Graham was working away so he couldn't come, and could her brother come instead? He was new to the neighbourhood and she wanted him to get to know some friendly people.

Of course!

Liz made Ange and Robert greeters for the night. They had to answer the door and give the newcomers a drink while she was juggling ovens and dishes and ingredients in the kitchen, and trying to get the starter right.

Ange came running in just as Liz had got to a crucial stage. Her face was alight. "It's him!" She hissed. "It's our hero! It's the brick-stealer." He's just shown up with Tally. It's Tally's brother. His name is Mitch. Tally brought a tray of mini baklavas, and Mitch brought a tray of various hand-made Moroccan almond confections. I've put them in the breakfast room. But it's our hero!" She looked at Liz, clear expectation in her eyes.

"Blimey. Yum – baklavas and almond thingies – they can come again!" Liz said.

"Liz! It's our hero!" Ange almost stamped her Gucci-shod foot.

Liz stopped herself from grinning. Ange was so easy to wind up.

"Did he bring my brick back, though?" she enquired.

"Oh! You're hopeless!" And Ange shot off down the hall to answer her husband's call.

The next visitor to the kitchen was Ronnie. "Anything I can do?"

"No, I'm fine, thanks. Got it all under control. Everything okay with you?"

"Everything's going swimmingly. Just to be clear. Everyone knows now. And I know you know who I am. And I thank you for respecting my wish not to know, even though you probably did know. What I mean is, thank you for pretending you didn't know."

Liz looked up in surprise. She fiddled with a bit of watercress.

"I don't underestimate you, Liz. I don't think you're nearly as scatty as you frequently make out."

Oh! Dang.

"In fact, I think you might have known from the beginning," Ronnie said. "However, it was obvious when you stopped tearing your shirt off in line dancing lessons when Danny joined. You're not going to take your shirt off in front of a man."

Liz lifted a glass and clinked it with Ronnie's before she started crumbling the Stilton.

"So, what about now?" Liz asked. "What's going to change? Robert and Hugh got together and looked into the situation as much as they were able without access to Graham's filing cabinet, and everything appears to be legal and above aboard and you can't get your property back."

"Legal, yes. I don't consider any of Graham's shenanigans 'above board', but good luck to him! Nothing's going to change. I have found that living like this with you all and allowing myself to simply be myself I have been happy for the first time for ages. Yes, I'm content to leave things as they are and I don't begrudge them their ill-gotten gains. I'm happy to be around my grandchildren, too. I'm entirely independent for the first time in my life. What more could I possibly want?"

Danny called and Ronnie went.

Yes, Liz thought as she shifted things around under the grill, the best revenge is to live happily. Although she was pretty certain revenge was something that had never crossed Ronnie's mind.

Ange came running along to say that Hugh and girlfriend weren't putting in an appearance, after all. Something had come up. Liz couldn't decide whether she was sad or glad. "Great! More room at the table," was her only comment. Ange nodded and ran off.

Finally, she'd got the starters under control. She yelled for a couple of tray-bearers; Jason and Danny came running. She loaded them up and took the last tray herself.

She stopped in the front room doorway for a moment taking in the scene.

The place was full of people all talking and laughing. It was the most satisfying feeling.

"Soooo…" Jason said as they piled in to their starters. "Who here has broken one of Philippe's windows?"

The laughter and chatter stopped, the clash of cutlery on crockery petered out, the sounds of Moocher slithering around under the table looking for dropped morsels was magnified in the vast silence that fell over the room.

"Uh…" someone said. "Pardon?"

"I'm just wondering exactly how many people have smashed a window of Philippe's."

Philippe shifted uncomfortably. "I don't need to know," he said.

"Just out of interest," Jason said. "Of course, we know Laurel has, but apart from her."

"I have not!" Laurel yelled. She jumped up, but Philippe grabbed her sleeve and tugging on it, he said, "I know you haven't. Stop worrying about it. I know you have not broken any of my windows."

She looked at him. Liz could see realisation slowly dawn on her that Philippe did indeed not think she had ever broken any of his windows. She flushed and sat down casting a grateful glance at him before lowering her lashes over her cheeks.

Oh-oh – that was on again, then, Liz thought, and smiled with satisfaction.

"Well," Jason said. "I'm waiting. This is just out of interest. Philippe isn't doing anything about it. I'm guessing there are a few people around this table who broke a window in order to give Laurel more work."

Whereupon Laurel squeaked. "No! Why would people do that?"

"Because they wanted to help and they thought Philippe could afford it. And now he's turning one of his restaurants into a gallery and wants someone to run it I'm guessing it's you who will be doing that and the windows will stop being smashed."

Laurel, unable to speak, turned to Philippe. It was his turn to flush. "I had been thinking of such a thing," he said. He glared at Jason, and then turned back to Laurel: "But I was going to wait for a more suitable time to ask you if you would run it for me. I really think we need fewer restaurants and more galleries and I can't think of anyone who is better suited to run it. Would you run it for me, please?"

Everyone waited breathlessly for the answer.

Laurel, her face one big grin, simply planted herself in his lap and wrapped her arms around his neck. He didn't seem to mind at all.

Jason gave it a beat before starting up again. He was like a terrier with a rat. "So, who here has broken one of Philippe's windows?"

"Oh, all right," Melanie said as if she couldn't keep it to herself any longer. "I broke a window."

That was astounding. Liz could never get over how you don't ever really know people. She wouldn't have guessed Melanie would do such a thing in a million years. But maybe she and Laurel had been greater friends than she'd realised.

"Why?" Laurel asked.

"So, you'd get the work. You wouldn't accept any help from anyone and you were getting thinner and thinner and more and more anxious. And I knew Philippe wouldn't mind." Melanie looked at Philippe. He smiled at her. No, he hadn't minded.

"I did one," Danny said.

Danny! What the hell?

"Danny?" Laurel queried.

"Well, this packing in the smokes isn't easy, you know. In fact, it's really, really hard and I've spent all these years happily smoking away and now I've spent a few days trying not smoke and it's *bloody hard*!"

They were all captivated by the normally mild Danny's vehemence.

"You've done incredibly well, Danny," Liz said. "You really have and I'm sorry I haven't given your efforts the attention they deserved. I should have made you a celebration cake or got you champagne or something."

"That's all right, Liz," he said. "I rewarded myself by breaking a window. It was in a good cause so I could totally justify it to myself, and it was remarkably liberating. I cleaned it all up myself afterwards, as well. I didn't want anyone to have an accident on my broken glass." He looked around a little nervously but a swelling round of applause brought him out in a smile.

Ronnie didn't stand up. He raised his hand and simply nodded when they looked at him. "Laurel found me in town when I was at my lowest." He didn't need to say more.

The silly smile on Philippe's face made Liz wonder if he'd known all this. Indeed, maybe he'd arranged it …

Ronnie grabbed Danny's hand and he sat down. They beamed at each other.

A few people around the table exchanged looks of surprise,

but then Tally coughed to indicate silence was required.

"Um. I might have broken a couple of windows," she said. She was staring down at her plate. "But I am very, very sorry I did. I wouldn't do such a thing again."

"But I don't even know you," Laurel said. "Why would you break Philippe's windows?"

Liz wondered if a woman scorned was really going to publicly declare her affair with everyone's favourite restauranteur thereby messing up her marriage, messing up Laurel's new-found happiness, and letting herself down in front of the step-children. She wondered if she should do something, provide a distraction, maybe leap up and scream 'Fire!' or maybe she should throw a brick at Tally, but she was the hostess of this social occasion. It didn't seem right to throw a brick at a guest.

And, anyway, Mitch had her brick.

Liz thought she heard Mitch mutter: "Honesty is not always the best policy. Sometimes it's merely inconsiderate." She saw Tally look at her brother, struggle with herself for a second, and then nod.

But she was on her feet now. She had to say something. "This was some time ago. It might even have been the first time your windows got broken. I, uh ... I was afraid there was a build-up of, uh, dangerous levels of ... uh, gas, in your restaurant, Philippe, that time when I was passing, and so I thought I'd better break the window and let it out before there was an explosion."

Good one!

"Okay," Philippe said. "Um. Thank you?"

Applause rang out. It had been a good performance. Tally actually did a little acknowledging dip of her head before sitting down. Liz was still watching her and she saw her mouth 'thank you' at Mitch.

What the hell was that all about?

Marcus and Sophie stood up looking smug.

Shock registered on Tally's face and her hand reached to cover her mouth.

Liz thought – no, surely not – they would have had to get to the restaurant quite far away at night.

Sophie said: "We just wish to point out that we are good children."

Marcus said: "Surrounded by bad adults."

They chorused: "We didn't do it!" And sat down to enthusiastic applause.

They were notching up credit to use against bad stuff they did in future. Very sensible.

"Can we count failed attempts?" Liz asked. "The brick got me on the rebound." She didn't mind the whole world laughing at her.

"I'm another failed attempt," Ange said. "I wanted to do it, but Liz wouldn't let me."

"What about you, Philippe? Did you break any of your own windows?" Liz asked, knowing full well he had. Everyone laughed. Of course, he hadn't! Silly Liz to even ask.

Liz looked at him and he looked at her. Then she suddenly realised, that Laurel might accept the others fooling about and breaking the odd window on her behalf, but she might not find it so acceptable if Philippe had. Especially with the whole gallery thing as well. So, she hastily added: "Of course you didn't. That would be plain silly!"

He shot her a look of gratitude.

"Anyway," She said, "let's toast Laurel's new career as gallery manager. I can't think of anyone better suited to the job!"

Moocher pranced around, yelping in tune with their cheers.

Chapter Forty-Nine
(Mapmaker)

Mapmaker was having a bad day. Work was proving particularly awkward at the moment. His aim to be a better, more optimistic and outgoing person was proving to be much more difficult to achieve than he'd ever imagined. It hadn't helped that Enid had been away for a while and he missed seeing her in Greg's.

He slogged his way home, forcing one foot in front of the other.

Was that Mr Grey he could see in the distance? He hoped not. Mr Grey regularly ribbed him about wanting a painting. He was obviously the type of person to judge on appearances. He simply didn't believe a nerdy guy like Mapmaker could afford one of his paintings. He would joke about putting him on the waiting list. Mapmaker would always say; "Yes, please do." And Mr Grey would go off laughing as if Mapmaker had just regaled him with some hilarious anecdote.

Today, Mapmaker felt particularly dispirited. He really needed a sign. He looked up at the sky. The moon was very bright tonight. Was that a sign? He tried to think that maybe Camille, the most consistent and important cheerleader in his life, was looking at the moon at the same time he was.

He was approaching number nine and could see the front room lit up. Once again there were loads of people in there all enjoying each other's company; and fine food, too if that was a leg of lamb he could see someone had just brought in on an enormous platter.

Bleak. That was his life. Bleak. He forced his feet to move towards his flat, but it was hard work. The desire to flop into the gutter and just switch off his consciousness was overwhelming. He stopped moving again – it was too hard to go on. His head was too heavy for his neck and faced downwards, staring at the ground not seeing it, when several unexpected things happened:

A gust of wind whistled down Malvern Road and his phone

beeped. Maybe it was a message from Camille! Just when he needed it! He whipped it from his pocket just as a piece of rubbish flew onto it and stuck on the screen. Impatiently, he snatched it away to see Camille's message.

A sudden onslaught of bitingly-cold rain slammed into him – Camille might as well have thrown a bucket of iced water over him. 'Pull yourself together!' she might have been saying.

But the text was a typical spammy message trying to sell him insurance. His spirits, which had suddenly rocketed skyward, just as suddenly plummeted to the earth.

He tried to flick the piece of rubbish from his hand but it wouldn't let go. It was wet and it was that kind of wrapper that is sort-of plasticky-paper so it clung to his hand. Grinding his teeth, he peeled it off his hand and, about to try to flick it away, he stopped and stared at it.

It *was* a message from Camille! Well, not exactly, but he would take anything he was given.

It was from a wrapper that had originally graced a packet of all-butter shortbread fingers. Camille's absolute favourite snack. It was her favourite brand, too. As he stared at it in the uncertain light with the rain bucketing down and the wind howling around his ears he felt an optimism that had been missing for a while. He smiled at the rubbish.

Mapmaker was so grateful he could barely contain himself. A slice of light fell onto the pavement next to him and he looked up to see the door of number nine had opened. In the doorway Liz Houston and her dog appeared. She invited him in to meet the neighbours.

He hesitated, his automatic reaction was to decline the invitation. But he knew Camille was pushing him; she had sent him a message; and, full of a new resolve, he accepted.

Chapter Fifty
(In from the cold)

They'd had a totally yummy concoction of Stilton, pears and watercress for starters and now Ange and Robert were bringing in enormous platters, held high, beautifully laid out legs of lamb dolloped with what she knew was a lentil, sun-dried tomato, garlic, wine, and mint mix – it smelled mouth-meltingly amazing! There were loads of side dishes, too. Just as she was about to inspect them all, she looked up and, in the glow of light from the bay window spilling out into the night, caught sight of the chap from one of the flats down the road. He was standing outside on the pavement, and looked as if he'd lost everything in his life that had any importance.

There was something about the way he stood, shoulders slumped, head down, that tore at her. It reminded her of going to a dog rescue place and seeing that dog in the corner, that one which had given up all hope. Awful.

She got up and made for the front door. Moocher came too. She had no idea what she was going to say to him when she opened the door. She didn't even know his name. By the time she got there he was looking at a scrap of paper in his hand. She saw him put it in his pocket when he registered he was no longer alone.

Her mouth opened of its own will, and said: "Do come in. Join us for supper. Meet some of your neighbours. You'd be doing me a favour and evening up the numbers." Oh, well done, mouth! She had no idea if the number thing was true or not, but it sounded good.

For a moment he hesitated as if trying to find a good excuse to refuse, but then he straightened, his shoulders went back, his head up, he smiled and stepped towards her. He appeared transformed. "Thank you so much," he said. "I would be delighted."

Liz grinned.

Moocher yelped and did a little dance on the spot.

They were delighted, too.

The end

Thank you for reading this book – if you have
the time to spare, a review would
be much appreciated.

Also, if you'd like news of my books there is space on my
website at: www.SusanAlison.com for your email address if you'd
like to subscribe to my newsletter.

First published in 2020
by Michael Villa Press

ISBN-13: 9798639798696

See artwork and books at www.SusanAlison.com; or search
for Susan Alison (one 'L') on Amazon or
Facebook, or @bordercollies on Twitter.

*Also by Susan Alison and **available now***:

Romantic Comedies:

White Lies series: Book 1: White Lies and Custard Creams
                           Book 2: White Lies and Stakeouts
Standalones: All His Own Hair
                           Out from Under the Polar Bear
                           New Year, New Hero

Urban Fantasy Novels:

Hounds Abroad, Book One, and Book Two

Books in Large Print:

White Lies and Custard Creams – romantic comedy
All His Own Hair – romantic comedy
'Sweet Peas & Dahlias' illustrated short stories
'Burglars R Us' illustrated short stories
Word Search, Sudoku, notebook, undated diary

Colouring Books – traditional line art:
Corgis, Cats, Border Collies, Greyhounds & Whippets
Christmas Canines

Colouring Books - greyscale:
Corgis, Border Collies, Greyhounds and Whippets, Cats

Illustrated Doggerel:
The Corgi Games
Woofs of Wisdom on Writing

Notebooks:
Various for scribbling, doodling, knitting, logbooks

Also by Susan Alison and **coming soon***:*

Romantic Comedies:

White Lies series: Book 3: White Lies and Sweetheart Scammers

Books in Large Print:

> White Lies and Stakeouts – (White Lies series, Book 2)
> Out From Under the Polar Bear
> New Year, New Hero
> Doggerel and Moggerel – illustrated

Colouring Books – greyscale

> Border Collies – Book Two

Illustrated Doggerel:

> A Christmas Corgi – an illustrated tale

* * * * *

Jill Mansell said of White Lies, Book One
ie: 'White Lies and Custard Creams':
"Susan Alison has written a lovely, quirky romp packed with off-the-wall characters – original, intriguing and great fun!"

* * * * *

Katie Fforde said of White Lies, Book Two
ie: 'White Lies and Stakeouts':
"Quirky, funny, full of wonderful characters you wish were your neighbours – this delightful book is
guaranteed to make you smile."

Susan Alison is the Katie Fforde Bursary Award winner for 2011.
She has won competition awards for short fiction and sold
numerous stories to commercial publications.

Her fiction concentrates on the relationships humans forge with
each other (and quite often with their dogs).

She is a freelance artist.

* * * * *

See artwork and books at www.SusanAlison.com;
or search for Susan Alison (one 'L') on Amazon
or Facebook, or @bordercollies on Twitter.

Printed in Great Britain
by Amazon

46452093R00127